WHO WANTS TO MARRY A *Millionaire?*

JESSIE J. HOLMES

Publisher's Note: This is a work of fiction. Names, characters, places, and incidents are a product of the author's imagination. Locales and public names are sometimes used for atmospheric purposes. Any resemblance to actual people, living or dead, or to businesses, companies, events, institutions, or locales is completely coincidental.

Interior Book Layout © 2017 BookDesignTemplates.com

Cover Design by Paper & Sage

Interior Design by Amber Saffen

Who Wants to Marry a Millionaire? / Jessie J. Holmes – 1st ed.

ISBN 978-1-7323289-0-7

To Dylan O'Brien:
It never would have worked between us.

Contents

DISCLAIMER

I'm not supposed to tell you this. I signed one of those "spill our secrets and we'll spill your guts" kind of documents, more commonly known as a confidentiality agreement.

Seriously though. I could go to jail. Or at least get a really hefty fine that I'd never be able to afford and then have to work three jobs to pay off, one of which is bound to be unsavory, forcing me to get mixed up in all kinds of illicit activity including changing my name to Starla and selling my baby. Or something.

My point is: I shouldn't tell you.

Will any of this stop me? No. Because I am a journalist. And as a journalist, I have the sacred duty of reporting the truth – at least as true as it can be coming from one highly biased perspective – and I am not one to shirk my duty. The world needs to know.

Well, that, and the fact that I'll lose my job if I don't write this piece consequently making it impossible to pay the fine I would never have gotten if I didn't write this in the first place…so it's a vicious circle. At least if I end up in prison – because of my future unsavory career – I will have gotten one of my articles on the cover of the top entertainment magazine in the country. Besides, my boss has her lawyers backing me up. And my boss might strongly resemble Meryl Streep's character in the Devil Wears Prada, which means her lawyers are bomb.

That being said, by reading this you are, in essence, a part of this. If you turn this page you are, of your own free will and choice, agreeing to never testify despite any perceived insight against my boss, her company, or me.

I feel like I should have this notarized or something. Oh well. "Consider this legally binding" will have to do.

With all due respect,

Paige Michaels

P.S. Consider this legally binding. (In case that wasn't clear before.)

Chapter $1

The tiny blue box sent my heart into a rhythmic dance as he knelt on one knee and opened it.

Holy freaking crap, that was a big rock.

The diamond caught the morning light and I was almost convinced he was sending an SOS signal instead of proposing. The gorgeous eyes I'd come to know so well were eager, ready for the answer we both knew was coming. I could just imagine the look on his face – on my face. Everyone watching would expect me to cry and squeal with joy. They would cheer and clap and pour champagne to celebrate. The thought filled me with anxiety. I was taking too long to answer. I knew exactly what to say, but I couldn't speak. I never expected it to go this far. I was supposed to get the story and get out.

I blame my editor, Carla. She's the one who started this. She's put me in this position. This was her doing. If she hadn't pulled me in for a yearly review I wouldn't be here. I remember walking into her office confident I was going to get a big fat raise, or at least a cost of living raise, for all my hard work my first year at *Look!*

"I'm going to have to let you go," Carla said. She was a statuesque blonde woman with a long straight nose and the kind of stare you rarely saw outside of celebrity magazines. It was the kind of stare that said, "I model in my spare time" to people she didn't know and said, "Mess this up and I'll make sure no one ever finds your body" to the people she did.

"What?" I blurted. I hadn't even sat down yet. In fact, my butt was halfway to the modern metal chair when she announced my termination consequently causing me to misjudge the distance and land on the floor instead. I jumped up, noticing her close her eyes as if asking the heavens for patience.

"Why?"

"You're an incredibly talented writer, but I feel you don't have the drive you need to succeed here."

"I don't understand." My voice felt thick and I took deep breaths through my nose pushing back sudden tears.

"Listen, Paige," she said, putting her hands together in front of her as if she was about to explain an extremely difficult concept to someone who didn't speak English. "You arrived in Manhattan a year ago, fresh out of college, bright-eyed and embarrassingly naive. Your college exposé on sorority rush week had people around here talking for weeks. We were thrilled to have you. Soon, though, you lost that investigative ambition you needed to become more than just a junior staff writer. Instead of seeking assignments you waited to be handed whatever was left."

"But I...I didn't know I was supposed to. This is my first job, I thought only senior writers got to choose assignments."

"Our most successful writers go after what they want. You didn't. You've become something of a drain on *Look!*"

Ouch.

"How can I be a drain? I have done everything I've ever been asked." I would not cry. I would not cry.

"That's all you do — just what you're asked. It's not enough to survive here. Not at *Look!* and definitely not in New York."

"But I..."

"I'm doing you a favor," she said, straightening the three lone pieces of paper she had on her desk. "You can go home to Tennessee —"

"Texas."

"— marry a nice cattle farmer and write picture books. Wouldn't that be nice?" She tilted her head and softened her voice as if she was speaking to the deranged.

I gazed behind her outside at the Manhattan streets. Her office overlooked hundreds of other skyscrapers, but in the far-left corner of the window, you could see Central Park. The leaves were just beginning to turn green after the harsh winter. I missed the color green.

My mom told me this would happen. She was of the mind-set I should get married and have children. Women shouldn't have careers. A woman's job was in the home.

How I longed to prove her wrong.

"Now, my assistant Marie already has your severance check. Your last paycheck will be directly deposited into your account —"

Two men standing on a large scaffolding against the building next door were changing its giant window cling billboard. I wondered if either of them would ever get fired for not taking the initiative. Maybe they should have put up a different billboard.

"You'll also be paid out your remaining vacation days, not that you have very many seeing as how —"

Going home to Austin for a while might be nice. I missed my family. At least they would sympathize. Well, mostly. My dad would say I was too good for that city anyway and he could line me up with a job at the local bank. My two older brothers always made fun of me for wanting to become a fashion and entertainment reporter. They'd get a kick out of this, that's for sure. Of course, my mom would be ecstatic saying how Paul Layton down the street was looking awfully handsome after his brutal divorce and how she was sure he didn't have that drinking problem anymore and didn't I just want to go over there to say hi and maybe offer to make him dinner?

"No," I said suddenly, interrupting Carla in the middle of saying something about my non-existent 401k.

She looked taken aback. "What do you mean 'no'?"

"I have to stay," I pleaded. "Give me another chance. I'll do better. Whatever it takes."

"I don't think —"

"You want initiative? I am *bursting* with initiative. Now that I know you're okay with me thinking up story ideas, I'll happily come to you with any ideas I might have!"

"That's really not the —"

"I have tons of ideas already. Really. Please just give me a chance."

"Paige —"

"Three. Let me pitch you three ideas and if you don't like any of them then I'll go collect my severance check from Marie, marry a farmer, and you'll never hear from me again."

She narrowed her heavily lined eyes. "Fine. Three."

At first, I was relieved. Then panicked. I didn't have three ideas. At least not three I thought would get me my job back. I was screwed.

Carla leaned back in her chair and folded her arms expectantly.

"Whenever you're ready," she said in a singsong voice, calling my bluff.

"Right." I straightened my jacket. Pacing would help.

"Prom is right around the corner," I said, turning back to her, my mind racing. I knew my next sentence was stupid, but it was like word vomit, I couldn't stop myself. "What if we do an in-depth look at why girls spend so much on dresses they only wear for a few hours?"

"You could ask the same thing about wedding dresses. There's no story there. Next."

"Okay." I rubbed my hands together feeling oddly like an evil mastermind who didn't actually have an evil plan. I wracked my brain for things I'd seen on *E!* the night before. "What about a day in the life of Emma Watson? Not many actresses have a degree from an Ivy League university. We could take a look at how it's affected her decision-making process with new projects!"

"No one cares. Last chance."

I stopped my pacing at the window and looked out knowing I had nothing left. Heck, my first two ideas were so boring I would have fired me. I'd miss it here. The two men had finished putting up the new billboard and were lowering themselves to the ground. It advertised a new reality TV show being aired in just a few weeks: *"Who Wants to Marry a Millionaire?"* My roommate, Jemma, found said "millionaire" desperately attractive. Right now, for instance, the billboard showed him with his hands in his jeans pockets as if he was a regular guy instead of a multi-millionaire. His brown eyes laughed at me and my failure. He seemed like the type of guy who would revel in other people's pain.

"Paige?" Carla prompted, but I ignored her.

What kind of man would star in a show like that anyway? It was some kind of game show where the contestants spent two weeks in California trying to complete three tasks in order to win a date with Lincoln Lockwood, a self-made, 28-year-old millionaire. At the end of ten days, Lincoln would propose to the winner and they'd get married on live TV. Jemma said the tasks didn't really matter. It all came down to your likability factor and, as someone annoyingly likable, she wanted to audition to be on the show. Unfortunately, she didn't have the money for the application. I told her it was stupid anyway. There was nothing "real" about reality TV.

"Paige, please." Carla sighed. "You have to understand what's really happening here. You're being let go."

"What's really happening…" I muttered, whirling back to Carla.

"What was that?" She looked like she regretted not having the Associate Editor fire me.

"What's real about reality TV? Nothing. We'll do an undercover expose on the newest reality dating show, '*Who Wants to Marry a Millionaire?*' We'll get a girl in there, have her play the part all the while writing a killer article exposing the *reality* of the show."

She blinked. For a second, I thought I was done. My pitch could have been a thousand times better. It should have been better. My heart sank.

"Hmm…" Carla pursed her lips in thought. She seemed to examine me with renewed interest. "That could work."

"It would totally work!" I agreed, enthusiastically as if I'd never doubted. I sank down on the chair, not even caring at how uncomfortable it was. "With the popularity of this show, this article would get read world-wide."

"Fine," she said, leaning forward and straightening her pen so it sat parallel to the three papers. I breathed a huge sigh of relief and sagged back into my chair, which only caused my butt to slide forward. I caught myself just before I fell off again and sat up straight.

"You'll be on probation until they announce whether or not you've been chosen."

"Wait, what?"

She continued as if I hadn't spoken. "Assuming you're chosen, we'll then evaluate what you'll need, funds and necessities, and develop a game plan for getting the story. Once you hand in the article, I'll assess it and determine if your writing is as good as I remember. Then, and only then, we will reevaluate your probation. If you're not chosen as a contestant, or if you're eliminated before you can satisfactorily finish the article, your probationary period will end, and you will be terminated, understood?"

"Me?" My eyebrows shot up. "I thought we'd get Abbie from Style or Lora, she's gorgeous, and *such* a fantastic writer."

"You wanted a chance," she said. "This is it. Don't mess it up."

My mouth hung open and she nodded in the direction of the door letting me know I was excused. Dazed, I walked to the door and pulled it open.

"Oh, and Paige?"

I stopped with one hand on the door and turned back to look at her.

"Get your severance check from Marie and use it for the application fee." She tilted her head to the side and grimaced. "And get your hair done while you're at it. Red is in right now, but we want you to look more like Christina Hendricks than Ronald McDonald."

"Right." I didn't even have it in me to be offended. Leaving her office, I grabbed the envelope Marie held out for me without meeting my eyes and tried not to resemble a zombie as I got on the elevator.

$$$

"Ahh!" My roommate, Jemma, couldn't stop screaming. "You're going to be on national TV! You're going to be a reality star! You're going to marry a millionaire!"

"I'm sorry," I said, narrowing my eyes at her. "Did you forget the part about how I lost my job?"

We were sprawled out on my bed. Or rather, I was sprawled out on my bed in my pajamas, eating raw cookie dough, and watching *His Girl Friday*. Jemma was perched on the edge of her bed looking like she was just asked to be the next Kate Middleton. She'd just gotten home from her day job as an assistant makeup artist and was about to head out again for her night job that kept her up until dawn and desperately exhausted.

She's a waitress. Not a hooker. I should have clarified that earlier.

"Oh, please." She pulled her long dark hair into a ponytail. "You haven't lost your job. You have the opportunity of a lifetime!"

"No, I don't. Jem, I have to *apply*. They're going to take one look at me and throw the application away."

"Shut up. You know you're gorgeous."

"Not gorgeous enough to compete with all the models that are going to apply. And as soon as I hear back from them that I'm not in, I won't have a job anymore."

"You'll be fine." She went to her makeshift dresser and exchanged the white shirt she wore for a black one. Only she could pull off a polyester black shirt and still look incredible. Where I was short and petite, she was tall and curvy. Anytime we were in public it was like I was invisible to everyone from grandpas to children staring at her. She hated it and more than once had told me she wished she looked like me. I would gladly trade. "You'll get your hair done. I'll do your makeup. You can get someone from *Look!* to take really amazing photos. The studio would be crazy not to pick you."

"Ugh!" I groaned and pulled a pillow over my head, muffling my next words. "I'm going to get fired. I hate my life."

"Paige Michaels. Get up."

I peeked over the corner of a pillow at Jemma who had her hands on her hips, visibly annoyed. I stood.

"Look around this place."

I looked.

Our studio apartment wasn't exactly nice. Or particularly clean. Two twin mattresses on the floor, beds unmade, took up the majority of the room. They were so close together Jemma often rolled over onto my bed without waking. Our dressers consisted of plastic drawer organizers, the kind you'd buy at Walmart to store your old DVDs. They were against the wall at the foot of our beds, an old TV precariously balanced on top. We had a fridge. Although, it was more of a mini-fridge and the freezer was only good for chilling water rather than making ice, but that was fine because we didn't have an oven, so all our food had to be fresh anyway. Our one and only window was in the corner and looked like it had somehow been forgotten during construction, so if we wanted to look outside we had to stand on top of a chair balanced on my mattress. Still…it was home. Or at least as homey as two just-out-of-college-girls could get in Manhattan.

"What am I supposed to be looking at?"

"This dump!" Emma threw up her hands. "We live in a dump!"

"It's not that bad," I said, unconvincingly, stepping sideways on my mattress to hide the pizza box I hadn't thrown out last week. (Yes, I have slept next to it for a week, and yes, I do I know how disgusting I am.)

"Paige. We use the radiator to cook Pop-Tarts."

"Your point?"

"This show. This stupid, shallow, and most-likely rigged reality show is your chance! You can get in there and get the story. No one does a better Valley Girl impression than you do."

I rolled my eyes.

"You'll be in a mansion in beautiful California. You'll have your own room. You'll probably get to travel and see the world. You'll have the attention of a freaking-hot millionaire! Yes, you'll be competing, but think of the fan base you'll have after this. Once you get the story, the real story, *Look!* won't be the only magazine who wants you as a writer. Thousands of people will follow your career after this. You'll have your pick of magazines. At the very least, you'll have credentials. *Real credentials.* More than just a list of hair products Taylor Swift uses. You can be a journalist and interview whoever the heck you want. We can move out of this crap shack and into a place that doesn't have six locks on the door."

"Okay…"

8

"Besides, what if…?" she trailed off.

"'What if' what?"

Jemma bit her bottom lip before she blurted, "What if by some random twist of fate, you actually fall in love? Wouldn't this all be worth it?"

I couldn't help myself. I smiled.

"You know," I said, folding my arms. "You really should give up that whole make-up artist thing and become a motivational speaker."

"So you'll do it? You'll apply?"

My stomach knotted, but I grinned. "I'll do it."

Jemma started jumping up and down.

"But I reserve the right to complain the *entire* time." I pointed a finger at her to emphasize my point. "And I'm not falling in love."

"Complain away my cynical friend," she said through her smile before grabbing hold of my finger and using it to pull me toward her for a bear hug.

California wouldn't be bad. A game show might even be fun. But under no circumstances was I falling in love on national TV. It just wasn't going to happen.

Chapter $2

Nope, definitely not fun. Three weeks had passed after I had submitted the application and I was spending my time breathing into a paper bag due to the fact that my acceptance letter still hadn't arrived.

"I'm going to –" *Inhale.*

"Have to –" *Exhale.*

"Move home –" *Inhale.*

"To Texas." *Exhale.*

Jemma rubbed my back trying to get me to calm down to no avail. The acceptance/rejection letters were supposed to arrive on Monday and when they didn't arrive Carla told me if I didn't have one by Friday I was fired. It was now Thursday, and I was certain I hadn't been chosen. After another bad day at the office - which now consisted of me trying not to spill coffee on Carla as I followed her from meeting to meeting taking notes - I'd run home and was unlocking our mailbox when Jemma literally crashed into me.

"Igotoffworkearlytocomecheck," she said in one breath.

My heaving breaths were my only response as I clawed through each piece of mail.

Junk.

Junk.

Junk.

Jemma.

Gum wrapper.

Junk.

Nothing.

"It's not here," I said so softly I wasn't sure Jemma heard me. I handed the handful of letters and flyers to Jemma and slumped against the wall of mailboxes.

She, too, combed through each piece of mail, pinching each piece ensuring nothing was stuck together.

It wasn't.

After finishing her thorough inspection, she grabbed my arm and pulled me up the stairs. It's a good thing she's my best friend because if anyone else had tried to stop me when I went to jump off the fifth floor landing I would have pulled them down with me.

Now here I was, ten minutes and one panic attack later and I still couldn't believe that I was fired. I don't get fired. I've never been fired before. Especially not for something that involved writing. The summer before college I worked as an assistant to this big shot in Austin and she said my daily task lists were the most beautiful thing she'd ever seen. I couldn't be fired. My Hail Mary should have come through. Why else would I have gone through all that trouble of coloring my hair and learning my fake backstory which was pretty much my actual backstory with the exception of being a journalist and having money. Reality TV Paige was an event planner. At least she would have been if I'd been chosen.

"Oh my gosh, my mom was right. I should have stayed in Texas and gotten married." I flopped onto Jemma's mattress-type bed. "I can't go into work tomorrow."

"Will you stop?" Jemma sat beside me and looked down at me. "You don't know for sure that you haven't been chosen."

"All that's missing is the rejection letter."

"Exactly." She slapped her knee for emphasis. "And until that letter comes I'm still holding out hope."

"At least one of us is." I sat up. "I guess I better call my parents and tell Mom she can't have her scrapbooking room anymore. Do you have someone in mind for a new roommate?"

"No!" Jemma jumped up, teetering unsteadily on the mattress before getting her footing. She pointed a finger at me. "You're not calling anyone or doing anything until that rejection letter comes. There's still hope!"

I stared at her like I stared at the women who walked around Times Square casting spells on everyone with red hair. I'd been cursed at least five times.

"Jemma, it's over." I stood and put my hands on her shoulders, finding it strangely comforting that she was the one freaking out now.

"I refuse to accept that it's over." But her eyes were filling with tears.

I nod sympathetically. "Why don't we watch *Dumb and Dumber* tonight before you go to work. Maybe that'll make you feel better?"

She sniffed. "Couldn't hurt."

We were about halfway through Jemma's favorite movie and about one Jim Carrey joke away from me sticking my head in the oven when someone knocked on the door. We waited a second to see if the person was at our door or our neighbor's, it's a really, *really* small apartment, but when we didn't hear our neighbor greet the guest I got up to answer it. Unbolting the six deadbolts, but leaving the chain in place, I opened the door and immediately went blind.

Flashing lights were going off and my vision was crowded with bright white circles. Jemma was at my side in an instant and slammed the door shut. Ferocious knocking and cries so loud it was almost as we didn't have a door at all.

"What the crap?" Jemma practically had to yell to be heard.

"I don't know." I rubbed my eyes trying to get the spots to go away. "I just opened the door and there were all these flashing lights. It's like someone put up a strobe light in the hallway. Or a photographer."

Confusion then excitement passed over Jemma's face. "Listen!" she squealed.

"To the screaming?" I yelled back. "Yeah, Helen Keller could hear that!"

"No! Listen to what they're saying!"

It didn't even occur to me that the maniacs in the hallway might be saying something. I listened, trying to make sense of the noise.

"Paige," Jemma said. "They're saying 'Paige!'"

"That's ridiculous." But even as I said it I could suddenly make out the word "Paige" through all the ruckus. "Why would they scream my name?"

"The show, stupid! The show!" Jemma put her hands on my shoulders and started shaking me even as she jumped up and down. "You made it in!"

"Wait...what?" I looked back and forth from the door to Jemma's beaming face. And soon I felt a smile creep onto mine. My hands shook as I undid the chain on the door. I looked back at Jemma's reassuring grin one last time and then opened the door.

$$$

"You could have at least thrown the pizza boxes away," Carla said, pushing her iPad aside. On it was displayed a news article with a picture of Jemma and I hugging, our closet-sized apartment in all its glory shining out in the background. The mess was quite a sight to see. I was pretty sure my mother would faint when she sees the photos. If she hasn't already. I didn't exactly tell her I was applying to be on TV.

And by "exactly" I mean at all. Zip. Zero. Nada.

Luckily for me, she and my dad were on a month-long cruise in the Mediterranean without cell service and wouldn't get back until the show was over. Thank heavens for small blessings.

"I didn't know a news crew was coming," I said trying to relax.

She sighed loudly and flipped through the papers I'd put on her desk. In addition to a news crew, several talk show hosts were there with their own personal entourages to capture the whole experience. I took Jemma's lead and jumped up and down screaming when they told me I'd been chosen. I actually started to tear up and one of the reporters looked at me like I was a child who'd just gotten her birthday wish. It's not that I was happy about being chosen - I mean, I was - but that had little to do with the tears. I was just grateful that I wasn't being fired and forced to move home.

Yet.

Before they left Jemma and I alone someone handed me a packet of papers, instructed me to read and initial each one and sign the final page. Legal reasons. Once I did that I would be officially part of the show. I went into work the next day with a smile so wide I looked like a maniac. Carla never showed up before nine, so I sat at my desk and read through each paper, initialing as I went along, until I came to page number eight and my heart sank.

Carla picked up the non-disclosure agreement, read through it once, twice, and then set it down and met my eyes.

"What's the problem?" she asked.

"Well, it's the uh – agreement," I stammered. "I can't write what goes on behind the scenes or I could get sued. *Look!* could get sued. We can't do this story."

Carla waved her hands in dismissal as she stood up. "We'll have our lawyers take a look and find a loophole."

"A loophole?" I asked, following her to the door.

"Of course," she said. "Finish signing the paperwork and make sure you've memorized your new backstory. You have to be as believable as possible. Use facts from your real life, like all the stuff about Tallahassee."

"Texas," I corrected as she herded me out of her office.

"And tell Marie to send Brett from Fashion up here. I have an assignment for him."

She started to close her office door, but I put my hand out to stop it. "Wait, I don't know what to do, where do we go from here? The producers said they start filming next Saturday and I need to be there before then."

"Marie will take care of the details." She started to close the door again but must have noticed the panic on my face because she hesitated and then put her hand on my shoulder in an almost motherly gesture. That is, if my mother were Hades' mistress.

"You made it in," she said. "That's all that matters."

I smiled weakly and thought I saw the faintest smile on her lips, until she said, "Just make sure you stay in." And shut the door.

$$$

Marie told me to only pack the essentials as all of my clothes would be provided for me. The fact that *Look!* would be choosing every outfit for me made me uncomfortable. But, as Jemma pointed out, at least I knew all the clothes would be top-tier designers. Apparently, Reality TV Paige made bank.

Jemma, being the true friend she is, insisted on dropping me off at the airport. If it were Jemma leaving, I would have been a true friend by calling her a cab and avoiding the extra hour stuck in airport traffic. But whatever.

"You'll call me when you get there?" Jemma said as she popped the trunk of her '97 Camry.

"Of course, Mom." I smiled sweetly as we got out of the car. She jiggled the trunk to get it open the rest of the way and yanked out my blue polka dot suitcase.

Jemma threw her arms around me in an awkwardly long hug. A moment later she let go, looked me in the eyes and said, "Don't forget what I told you."

"Don't put out unless he buys me two desserts?" I joked.

"Get the story, but don't be afraid to have some fun."

"This is work for me, Jemma. It's not supposed to be fun."

"Oh, now honey," she said with a wink. "Life is work, but that doesn't mean it's not fun."

We kissed each other on the cheek and after flipping off the guy in the car behind her laying on his horn, she drove away. I watched until her car got lost in the sea of traffic and then made my way inside.

After making my way through line after line I finally boarded the plane and cursed when I saw my seat. Marie booked me a middle seat. I knew that woman hated me.

I had just sat down next to a squat man with a handlebar mustache when someone nudged me from behind. My jaw almost dropped when I turned and saw a gorgeous blonde woman sliding into the seat next to mine. Her hair looked like she'd just finished filming a shampoo commercial and her face was annoyingly perfect with high cheekbones and bright green eyes.

"Excuse me," she said politely. "I know it's a terrible bother, but I noticed you're not using the space under the seat in front of you. Do you mind if I put my bag there?" She held up a tiny square purse. Prada. If I had a Prada bag I hold it in my lap for ten hours before letting it touch an airplane's floor.

"Uh...sure," I said, moving my feet slightly so she could slide her bag under the seat.

"You're such a doll, thanks," she said sitting up and buckled her seat belt. "I know it's always a pain sitting in the middle so if you ever want to stretch your legs or anything just let me know. I'll be happy to switch with you for a while. It's a long flight."

No. A woman who looked like Hollywood Barbie could not *also* be nice. It just wasn't fair to the rest of us mortals.

"Um...thanks," I replied, not sure what to say.

"No problem." She then reached into the bag still sitting on her lap and pulled out a book.

A book.

A *book!*

It wasn't even an autobiography by some random famous person who only wrote it because that's apparently a thing now. No, it was Stieg Larsson. I tried to read Stieg Larsson once and got so confused by the multitude of words over eight characters that I gave up after thirteen pages.

I had misjudged Barbie.

I smiled at her as if this small act somehow redeemed me of all my silent stereotypical judgements.

The majority of the flight was spent in silence in which Barbie only looked up from her book once to politely order a ginger ale. I read and reread my backstory five times and then went through the information Marie had supplied me with about Lincoln Lockwood.

He'd started his first company when he was nineteen and by twenty-one had two additional start-ups to his name. The app he'd designed allowed women and men to match what was currently in their closet with items in nearby stores. They could filter out what item they were looking for and the amount they wanted to spend, and fashion designers would put an outfit together for them from nearby products. Lincoln said he'd built it because he couldn't tell what looked good together and what didn't. He eventually sold the company and went in an entirely new direction creating an app that allowed underprivileged children to learn to code by playing video games. That venture led to him starting a youth center and multiple charities around the country, eventually being hailed as International Entrepreneur of the Year and one of the top philanthropists in the US.

Not a bad catch.

When we were about to land, Barbie put down her book and said, "Forgive me if this is intrusive, but you are *so* pretty."

It took me a minute to realize she was talking to me. "Oh, well, thank you."

"Do you model?"

I let out a harsh laugh. "No."

She mistook my laugh for insecurity. "You should look into it! You have a classic 1940's look."

"I'm too short to be a model."

"Oh, that hardly matters anymore. Here," she leaned over me and grabbed her purse, "let me give you my agent's card. She's amazing. She got me started."

"You're a model?" I didn't know why I sounded surprised.

"Yes, it's fabulous!" she practically squealed. "I started when I was 17 and it has been the highlight of my life. I've been all over the world for shoots. I've even been featured in some of the top magazines."

"That's great." My voice came out flatter than I'd intended.

"Here." She handed me a business card. I thanked her but didn't bother looking at it before I tucked it into my pocket.

"So is that why you're heading to LA? For another photoshoot?"

Barbie giggled. "No, I'm actually going to meet my fiancé. Well, he's not technically my fiancé yet, but he will be soon."

"That's great. Congratulations."

The plane landed, and we taxied around the runway. Barbie, although perfectly nice, sure liked to chat. I was glad she'd been so interested in her book during the flight otherwise I might have made a terrorist threat just to get off the plane. I've never heard someone talk so much and I was a journalist.

Barbie and I got off the plane together, but instead of going our separate ways like you do with any other person you meet on a plane, she stuck to my side like Velcro until we reached the baggage claim. Finally, on the escalator down, I said, "Well it was nice to meet you."

"You too! Oh my gosh, how rude of me! Here I've been prattling on and on and I never even asked your name."

I smiled. "It's Paige."

"Mine's Amelia." She stuck out her hand and I shook it.

We reached the bottom of the escalator and I scanned the crowd looking for a sign with my name. The producers had said someone would meet me here and take me to Mr. Lockwood's residence. Yes, they actually used the word "residence."

I finally spotted someone in a white shirt and tie holding a sign with my name on it. I grinned in relief and headed his direction, only vaguely aware of Amelia heading the same direction. I stopped when I reached the man and pointed to his sign, "That's me."

"Pleasure to meet you, Miss Michaels." He nodded at me and then focused on someone behind me. "And you must be Miss Gregory."

I turned to see Amelia standing behind me with a plastic smile on her face. She'd never looked more like a Barbie.

"Come with me, if you please," the man said and headed outside.

"You mean both of us?" Amelia said.

"Yes. Please." He gestured to a black sedan and Amelia and I followed him, neither one of us quite sure what to think. When we reached the car, the man opened the door for us. Amelia and I awkwardly looked at one another.

"I'm sorry," Amelia finally said to the man. "I think there's been some confusion. I'm headed to Beverly Glen."

"Yes." He nodded.

Amelia looked at him expectantly, but when he didn't offer anything more she pointed to me and said, "She's not."

"Actually," I said. "I am."

The man nodded enthusiastically. "Yes, you are both contestants."

Amelia sneered. "Her?"

"*Her* name is Paige. Remember? Your bestie from the plane?" I snapped.

Amelia made a sound somewhere between a scoff and a snort as she rolled her eyes and climbed into the car.

"This is going to be fun," I mumbled.

Chapter $3

It took us just over an hour to get from the airport to Mr. Lockwood's residence.

We pulled up to a gate larger than the one around Buckingham Palace. As we waited for the guard to verify the driver's identity, Amelia turned to me.

"I can't believe you're a contestant too," she said. "Why didn't you tell me?"

"Oh, you mean in the five minutes your word vomit stopped spewing I was supposed to violate my confidentiality agreement and tell a complete stranger that I was competing on a new reality TV show called '*Who Wants to Marry a Millionaire?*'"

"You should have said something."

"Why?"

"It doesn't matter," she said, folding her arms and staring out the window. "You'll be eliminated in the first round anyway."

I ignored her, or at least pretended to, as the driver was allowed through the gate and drove another mile through twisting, tree-lined streets. He pulled up behind several trailers that looked like they were made for rock stars. We got out of the car and were led past them until we reached the driveway.

That's when I decided I wanted to go home. *Home* home to Texas. I wanted to crawl into my mama's arms and have her shield me from the rest of the world because I clearly wasn't cut out for this.

The so-called driveway was big enough for two rows of five cars to park side-by-side, but every inch of it was covered with lighting equipment and cameras larger than my ten-year-old nephew. Three rows of desks, the kind you'd see in a college classroom, were neatly lined up facing the garage doors. On each desk sat a tablet slightly smaller than an iPad. Women, each one prettier than the last, stood interspersed throughout the desks looking warily at the tablets.

Amelia, not the least bit intimidated by the scene before us, walked ahead of me and was directed to a desk in the front row.

I just stood by the trailers wondering what I'd gotten myself into. Why were there so many women here? I thought there were only five contestants.

"Take your seat," a stout woman wearing a headset hissed to me. Not knowing which desk was mine, I sat down in the one nearest to me, and tried not to look nervous. At the front a man was holding up the tablet seemingly explaining something. Another man did the same to the woman sitting next to her.

"What're they doing?" I asked the girl who'd just taken the seat next to mine, a blonde (surprise) girl wearing a yellow dress so short I could practically see her hipbone. She shot me a look so nasty I recoiled. I mean, I literally jumped backward. And because the universe hates me, I knocked the tablet off my desk and watched in horror as it crashed to the ground a few feet away, shattering the screen. I squeezed my eyes shut hoping that everyone within a three-mile radius had gone temporarily deaf so no one would notice.

"Here," someone said, and I peeked to see a man pick up the tablet. He pressed a bit on the shattered screen and it lit up. "I think it might still work."

"Thanks," I said, my voice barely above a whisper.

"Happens all the time." His bright smile lit up his face. He was cute. The kind of cute girls fought over in high school. He had light brown hair, a day's worth of stubble, and an air of confidence that came from years of leadership. He was well-dressed in dark wash jeans and a blue sport coat over a white button-down shirt.

"Really?" I said. "Do you often have women sitting in your driveway tossing tablets around? Because I hate to be the one to tell you this, but that's not normal."

He barked out a laugh and another man came over. He looked at me suspiciously and leaned in to whisper something, but my knight-in-shining-armor waved him away. "I've got her, Paulo, you can go help the next one."

Paulo didn't seem particularly happy with this answer, but he moved past me to help Nasty Look Girl.

He set the tablet on the table in front of me then took my hand and placed it on the screen. Resisting the urge to pull away, I raised an eyebrow said, "Do I get to know what's going on?"

"Of course," he said looking directly at me for the first time. He crouched down to my level and spoke as if he were revealing a secret. "This is a lie detector test."

"Wait...what?" I jerked my hand off the screen as my evaluation of him halted.

"Lie detector test," he repeated. "Before you can get into the mansion you have to pass the test."

"Please tell me you're joking."

"Nope." He shrugged and gave me a lopsided smile that made the cutest dimple appear. I had the overwhelming urge to touch it. "If you've got nothing to hide you have nothing to worry about."

"You just put your hand here." He tapped the broken screen and it lit up with the outline of a hand. He placed his hand on the broken screen and must have seen my worried look because he said, "Don't worry, the screen won't cut your hand, I checked it." He held up his scratch-free hand as proof.

"Thanks," I managed to squeak.

"Five minutes, everyone! Five minutes!" someone yelled. "Andy! Come on, you're up!"

Andy looked back at me, winked, and said, "Good luck" before walking to the top of the driveway where half the cameras were pointed.

I was still dazed when I heard someone call out, "Rolling in five, four…" I looked around wildly wondering if I was going to get any directions. Was I just supposed to sit there?

"Welcome to the qualifying rounds!" Andy said in an overly dramatic tone like he was a radio announcer. "We're here with thirty beautiful women who are all vying for the chance to win the heart of none other than Lincoln Lockwood. And this is their first test."

Oh, please tell me he was kidding.

"It's easy to get caught up in the glitz and glamour of Hollywood. So many people are after their five minutes of fame that they forget what's truly important. We are here today to make sure these ladies are here for the right reasons. Before anyone becomes a contestant and enters the house she has to pass a lie detector test."

I couldn't believe what I was hearing. I wasn't technically even *a contestant* until I got in the house. From the murmurs heard throughout the desks, I wasn't the only one who'd misunderstood.

"That's right, ladies," Andy said with a mischievous grin. "It's like a giant game of Truth or Dare. I dare you to try to lie."

Oh, crap.

"The palm of your hand is to remain flat against the screen of the tablet. I will ask a series of questions to which you will respond with a simple 'yes' or 'no.' At no time during this test are you to remove your hand from the lie detector. If you do so, an alarm will sound, and you will be disqualified. The same alarm will sound should any of you be caught lying. Please remember that your honest answers to these questions will be evaluated after the final question. The contestants will then be announced and allowed to enter the house."

Super. Not only did I have to take a lie detector test, but every time I lied an alarm would go off. I guess I was moving home after all.

"No need to be nervous, ladies," Andy said, now looking directly at us. Directly at me. "If you've got nothing to hide, you've got nothing to worry about."

"Cut!" A man rushed up to Andy. "Perfect, that was great." He motioned for the cameras to move to their new positions and began directing several people to different places around the driveway.

I sat up straighter as a scraggly man with an untamed beard approached me with a long cable. Luckily he strode right past me, dragging the wires behind him, and I let out a sigh of relief. I waited for Andy to come back over to me. He must have known I was a reporter. Why else would he have stared at me specifically when he mentioned not having anything to hide?

I debated standing up and leaving before the test even began. At least it would save me some embarrassment. Just as I made my decision the director yelled something unintelligible and the staff scurried to get into place.

Andy scanned our faces, standing in the same position as when he made the intro. "Ladies," he said. "Please place your hands on the detection devices."

My hand shook as I did what he asked. I should make a run for it. Now. Before he started asking questions.

"With your palm firmly pressed against the glass, please answer 'yes' or 'no' to the following question: Do you know who Mr. Lincoln Lockwood is?"

"Yes."

"Yes."

"Yes."

I don't know why I was surprised that we didn't all answer at once. I guess I assumed since we were being treated like drones that we would act like drones. I echoed my own affirmative answer.

"Would you be here if Mr. Lockwood wasn't a millionaire?"

Several silent seconds passed before the first person answered, "Yes" and the alarm didn't go off. She was telling the truth.

Another woman said, "No" which seemed to give the others confidence because they almost all responded "no" as well with a few smatterings of "yes" thrown in. I responded with my own "no" but assumed it was for an entirely different reason than the other women. I wouldn't be here because there wouldn't be a reality TV show to be on which means that there wouldn't be a story.

Andy continued, "Would you be willing to sign a prenuptial agreement?"

I didn't even hesitate for that one and said, "Yes." If only they were all that easy.

I heard several other women say "yes" as well, but when the woman who had given me the evil eye said "yes" her device started to wail. Andy gave her a sympathetic look and then motioned for two men in black suits to escort her out. Out where I wasn't quite sure since we were already in the driveway.

Andy continued his line of questioning and most of it was easy to answer like "have you ever committed a felony" although three women did get sent packing for lying on that one. When Andy said he had reached his final question I couldn't help but breathe a sigh of relief.

"Do you believe you could fall in love on this show?"

"Yes." The answers were almost immediate, some followed by giggles and furious blushing. I watched the other women with awe wondering how anyone could believe she would fall in love on TV. Two women answered no and even though the alarm didn't sound, they were escorted out. My internal debate about answering "no" came to an abrupt halt. It was clear there was only one correct answer to this question.

A fact that became increasingly apparent as I realized I was the only one who hadn't yet answered the question. The remaining women turned in their seats to look at me and Andy raised his eyebrows expectantly.

Here we go.

"Yes," I said clearly, hoping against hope that the lie detector didn't pick up on my trembling hand. The women all turned back around to look at Andy and I held my breath, waiting for the alarm to go off.

"Congratulations, ladies," Andy said, holding out his hands like he was welcoming us into some elite club.

The alarm still didn't go off. In awe, I stared at my hand and the screen glowing beneath it.

"If you will all please follow me," Andy said and led us through a gate next to the driveway. In a daze I followed the group of women, cameras, and staff through the gate, casting backward glances at my desk and the device sitting on top of it.

Nothing. It didn't make a single beep.

Still in awe, I barely noticed the stone path that led from the gate to the front of the house until we reached the front door. Although the word "door" didn't seem to describe the giant monstrosity in front of us. It was an opening big enough for Hagrid to walk through. Andy waited until we were all gathered on the porch and the cameras were trained on him before he spoke again.

"It's my pleasure," he said with the same dramatic flair he'd used to introduce the show, "to welcome you into the home of Mr. Lincoln Lockwood."

He turned the knob of the massive wooden slab and let the door swing open.

Gasps immediately followed his grand reveal and the women hurried past him into the foyer, cameras moving with them, capturing every expression. I stood, alone except for Andy, in the door's entrance staring slack-jawed at the scene before me. The ceilings were as high as skyscrapers and large windows allowed brilliant sunlight to stream through and catch the crystal chandelier. High heels clicked, echoing across the beautiful cream-colored tile floor as the women explored the space.

I just stood there. In the entrance. Wondering if my entire apartment building would fit in this foyer.

I was pretty sure it would.

"Are you going inside?" Andy said normally instead of the dramatic voice he had when on camera.

"Oh." I shook my head to clear dazed look from my face. "Yes."

But I still hesitated knowing that the second I crossed that threshold there was no going back. I was in this competition, show, contest, whatever, to get the real story and launch my career as a journalist. Now was my last chance to leave.

I jumped as I felt hands on my shoulders and Andy's voice whispered in my ear. "You can't get anywhere if you never take the first step."

And then he pushed me toward my future.

Chapter $4

Out of the thirty women who'd arrived, only ten remained after the lie detector test. I'm not sure why I wasn't eliminated, but I will thank the heavens and the earth that my lie detector's screen was shattered. I was confident I'd broken it. The producers, Andy being one of them, gave us a whole ten minutes to introduce ourselves to the other women. That pretty much meant that I got names, faces and whatever absurd thing they did for work (one was a balloon artist), before being led on the world's quickest tour of the house-slash-palace. Afterward, one of the underlings - those adorable intern go-getters who still think that if they work hard they'll get somewhere in life - showed me to a room at the end of a looooong hallway and left me to unpack.

Honestly, my room was a bit of a disappointment after seeing the rest of the house which not only contained an indoor swimming pool and basketball court, but also held a movie theater and a bowling alley, all of which were in the central part of the house. We weren't allowed to enter the north wing because Mr. Lockwood required his privacy.

If you asked me he didn't want that much privacy if he was willing to broadcast his love life on national television. But whatever.

It seemed Marie had already sent my things because there were two large suitcases marked with the initials P.M. next to one of two queen-sized beds. I paused halfway to the bed. Two beds?

"Hi!" I cringed at the sound of a Disney princess voice and turned to face her.

"I'm Peggy," she said, eagerly holding out her hand. I shook it cautiously. She even looked like a Disney princess with her golden hair pinned back on one side and flawless porcelain skin.

"Paige," I said and tried to smile even though I was groaning inside. 50,000 square feet and they didn't think to put in a few more bedrooms? Get rid of the basketball court and put a couple there. You can play in the driveway like a normal person. I cursed Jemma for putting the "your own room" idea into my head.

"I guess we're going to be roomies, huh?" She shrugged and went over to the bed nearest the window and heaved her suitcase on top. "This is going to be so much fun!"

"Yeah," I said because it was something to say.

"I mean, this is such a great idea to have a contest for Lincoln's love," Peggy said and began unpacking. "It must be so hard to date when everyone knows your net worth. He's probably been so lonely for so long and now he has the perfect opportunity to find his soul mate. Of course, I hope it's me, but there are so many amazing women here that I'm sure whoever he chooses will be perfect for him. We're going to have so much fun getting to know one another! I'm sure all us girls will become the best of friends."

I gaped. She was acting like we were rushing a sorority, not trying to win the heart of a millionaire while thousands of people watched and judged our every move. Realizing my jaw was open, I snapped it shut and started to unpack my own things. Peggy chattered non-stop for the next hour without any encouragement. I could have been deaf, dumb, and blind and she still wouldn't have stopped talking. It was only when I turned off the lamp next to my bed that she said, "Oh, are you tired? I guess it is getting pretty late. Talk to you in the morning!"

"Can't wait," I said dryly and shut my eyes, grateful for the silence.

$$$

As much as she talked, I admitted I did like one fact about my roommate: she slept in late. She was still dead asleep by the time I got ready and made my way downstairs to the kitchen. The kitchen was a full chef's kitchen, the center island was ten square feet next to what I learned was called a breakfast nook, and it opened into a family-type room filled with low, modern leather couches and huge windows overlooking the rolling hills of the estate. Coffee table books were lying on glass side tables acting as if someone had actually read them rather than bought them for the sole purpose of decorating a table. Nearly every seat was occupied by my fellow contestants, each eating a meager breakfast.

I turned to the array of food on the island and my heart sank.

Do you know what I picture when I hear the word breakfast? Pancakes, eggs, bacon, French toast, waffles, sausage, scones, muffins, hash browns and on and on and on. Do you know what Hollywood means when they say "breakfast?"

Oats. Fruit. Yogurt. Skim milk.

Skim milk. AKA white water.

The sight of the overly healthy food so early in the morning made me seriously consider going upstairs, packing my things, and demanding a ride to the airport. I was told all meals were included during the competition. All meals. Not all fake snacks.

No. I wasn't going to let this ruin my time here. I was incredibly lucky to still have a job. I was going to get the story even if it meant I was hungry the whole time.

My stomach grumbled in protest.

I poured myself a glass of cucumber water (why can't people leave well enough alone?), grabbed an apple, and took a seat on the nearest couch next to a girl on her phone.

That girl? Yeah, turned out it was Amelia, my friend from the airplane. I didn't realize she had made it through the lie detector round. She gave me the up-and-down-you're-so-pathetic-you're-not-even-close-to-being-competition look and then went back to texting while drinking a dirt-colored drink I'm positive tasted even worse than it looked.

At least she wasn't my roommate.

It was fairly quiet in the room, each girl on her phone pretending to be patient as we waited for instructions on what to do next. Footsteps sounded in the hallway and everyone's heads whipped to see who it was. But it was just Peggy. She waltzed into home base looking as fresh-faced and perky as she had last night. Birds probably serenaded her as she got dressed this morning.

Twenty minutes later, the time filled with Peggy's non-stop commentary on every breakfast item and popular breakfast items in other cultures, Andy and a woman I'd never seen entered from the forbidden north side. Andy looked just as sharp as he had yesterday in chinos and a light blue button-down. The woman wore all black and looked like she was about to announce who pulled the sword from the stone.

"Ladies!" the woman called, unnecessarily, as we were all already looking at her. She glanced around, her tiny frame a stark contrast to Andy's towering figure. Once satisfied all attention was on her, she smoothed her pixie cut before making her announcement.

"My name is Wanda Reynolds and I, along with Andrew Warner, are the producers of *Who Wants to Marry a Millionaire?* We'd like to thank you all for your honesty and congratulate you for surviving the first night." Polite chuckles sounded throughout the room. "But don't get too comfortable, as five more of you will be leaving us before the end of the day."

I watched as the girls around the room exchanged anxious glances.

"I'm glad to see you're all dressed and ready because we have a busy day ahead of us. The busses will take you to the warehouse where we will film the interview round in front of a live audience. Mr. Lockwood will ask questions and eliminate you based upon your answers. Cameras will arrive in 30 minutes." She pivoted on one foot and left the way she'd come.

The room went deadly silent. Seriously. It was like she had just stated that Bloomingdale's was going out of business.

The second she was out of sight it was mayhem as nine girls literally ran out of the kitchen-dash-family room-dash-couch area. Bare feet were heard smacking on the tile staircase as they scurried to their rooms.

I watched them go, my mouth open, and when I looked around the room I realized I was alone.

"Aren't you going to hurry upstairs?" Andy asked.

Well, *almost* alone.

I glanced behind me, but everyone else had left. Andy sat in an uncomfortable-looking armchair next to the spot Amelia had just vacated.

"Am I supposed to be doing something?" I asked.

He chuckled.

"No," I said, "I'm serious. Were there some instructions given this morning or something that I missed? I didn't think I'd slept in too late, my roommate was even still asleep, but if I missed something –"

"No," Andy interrupted. "You didn't miss anything. They're all just going to get ready."

I blinked. "Ready for what?"

It was Andy's turn to look confused. "Ready for the interview round. Ready to meet Lincoln."

"Oh." Of course they were. I probably should too. I glanced down at my simple, yet pricey pink sundress and platform sandals. I thought about the rest of my shoes, in a neat line in the closet upstairs. Marie, or whoever, had chosen well. It seemed that Carla didn't want to leave anything to chance because there was also a pocket-sized Lookbook detailing every outfit down to the last accessory. I'd followed its directions down to the oversized flower-shaped ring on my middle finger. I could just imagine her seeing me on TV and firing me for defying her instructions.

Andy broke through my thoughts. "You don't seem concerned."

"Well, it's not like I don't care," I stammered. "I just assumed that whatever we wore to breakfast would be what we wore to meet Lincoln – I mean, Mr. Lockwood. I didn't think I'd have time to change."

Laugh-lines appeared at the corner of his eyes, but he didn't say anything.

"I mean," I said, unable to think of my next words. Why did he have to look at me like that? "Should I? Go change?"

"No," he said still staring. "You look great."

His compliment did nothing to ease my nerves. Nerves I now had because everyone was freaking out and I hadn't realized that I obviously needed to change clothes and maybe I should have worn the Stella McCartney halter top and oh my gosh I was going to meet Lincoln Lockwood who had to like me enough to keep me around so I could write my article and what if I was sent home then I'd have to go back to Texas and marry a farmer and have ten kids and --

"Are you okay?" Andy asked.

"What?" I mentally shook myself.

"You look a little...worried."

"Oh, yeah, I mean I'm fine, of course."

"Okay," he said this like he didn't believe me.

"I'm Paige Michaels," I said trying to distract myself.

"Andy," he said shaking my outstretched hand.

"So what do you do, Andy?"

He looked at me with laughter in his eyes and a second later I realized my mistake. "Oh. Right. You're the producer."

"And the host," he offered.

"And the host," I repeated. "I'm sorry, I must be more nervous than I thought."

"I'm sure. Paige Michaels," he mused. "I remember your profile. You're from somewhere in Texas, right?"

"Austin. Kind of. We're actually about an hour outside Austin in a tiny town no one's ever heard of."

"That explains the small-town charm."

I blushed. "If making an idiot out of myself classifies as 'small town.'"

"No, it's endearing. Good strategy." He grinned.

Strategy? Like I'd planned to act like I didn't have a clue?

"What got you into television?" I needed to change the subject.

Andy leaned back in his chair. "Lincoln, actually. We were buddies in college."

Before I could respond, Wanda's stilettos announced her arrival. Andy stood up to greet her and I followed suit.

"Andy!" she barked once we were in sight. "Are you coming?"

"On my way," he said. He mouthed sorry to me and followed Wanda down the hall.

I checked the time on my phone. I still had twenty minutes. I sat back down, nervously tapping my shoe against the floor, debating changing them. But Carla/Marie/Whoever was right. These shoes did go best with this dress. The fourth time I pulled my phone out to check the time I got a text from Carla.

Have you met Mr. Moneybags, yet?

I typed out a quick response.

Soon.

Hurry up and meet him so you can get your story.

It's only day 1.

Which means you have one less day to get the scoop.

Knowing she was right, I opened up my Notes app and started writing down descriptions of the things I'd seen so far. After describing, in detail, the entrance hall with its wood-paneled walls and abstract artwork, I sighed and turned my phone off. We had about ten more minutes before we would start to film. Ten minutes I could sit here impatiently waiting, making myself more nervous by the minute, or ten minutes I could wander around the "off limits" part of the house. I got up and peeked down the hall which Wanda and Andy had disappeared. Only a few feet away were open double doors that led outside. I glimpsed the pool as I passed but continued down the hall. All the doors were closed and every turned corner led to more hallways and staircases. I stopped to listen at one of the doors.

Nothing. I opened it as quietly as I could and listened, but the only thing on the other side was silence. My hand patted the inside wall looking for a switch. My anxious heartbeat thudded in my ears as my fingers closed around the switch and I flipped it on.

It was a bathroom.

A half-bath to be exact with a cute little pedestal sink and fuzzy green rug. It figured that the first thing I found was the place things go to die.

Disappointed, I turned off the light and closed the door. I went to retrace my path to the back doors, but nearly jumped out of my skin when someone blocked my path.

"Holy –" I gasped, putting my hands to my chest as if that would be enough to prevent a heart attack. The man in front of me, dressed in jeans and a dark blazer I immediately knew must have cost more than my first car, frowned and put his hands in his pockets.

"May I help you?"

"Right," I said. "Sorry, I was just looking for the bathroom."

"You didn't use it."

"No, I, uh…" How long had he been standing there? "I just wanted to know where it was. You know, for future reference."

He raised an eyebrow. I smoothed my dress and frantically tried to come up with a change of subject.

"Hugo Boss." I gestured at his blazer. "Nice."

"Thank you. How did you –"

Crap. I forgot that TV Paige was an event planner. Not a journalist at a fashion magazine.

I shrugged nonchalantly and told part of the truth. "I'm obsessed with fashion."

He studied me for a moment longer and then said, "I assume you're one of the contestants? I believe they're loading the busses. Let me show you to the driveway. I'd hate for you to get lost."

"That's so kind of you," I said innocently and followed him through a maze of hallways decorated with modern sculptures and bright, colorful photographs of…shapes.

"I believe the contestants are meeting just outside." The man pointed to the massive front door.

"Right. Thanks again." Before he could reply I hurried through the door. Wanda glared at me when I reached them, even though I doubted I was that late, and pointed to the open doors of the tour bus. I took a seat in front of a pair of dark-haired girls whose features were so similar I nicknamed them Giggle Twins.

"Is that him? I can't tell from here." One of them whispered. I looked out the window to see who she was talking about. At the opposite end of the driveway the man I'd run into was standing next to a black sedan talking to Andy.

The other girl squealed and started giggling. "Yes! That's him!"

No. They couldn't be talking about *him*.

"Yes, yes, Mr. Lockwood is very pretty." Wanda took a seat at the front of the bus and the doors closed behind her. "But don't get too excited. Remember that only five of you will get to meet him."

That was Mr. Lockwood? *Lincoln Lockwood?*

My hands covered my face in embarrassment.

Of course. The Hugo Boss jacket should have tipped me off. He looked slightly different than he did in the promotional ads. His wavy black hair was longer and had that just-woke-up-but-still-amazing look to it and there was a day's worth of stubble on his face. It still didn't excuse not recognizing him.

My first interaction with the star of the show and we'd talked about the bathroom.

I shouldn't have unpacked last night. It would have saved me some time.

The bus pulled up to a large concrete building and we filed off. We all shuffled through non-descript metal doors and through an unusually wide hallway until we stood looking at a black platform. I was surprised to see the studio audience was already seated and chatting with the inevitable excitement of those who were about to witness celebrities in action. Ten wooden barstools were lined up at the front of the stage, close to the audience, and a large black curtain hid one side of the stage. Looking at the scene from backstage reminded me of the many choir concerts I'd performed in during high school. The thought filled me with dread.

Wanda gave us the extremely helpful instructions of "take a seat when he says your name" before she left us standing clumped in a corner. We barely had a chance to breathe before our eyes were seared as the stage lights came on. I was still seeing white spots when I heard Andy speak.

"Ready when you are, Tom."

A man ran the length of the bleachers in front of the audience waving a giant sign that I'm sure said something like, "shut up," because they quieted immediately. Andy straightened his back and upon some signal started talking in his announcer voice.

"Thanks for joining us on *Who Wants to Marry a Millionaire?* I'm excited to introduce you to the ten honest women who passed the lie detector test with flying colors!" He swept a hand in our direction and the cameras rotated toward us. Andy moved to stand at an angle where another camera was trained on him. "Let's welcome Amelia."

The audience cheered as she strode to her stool like a model. Then again, I guess she was a model, so I really couldn't judge her for that.

He called Carmen next, followed by the Giggle Twins and Peggy. He introduced us one by one until we were all seated. My name was the last to be called and I was forced to sit on the stool farthest from the curtain. I crossed my legs in what I hoped was a semi-ladylike manner.

"We will all get to know them better as Mr. Lockwood asks them questions submitted by the audience," Andy said. "The questions will be to the entire group. Mr. Lockwood will rate their answer on a one to ten scale, ten being exactly what he wanted to hear. At the end of the round the contestants with the five lowest scores will be eliminated; however, Mr. Lockwood has the ability to eliminate any contestant at any time.

"Let's get started." Andy walked past the black curtain and a moment later the crowd cheered.

"Hi, everyone," I recognized the voice from earlier, "I'm Lincoln Lockwood. Is everyone ready to help me choose my future wife?"

The audience cheered and clapped, a couple women calling out "choose me!" It was like an electric current ran through the ten of us onstage. Posture straightened, hair was fluffed, coy smiles were directed at the camera. All eyes were drilling holes into the side curtain waiting for it to be pulled back. A moment later, Andy came into view, stopping to stand on a red 'x' a few feet from the curtain. He turned to us and gave us a mischievous smile.

"Oh," he said and playfully bumped his forehead with his hand, "I forgot something. You won't be able to see him or his reactions… and *he* won't be able to see you."

Chapter $5

If jaw drops were audible, I'm pretty sure there would have been one loud *klunk* as this new development sank in. While it was unexpected based on what we'd been told, it wasn't wholly surprising to me. This was a game show. Twists and turns were part of the so-called fun. I looked down the line at the other contestants and noted that they did *not* look happy. Several of them were grimacing and a couple were looking down at their outfits like they'd just spilled red wine down the front. I doubted they would wear the same dress again on TV which meant all of them had just wasted one of their best outfits. I suddenly appreciated Andy's comment about my sundress. Sure, it was more casual than the other girls' dresses, but it also wasn't even in my top five best outfits.

"That's right," Andy turned back to the audience, "this round is based on answers alone. We don't want Mr. Lockwood's heart to be swayed by beauty."

Once again, a man ran down the length of the bleachers holding up a sign. If it said "laugh" it wasn't doing any good. Some of the audience politely chuckled, but the majority looked bored. Andy seemed to notice because he decided to dive right in to the interview.

"Mr. Lockwood, do you have your questions ready?"

"I'm ready," Mr. Lockwood replied.

"Be sure to pay attention to each answer. One of these women is your future wife. You want to get this right."

"I'm sure with the audience's help, we'll manage." The audience cheered at this without any help from the man with the sign.

"Let's begin!" Right as he spoke the words I noticed a glow out of my peripheral vision and looked behind me. What I'd thought was a wall turned out to be a screen. It had been lit and about halfway up the screen there was a row of ten animated canvas bags. I turned back to the crowd and noticed a few of them pointing to a spot just above my head and the scene sunk in. An empty bag with a dollar sign on it, the kind a robber would use, was hovering over my head. I rolled my eyes. They were probably going to keep score in some cheesy way like filling the bag up with money.

"Question one will be directed to all contestants. You have one minute to answer." Andy sounded way too excited.

As a journalist I was used to asking the questions. I wasn't sure I was going to like being on this side of the interview. Already, my back hurt from not having any support and I tried to sit as straight as possible without looking prissy. The last thing I needed was for Carla to scold me for slumping like a millennial. Even if I was a millennial.

My stomach clenched, and my knees started shaking. I adjusted my position so it would be less noticeable, but the shaking just got worse. It looked like I was doing it on purpose. I was going to be labeled as the child who couldn't sit still. I flexed my leg muscles several times and the shaking started to slow.

"Ladies, thank you for coming." Lincoln said as if he was welcoming us to brunch. "I hope you're as excited to be here as I am excited to have you. What made you enter this competition?"

Amelia spoke first. "You, of course!"

The audience laughed. Once they had quieted she continued, "I've always thought you were amazing. You started your own company at nineteen because you wanted to provide children with a place of refuge. Within ten years you've have made it into the conglomerate it is today. You've been such an inspiration. Even though I have a good career as a model I have really always wanted to start a charity for adoption. When I heard about your latest project, Love Is, a charity to help couples afford the costs of adoption I just swooned. I knew right then that you were the man I wanted to marry. I applied to *Who Wants to Marry a Millionaire?* immediately."

Everyone clapped, and she even got a couple catcalls. The sound of coins dropping into a jar sounded through the loud speaker. I looked at the screen and, just like I'd predicted, gold coins dropped into the bag and a number appeared on the front. Nine. She'd gotten nine points.

The girl next to her spoke and as each answer was given it got closer and closer to my turn. I cursed the sixth girl for stealing the answer I'd planned on giving. Granted, "my parents convinced me this was my chance to find true love and I needed to go win your heart" wasn't incredibly original or interesting, but she still got five points.

Lincoln repeated the question before I could speak. "And contestant number ten, what got you here today?"

I said the first thing that came to mind. "A bus."

Everyone laughed, including my competitors, but an awkward silence filled the studio as they waited for me to say something else. I didn't. I couldn't. It was like someone had taken away my ability to speak. I tried, I really did! But every time I opened my mouth I couldn't make a sound. I finally just smiled politely until the longest minute in the history of the world was over and Andy hopped back in front of the camera. Hopefully they'd edit my answer out.

"I love girls with a sense of humor." His laugh almost sounded genuine. I heard the computerized coins drop and I looked back. Five. I sighed with relief. Even though it was the worst answer known to man, he'd still given me five points. Bless him.

"Let's continue," Andy said, turning it back over to Lincoln.

"If you could go anywhere, where would you go and why?" Lincoln asked.

I didn't have any more problems answering his questions. Most of the time I gave a non-answer like, "Who doesn't like hang gliding?" and "It was *such* an experience." One of the perks of being a reporter is that you know when the person you're interviewing is side-stepping the subject. It comes in handy when the tables are turned and you're asked questions you don't want to answer.

On and on it went until we'd been asked two hours of questions from "What is your most embarrassing moment?" to "What do you consider a deal breaker in a relationship?" Every girl was asked the same number of individual questions and halfway in one girl started crying because she was in ninth place. When we reached the last question, I was no longer nervous. I was in fourth place and it seemed unlikely I'd be eliminated with only one question left. I just wanted a cheeseburger and a nap.

"One last question for the group. None of you have officially met me. So why do you want to marry me?"

I was so focused on my growling stomach that I barely heard the other girls' answers. When it was Peggy's turn, her voice jolted me out of my reverie and I realized I only had one more person before it was my turn. I considered his question. Why did I want to marry him?

Peggy giggled before she finished by saying, "And it doesn't hurt that you're handsome." Her answer got her a perfect score and suddenly the audience was on their feet, cheering as the coins dropped. I looked at the screen and saw she'd bumped me from fourth place. I tried to relax my shoulders. I was still fifth. It didn't matter that the girl sitting next to me was in sixth and only two points behind me. She'd have to get at least three, but if I got at least a three then I would still be ahead of her. I was fine. I was still here. Her answer would be stupid and I'd be in the final five. It would be fine.

"Rachel, what do you think?" Andy asked her. "Why do you want to marry Lincoln?"

"A few years ago I had a best friend who was one of the most amazing men I'd ever met. He was kind and generous. He was the type of person who would not only give you the shirt off his back but would take you to the store and buy you several more." Rachel's voice cracked a little. "He died last year."

The audience said "ohh" in such a synchronous way I almost thought the running man had decided to run around with a sympathy sign.

41

"Months after he passed I saw an interview of Lincoln on TV. He immediately reminded me of my friend. It made me want to see him more, so I started watching every interview and reading every article. I realized that Lincoln was the same type of person as my friend. You could see it in his eyes. Knowing what kind of man he is, who wouldn't want to marry him?"

An audible swoon-like sigh spread through the room and a few people clapped. When enough time had passed, Andy said, "That was beautiful. Thank you, Rachel. Let's see what Lincoln thinks."

My heart sank with each coin's *clink*. They finished falling into the bag and just like that I was in sixth place. Ten. I could barely believe it. She was eight points ahead of me.

No.

My life flashed before my eyes. Okay, not really, but my career sure did. My name on the cover of *Look!* My corner office with a personal assistant just outside the door. The VIP treatment at New York Fashion Week. It was all gone in a flash. I was never going to become an award-winning journalist. I was going to be fired and I'd never find another job because word would get out that I'd been fired from the top fashion magazine in the country. Everything I'd worked for – starting an e-zine for my high school, middle of the night tampon runs for my so-called sorority sisters, the haranguing I'd endured in the Student Union when said sorority sisters saw the article I'd written on the front page of the local paper – it was all for nothing.

"Paige?" Andy said and from the tone of his voice it didn't sound like the first time he'd said it. Everyone was quiet and waiting for me to answer. And it had to be good. Really good. I had to get a nine in order to get back into fifth place. Think, Paige, think. Why did I want to marry Lincoln? Money? Looks? The alimony that would come from our inevitable divorce? The answer was simple, really. I didn't. No part of me had any desire to marry Lincoln.

"Paige." Andy's voice was a little firmer and I froze as I looked into the audience. I'd been silent for too long. I needed to say something. Anything. Pausing this long did not look good. At this point it couldn't even be described as a pause. It was silence. Complete, humiliating silence.

Say something. Say anything.

"I don't."

ANYTHING BUT THAT!

I silently swore. I had just guaranteed my departure.

Gasps sounded from the audience and even Andy's mouth fell open. He looked between me and the camera. Me and the camera. Then he closed his mouth, smiled as if I hadn't just given the worst answer in the world, and opened it to speak when I interrupted him.

"What I mean to say is that I don't – yet. I've never been particularly good at the whole dating thing, but I feel strongly about getting to know someone before committing to him. Everything Lincoln has done and accomplished is truly admirable. It's clear to me that he's a good person. But just because he's good doesn't mean that he and I will be compatible." I saw a few heads nodding in the audience. "My friend wanted me to come on this show. She knew that I admired Lincoln and she pushed me to take a chance. So I did. I took a chance to get to know 'The Most Eligible Bachelor of 2017.' I was excited to find out more about the 'Entrepreneur of the Decade.' Through the whole application process and the awe of being chosen, I've realized something. I don't want to fall in love with Lincoln Lockwood, the business mogul. I want to fall in love with Lincoln Lockwood, the man who isn't defined by a title, but defined by his heart. So I don't want to marry Lincoln Lockwood – *yet.*"

I took a shaky breath as Andy turned to the clapping audience. A few people stood and whistled, but the majority clapped from their seats. Andy didn't have to prompt Lincoln to give me a score. I glanced over my shoulder and watched as eight coins fell into my bag.

Eight. Which meant…

Rachel and I were tied for fifth place. I almost burst into tears. Tied was good, right? They'd keep us both, right? Right? They'd have six contestants instead of five? Right?!?!

The three lowest scoring girls were weeping into their hands. The fourth girl looked so murderous that I calculated how long it would take me to run to the exit in my wedge sandals.

Andy had moved to Lincoln's side of the curtain and was speaking again. I tried to focus.

"—an unexpected tie, which means you have quite a choice to make tonight." Andy came back into view and looked directly into the camera. "Who will be sent home? Rachel or Paige? Tonight, Lincoln will choose, but then it's your turn. America, get ready to vote for the woman you think should become Lincoln's future wife. See you next time on *Who Wants to Marry a Millionaire?*"

$$$

Once we were back at the house Wanda gathered us in the kitchen-slash-living area which I was beginning to think of as "home base" to tell us the plan for tonight. The five – no, four – lowest scoring girls hadn't been sent home yet. It seemed like that Lincoln still got to meet all of us. I stood in the back as Wanda talked and checked my phone. I had six texts from Jemma and one from Carla. I opened hers first.

> **Since Marie didn't book you a flight back today, I'm assuming you made it past the qualifying round. Congrats. Don't screw it up.**

That definitely didn't require a response. I'd wait to see if I was going to be sent home first. I couldn't wait to hear what she had to say about my interview.

"—at 7:00 p.m." Wanda's voice brought me back to the present. "It's formal, so be sure to dress appropriately."

"Is that when dinner is?" I whispered to the girl next to me.

She gave me a crusty look and said, "No, that's when we get one-on-one time with Lincoln before he sends people home."

"Okay, but what did she say about dinner?"

She gave me a disgusted look and stepped away from me.

"—you talk to him," Wanda finished. "Get some rest and we'll see you all for your grand entrance promptly at seven."

Everyone headed upstairs and I shuffled after them, my stomach growling. Was I the only one who cared about dinner?

44

Peggy was already in our room by the time I got there.

"I'm going to take a bath!" she announced the second I walked inside. "Do you need anything from the restroom?"

I waved a hand dismissively. "No, you go ahead."

"Great, thanks!" She shut the door behind her.

My stomach growled, and I clutched at it wondering if Marie had packed me any food. I looked at Jemma's texts to distract myself.

Call me. I'm DYING!

You're ignoring me aren't you. :(

If you don't call me soon, I'm throwing all your stuff out the window.

I looked at the time, but it was three hours later there and she'd still be at work. I quickly wrote back:

That window is smaller than a doggy door. I'd like to see you try.

I wasn't supposed to be downstairs for two more hours. Two more hours and I could be headed home. Without dinner. Ugh. It was like being grounded, but worse. Instead of losing my phone privileges, I lost my job. I shouldn't think about it. I was going to give myself an ulcer. At least that's what my mom always said whenever I told her all my worries. Glancing around the room I saw my laptop sticking out from my bag.

I opened a new document and began to type:

Aslkdfja;lskdjfalksjdfkaj;sf

I stared at my screen and deleted the letters. I could do this. Carla even said I was talented. That had to mean something, right?

The only thing real about reality TV is the lack of food.

No.

The only thing real about reality TV is the misuse of the word "luncheon."

Okay. I needed to try harder.

Aslkdfja;lskdjfalksjdfkaj;sf

That wasn't working. I closed my laptop. Other than my not-so-adventurous bathroom escapades this morning I had done nothing in the way of investigative journalism. I laid back on the pillows and twisted my hair around my fingers. I had to wait until we were all together again before I could find anything out. I wondered if Amelia was randomly chosen. If I had to guess I'd say she was. She seemed pretty sincere on the plane. And she was definitely surprised when she learned I was a contestant too. Maybe all the contestants were just like me - plucked from a stack of applications. I wondered if I could get my hands on all the applications that weren't picked. Could I get Andy to somehow give them to me? I pictured myself flirting with Andy and laughed out loud. That would be a joke.

Somewhere along the way my thoughts drifted, and I fell asleep.

$$$

"Paige? Paige?"

I blinked, realizing that I'd fallen asleep and swung my legs off the bed.

"What time is it?" I asked Peggy.

"Just after six o'clock. You should probably start getting ready."

I looked at her, completely dazzling in a shimmering gold gown with her hair pulled up, and I blanched.

"I slept for *an hour?*" I screeched and ran to the closet, thumbing through all the gowns.

"I'm sorry I didn't wake you sooner," Peggy said wringing her hands. "I thought you'd set an alarm and I didn't want to wake you up before it went off."

"No, it's fine. Thank you for waking me up." I held two dresses up side-by-side to compare them, before deciding on the black one.

"I'm going to head downstairs and see if I can find a snack before we start filming. Do you need any help before I go?"

"No, thank you." I paused in the middle of digging through my jewelry to shoot her a grateful smile as she left.

After showering faster than the Flash on fire, I did my makeup and curled my hair. Fortunately, my personal Lookbook allowed me to finish dressing in record time.

6:54. Just in time.

I allowed myself thirty seconds to admire (and double check) myself in the mirror. My hair wasn't as fancy as I had planned, but the chandelier earrings seemed to kick the low chignon up a notch. The simple, black Elie Saab gown with a lace bodice and flutter sleeves fit perfectly. Open-toed gold stilettos peeked out from beneath the floor-length skirt and the crystals on the heels made it look like I'd walked through a pile of glitter. I smoothed the dress one last time before heading downstairs.

I went straight to home base, but no one was there. Where had they said to meet? I turned the corner and found myself walking aimlessly down hallways trying to find the group. Were we supposed to be outside? Maybe I should start opening random doors. I knew I wasn't in the private part of the house, but this morning's encounter had left me skittish.

Sighing, I turned another corner and ran straight into someone's chest. I screamed before I could stop myself and took a step back, tripping over the hem of my dress. He caught me by the arms and steadied me.

"Andy," I said breathlessly, trying to calm my racing heart.

"Paige," he said and resumed tying his bowtie. I looked him up and down admiring his sleek black tux. He looked *good*.

"Shouldn't you be watching the intros?" he asked.

"I can't find anyone."

"They're just on the back deck." I looked at him blankly. "Outside the kitchen?"

"Oh, of course," I said and then gave him a sheepish look. "Mind if I follow you there?"

He jerked his head in a "follow me" gesture and we walked down another hall through a set of double doors and we were there. Andy pointed toward the others, indicating where I should go, and I nodded my thanks. Everyone stared at me as I hurried over and Amelia whispered something to the girl sitting next to her. Wanda stood in front of us gripping her phone to the point I thought the screen might shatter.

"Thank you for gracing us with your presence," Wanda clucked.

I waved a hand dismissively. "Please, the pleasure is all mine."

She glowered.

"You each have five minutes to be alone with him. Peggy, you'll go first." Andy led Peggy past the palm trees and the rest of us sat around the large wooden table to wait.

I was last once again. I spent the next forty-five minutes impatiently tapping my foot and imagining what we were going to have for breakfast the next day. My stomach cramped in pain from barely eating anything. One of the girls complained it was too cold so they turned on the outdoor heaters. I was slowly baking and estimated I would be fully cooked just before dawn. Peggy made friends with girls sitting across the room from me, so not only did I not have anyone to talk to, but I didn't have a shield from the daggers Amelia kept sending my way. My mood was worsening by the second.

I was tired. I was hungry. I was worried sick about being sent home. I was not cut out for reality TV.

When Wanda told me it was my turn, I was so hangry she had to remind me to smile. I did but based on her expression I believe it came off as menacing. I took a deep breath before I took the same stone path the others had taken behind some trees. I ignored my stomach and reminded myself that I had to be charming and not even hint at the fact I might be going home soon. I had to act like I belonged here.

"Hi," I said when I reached Lincoln. I saw the signal and knew the cameras were on me. He gave me a hug and then we sat down on the plush couch.

"It's Paige, right?" he asked.

"Yes," I said. "Paige Michaels. Remind me of your name?"

He chuckled politely. "Lincoln Lockwood. You might have heard of me."

I pretended to think. "I'm not sure, what is it that you do again?"

"I'm an entrepreneur," he said his smile just as dazzling as it had been that morning, but something about it made me think he looked plastic.

"Ooh," I shook my head in mock disappointment, "code for 'unemployed.'"

He laughed. "Then what do you do for work?"

"Ugh. I hate talking about work." I groaned dramatically so he knew I was kidding. I turned so my knees practically touched his. "Let's talk about something more interesting. Describe yourself in five words or less."

"What? I can't –" He laughed nervously.

"It's not that hard," I teased.

"Then you go first."

I held up a fist and counted down on my fingers. "Event planner. Southern. Manhattan. Hungry."

He grinned, genuinely this time, and I could practically see his guard fall.

"You chose 'hungry' as a word that describes yourself?"

I shrugged. "It's a perpetual problem. Now it's your turn."

He thought for a moment before copying my gesture of counting down. "Businessman. Artist. World traveler. Soccer. Intrigued."

"That's six words."

"The first five described me. The last one describes how I feel about you."

Chapter $6

An incredibly long thirty minutes later we stood in a line by the pool, waiting for Lincoln to send five of us home. The four lowest scoring girls were off to one side fighting back tears. Rachel and I stood in the middle, the four top-scoring on our other side. I looked around trying to find something mildly interesting to focus on. Wanda stood about ten feet away wearing lime green stilettos talking to a man setting up a giant light. My eyes zoomed in and tried to figure out whose design the shoes were even though I wasn't close enough to see the stitching or a trademark. Seconds later, I was distracted by a pair of black doc martens. My eyes traveled up the length of the man coming to stand next to Wanda.

Dang.

Tiny gasps and giggles escaped our group as he stopped at Wanda's side with his hands in his pockets. Lincoln looked like he'd just come from a photo shoot. Although, I guessed it was possible he had. His crisp white shirt was tucked into faded dark jeans and he wore a linen jacket that probably cost more than my rent. Andy joined him then. He was in a tailored black suit that fit so well my head tilted a little to one side. The top button of his shirt was undone showing off his deep tan and I gave thanks to the sun for not burning him the way it burned me. It would be a shame to ruin that skin. Lincoln muttered something to Andy that made him let loose a bark of laughter, then turned his back to us not at all concerned that ten women were salivating over him. Over both of them.

"Ladies, stop fidgeting!" Wanda yelled. We stilled as the cameras began filming. They panned our faces before coming to a stop on Andy.

As Andy finished his intro he looked to Lincoln. "You've met a lot of amazing women, Lincoln, and you'll be more compatible with some than others. America voted and tonight we say goodbye to five amazing women." He folded his hands in front of him and hung his head for a moment.

Crap, he made it sound like we were dying. Or being executed.

Or losing our jobs.

I choked back the urge to cry.

"Michelle, Anna, Lynda, Wendy, thank you for being a part of the show. It's been lovely to meet each of you. Please take a moment to say goodbye to Lincoln." He stood aside and gestured to Lincoln.

The whole ordeal was too much to handle for a woman with choppy blonde hair – Michelle, I think? She burst into sobs and ran into the house. No one made a move to follow her and this did nothing to ease my nerves.

Before the door had closed behind Michelle, another girl, whose name I couldn't remember, burst into heaving sobs. She launched herself forward and threw her arms around a startled Lincoln. He did his best to console her as she sobbed into his neck, awkwardly patting her back and shooting Andy "help me" looks. Andy had a look of concern on his face, but I couldn't tell if it was genuine. Part of me thought he was probably laughing inside. After a moment Andy gently pried her arms from Lincoln and she directed her pleas to him, muttering unintelligible words and ignoring the snot leaking out her nose.

It took several minutes for them to placate her to the point a few of the techs could lead her back into the house, but as soon as she was gone the next girl was already by Lincoln. Unlike the girl before she simply smiled, gave Lincoln a hug goodbye and left. Not a tear shed. I kind of wished she'd stayed instead of Amelia. Lincoln said goodbye to the last woman before Andy turned to the four girls on my left.

"Cut!" Wanda called out before he could open his mouth. My heart kicked into overdrive. Were they bringing someone back? "That was perfect. Let's get it once more for safety."

Never mind.

They ended up not only filming the goodbyes one more time but three more times. Each time Wanda directed them to repeat exactly what they'd done before. It was ridiculous considering it was "perfect" the first time. I felt bad for the women having to leave and come back several more times. Michelle didn't return, but the girl who'd cried and cried continued sobbing through all three takes. It was like witnessing someone's most embarrassing moment over and over. Every time she threw her arms around Lincoln, I imagined my exit and prayed I wouldn't cry. The world would think I was heartbroken when really it was because I was fired. By the time they were ready to move on, I was such a bundle of nerves I felt like I might puke, then faint and then wake up only to puke again.

Andy's voice yanked me out of my panic attack and I tried to hear through the pounding in my ears.

"Amelia, Carmen, Bunny, Peggy." He nodded to each of them in turn, all standing in perfect confidence. "Congratulations on making it into the top five. The four of you may go wait on the terrace."

Once they'd taken their places on the terrace, overlooking us like the four horsemen, Lincoln came to stand in front of Rachel and me. Andy removed two black envelopes from his suit jacket and grimly handed them to Lincoln.

Andy focused his solemn gaze on us. "The original plan was whoever scored the lowest on today's interview would be leaving us tonight, but this is a unique situation," he explained. "You both did well ending up with the same number of points. When Lincoln hands you the envelopes, you'll take turns opening them. Inside it will either be empty or there will be a plane ticket home. Paige will go first."

Lincoln stepped forward. "I want you to know that no matter who stays and who goes, I think you're both really amazing women."

Except for the woman who goes. She's less amazing. Let's face it.

Trying to stop my hands from shaking, I took the envelope. Your mind is stronger than your body, right? I commanded my hands to just stop trembling until I could open the envelope. Thirty-seconds. Tops.

Epic fail. My pale skin was a stark contrast to the black matte and it was painfully obvious that my fingers were vibrating like an earthquake. Hopefully, the cameras weren't zoomed in on my hands. I slid my forefinger under the flap and held my breath as the paper tore. I glimpsed a streak of white and my heart dropped, but when the envelope lay flat in my hand I realized it wasn't a plane ticket at all. A single word was written on the flap of the envelope in sparkly white marker:

Intrigued?

I didn't have time to process Lincoln's message, because Rachel was already tearing her envelope open with a vengeance. Upon viewing the plane ticket inside she roared ferociously. Cringing, I leaned away from her. She sounded like an angry elephant. I looked to Lincoln and Andy for direction, but they seemed equally shocked at her outburst. She began yelling obscenities at Lincoln. He backed up with pure terror in his eyes and the cameramen closed in on us capture every expression.

"Rachel, I –" but he couldn't get a word out. Rachel was screaming at him, interspersing her curses with half-sobs and declarations about how she loved him, but she was too good for him and he'd never find another woman like her.

With each word, she got closer and closer to him. Lincoln continued stepping back with a smile mixed with sympathy and fear. He was at the edge of the pool before Andy intervened. He tried to separate the two, but Rachel slapped him away. I frantically looked around until I found Wanda, who was jerking her head in a way that told me to get involved. I gave her an exasperated look. Wasn't it part of the producer's job to contain the crazies? At least she was getting paid to deal with overreactions. Shaking my head, I channeled my mom and purposefully strode toward the fight and put a hand on the woman's shoulder.

"Hey!" I yelled to be heard over her tirade. "Stop!"

Ugh. I groaned inwardly. I even sounded like my mom. Ignoring the revelation, I yanked on Rachel's shoulder and stepped between her and Lincoln. Putting my hands up as if calming a wild animal, I said in a soothing voice, "You're being filmed right now."

Realization dawned, and she momentarily stopped screaming, choosing instead to quietly seethe. Andy let out a tiny sigh of relief, but the cameramen didn't stop filming.

"That's it," I said to her, knowing I'd found her weak spot. No one wants to look crazy on national TV. Although I was pretty sure that ship had sailed. My eyes darted purposefully between her and the camera. "Just breathe. He's not worth it."

She took a deep breath and stepped back. The anger in her eyes flickered and she nodded as I talked.

"This isn't you," I said, even though for all I knew this was her reasonable side. "The stress of this competition is making you crazy. You're right. You're too good for this. He's not worth it."

Wanda started to speak, but I shot her a glare and she closed her mouth.

"But what am I going to do?" Rachel's rage was replaced with black mascara tears and she could barely speak through her sobs. "I - left - every - everything to come - here."

I nodded sympathetically because that's how you deal with crazy people. "I know it's hard, but you're strong. You're going to go home and meet some wonderful man who's going to love you more than Lincoln ever could."

Her sobs quieted, and she muttered to herself as she backed away. I nodded at the techs who had consoled the last girl and they hurried over. She allowed one of them to take her arm and lead her toward the house.

Those of us remaining, including all but one cameraman who'd followed her, heaved a collective sigh. I faced Andy and Lincoln, let my shoulders slump and the relief sink in. Rachel was gone. I could stay. I wasn't going to lose my job. At least not yet.

"Looks like you dodged a bullet there," Andy said to Lincoln under his breath.

"I'm definitely glad I chose you, Paige," Lincoln said, and then his eyes widened as he saw something behind me.

I turned just in time to see Rachel rushing toward me, screaming, "You planned this! You manipulative little –"

Andy stepped forward to shield me, but Rachel's wrath had given her super strength and she plowed into us, pushing Andy and me over the edge into the pool.

$$$

A shuffling noise woke me in the middle of the night. I'd gone to bed immediately following the elimination, too wet and exhausted to wait around for another quinoa dinner. I squinted at the blurred red numbers on the alarm clock. 2:00 a.m. I rolled over, trying to ignore the noise, assuming it was Peggy getting up to use the bathroom. When I didn't hear the bathroom door close, I reluctantly peeked over at her bed.

And screamed.

"What the –" I yelled, scrambling into a sitting position and clutching the covers. "What are you doing?"

Peggy was leaning over the edge of my bed watching me sleep.

"I didn't mean to wake you," she said in the same tone as that kid from The Sixth Sense. Goosebumps ran across my skin and I shoved my back against the headboard.

"What are you doing? Why were you standing over me while I slept?"

"It didn't wake you last night."

"This is the second night you've done this?" I screeched. I was living in a Stephen King novel with a Disney princess as the main character.

"You're pretty when you sleep," she said, her voice still that flat creepy tone.

No. Freaking. Way.

I clambered off the opposite side of the bed, keeping a good five feet between us, scooped the down comforter into my arms and grabbed a pillow. Without another word, I went into the bathroom, locked the door behind me, and made myself a makeshift bed in the claw foot tub.

Despite my awkward sleeping arrangements, I must have dozed off at some point because I woke to Peggy knocking on the bathroom door.

"Paige? I don't mean to be a bother, but you've been in there a really long time and I still need to get ready." Her voice was back to its normal sing-song nature.

I got out of the bathtub, stretching my stiff muscles while I gathered my bedding, and opened the door. She blanched when she saw me.

"What happened to you?"

"You're kidding, right?" My voice was hoarse and venomous.

"No," she shook her head, astonished. "What happened?"

"I woke up to Chuckie watching me sleep." I pushed past her into the bedroom and dumped the blanket and pillow on my bed.

"Oh no." She wrung her hands. "I was afraid this would happen."

"What would happen?" I spat.

"Sometimes I sleepwalk - or talk - and do odd things in the middle of the night. My roommates in college used to lock their bedroom doors at night. I've lived on my own for the past couple years, so it barely crossed my mind that it might happen when I came here. I'm sorry if I scared you."

"Scared me?" I slammed the closet door shut after grabbing what I needed. "You terrified me. How would you feel if you woke up to find a complete stranger standing over you looking like she was contemplating how to get away with murder?"

Peggy winced. "I wouldn't be very happy. I'm completely asleep when it happens so I never remember what I did."

I almost felt bad for her. I probably would have if I'd gotten a good night's sleep.

"It's fine," I said because I didn't know how else to respond. Of course, my roommate was a sleep-psycho. That's just my life.

"I'm sorry."

"It's not your fault." Unless I ended up smothered with a pillow. I took my things into the bathroom. "You don't mind if I shower first, right?"

I didn't wait for an answer, just shut the door behind me.

$$$

Breakfast was another array of fruit and protein smoothies. I chose a pink smoothie thinking it was the safest bet, but it ended up tasting like Pepto Bismol. I was so hungry I forced myself to swallow at least half of it before my gag reflex took over.

"Ladies," Wanda said, coming into Home Base, "In exactly one hour we will start preparing for the first task. All of you should be familiar with the rules, but to refresh your memory there will be three group tasks. The winner of each task is automatically safe for that round and will be awarded a date with Lincoln. The first task will be rated all or nothing, no points will be awarded. The winner will be safe from elimination and the other four contestants will remain on equal footing. The second task is viewer based. The viewers will score each of you as they watch your progress throughout the race. The lowest score will be eliminated. The third task only allows the first three that finish to move on. There will then be the final task. The final three contestants will each get ready for her potential wedding and the lucky bride will be announced during a live airing of the final episode. Meet in the driveway in twenty minutes."

All of us were quiet and somber. My stomach twisted in a way that had nothing to do with hunger. Even though Lincoln said I intrigued him, that didn't necessarily mean I was safe. I needed to make the most of my time here. If I could find enough dirt before the next elimination, I might be able to keep my job even if I came in last.

Most everyone, including the cameras, followed Wanda when she left. Only one other girl remained, and she was eating a mound of honeydew at the counter. I headed over hoping she was in a secret-sharing mood.

"I'm Paige," I said and shook her hand.

"Carmen," she said with a smile. Carmen's name fit her perfectly. Her hair was the color of brown-sugar with blonde woven throughout and her brown eyes were flecked with gold. "Where are you from Paige?"

"Manhattan," I replied. "You?"

"Oh, I just love New York. The fashion alone is to die for!" She squealed like a teenage girl who'd just gotten asked on her first date. "I'm from Southern Florida. Are you nervous about the first task?"

"A little. This is all new to me." I sighed dramatically and lowered my voice conspiratorially. "Sometimes I wonder if I'm here for the right reasons, you know?"

"You're gorgeous. The gorgeous ones always do well on TV," she assured me with a warm smile. "So, where are you from?"

I blinked, wondering if she was kidding. "Manhattan," I repeated.

"Oh, I just love New York. The fashion alone is to die for!"

I tilted my head. Maybe she was just nervous. There were four other women to remember, after all, and she seemed genuine and friendly.

"I'm a bit fashion-obsessed myself," I said, deciding to write the whole thing off and be direct. "What made you decide to enter the competition?"

"Oh, I'm a *huge* fan of reality TV. Have you seen the one where couples are put on an island and have to capture all the buffalo?"

My eyebrows shot up. "Can't say that I have."

"It's amazing! But even if we didn't give totally honest answers during the interview, we all know why we're really here." She glanced around and then her voice dropped. "Did you see that Lincoln was ranked number fifty-one on the list of richest men in America?"

"I didn't."

"It's hard to believe a millionaire with a butt as cute as his is single." Carmen winked.

"It's a rare phenomenon, that's for sur—" I stopped as Carmen stood up. I assumed she needed another drink or something, but she adjusted her skirt and walked away as if we hadn't been talking at all.

I watched her leave home base without a backward glance, stunned at the abrupt ending to our conversation. Flummoxed, I realized that now Carmen had left I was alone once again with another fifteen minutes to kill. I plopped down on a couch and called Jemma.

"Hello?" A sleepy voice answered.

"Oh, Jemma, I'm sorry." I slapped my forehead. "I totally forgot you'd be asleep right now."

"Paige?"

"Yeah, it's me," I said. "But go back to sleep, I'll call you later."

"Don't be ridiculous," she said, now sounding fully awake. "I haven't heard anything from you and I've sent you a billion texts. Tell me everything."

I filled her in on my awkward run-in with Lincoln while snooping and the elimination the day before. When I told her I was pushed into the pool she laughed so hard I could just picture her rolling around on the floor.

She finally calmed down. "I cannot wait to see the first episode tonight. Only you could make sarcasm seem intriguing."

"Let's hope America finds me as intriguing as he does. I need this to work."

"It'll work," Jemma insisted. "Who wouldn't fall in love with you?"

I looked around the room to make sure I was still alone. "I don't want him to fall in love with me. I want him to keep me around long enough for me to get my story."

"That'll work too."

I heard Wanda's voice in the distance.

"Gotta run," I said in a low voice. "We're about to film the first task."

"Text me when it's over!"

Chapter $7

Obstacle courses are fun!

At least that's what I kept telling myself as I toed the red line painted on the grass. We all stood on one side of a football field looking down the length of it at a giant red and yellow inflatable death trap advertised as an obstacle course. On the other side of the inflatable was an above ground pool where I was supposed to fish out a key that would unlock a door to what looked like a concrete box where, where yet another challenge lay. After that there was a maze of some kind, then something involving food – which was the only part of this course that I was a fan of – and then finally trivia. Lincoln waited at the opposite end of the field and the first one to reach him would win the first date. The whole thing practically guaranteed viewers would give you an unfortunate, but clever, nickname to haunt you through the rest of the show.

My competitors were stretching and running in place to warm up, whereas I was preoccupied staring at my neon yellow yoga pants and bare feet. Of course, the only redhead got neon yellow. At least the cameras wouldn't be able to capture my expression because my ghostly pale face would be totally washed out. The other four girls wore nearly identical outfits except for each pair of pants was a different color neon.

Wanda assured us that because of the complexity of this task, it would only be filmed once. I tried to be grateful I wouldn't have to embarrass myself multiple times just so they could get the right angle, but a part of me was certain it would take approximately thirty seconds for me to do something stupid, consequently embarrassing me to the point I'd want to dig a hole and live like a hobbit for the rest of my life.

"Ready?" Wanda called.

I looked over my shoulder. Andy stood next to her, in light-colored jeans and a striped buttoned up shirt, not bothering to contain his glee at my discomfort. Why he was singling me out I had no idea. I grumbled as the others took their spots next to me. Bunny's foot was inching forward, almost at the red line, ready to cross it as soon as the shots rang out. The cameras took a few minutes to pan each of our faces – Amelia's determined, Bunny's nervous, Peggy's eager, Carmen's bored, and mine…well, we don't need to talk about that – before Wanda fired one of those guns used at horse races.

Reminding myself that my career was at risk, I booked it toward the inflatable. I groaned as I saw the rope handholds we needed to use to climb up a sloped side, like running up a playground's slide. Gritting my teeth, I jumped onto the death trap without a moment's hesitation. I stumbled, losing my footing on the slick vinyl, but managed to grasp one of the ropes and pull myself up.

Amelia and Peggy were ahead of me, but I was just grateful I hadn't fallen. The vinyl was hot from the afternoon sun and my bare feet kept slipping to the point I was only using my upper body strength. Which, admittedly, wasn't a whole lot. Luckily the climb wasn't long, and I was soon at the top and sliding down the other side on my stomach. I'd just gotten up when Bunny slid into my legs, knocking my feet out from under me and we fell in a heap. She "accidentally" elbowed me in the ribs while trying to stand up and then she was rushing forward to the tube we had to climb through.

I made a noise somewhere between a growl and a groan and hurried after her. Settling on my hands and knees, I made my way through the tunnel, the vinyl pressing against me from every side. I felt like I was being hugged by the giant marshmallow from Ghostbusters. Barely able to breathe, I hoped against hope that the inflatable didn't suddenly pop and leave me inside to suffocate. (It's a legit worry, okay?)

Once out of the tunnel I stood on the edge of a giant square pit with foam at the bottom and a wire above me. I watched as the other girls zoomed across the pit holding tight to a bar that was dangling the wire. It appeared to be a zip line. I pretended I wasn't afraid, if only for the cameras, and grabbed the bar above my head. Swearing worse than my Uncle Mike, I launched myself off the edge and flew across the foam pit. I must have closed my eyes at some point because I didn't realize I was at the end until I came to a sudden stop. The force jerked me backward making me lose my grip and causing me to teeter on the edge.

Somehow my feet managed to balance my body and I slid down the other side into the pool. The cool water felt amazing on my hot skin and my head broke the surface just in time to see Amelia hop out and run, soaking wet, to what had looked like a big concrete box from far away. It now just looked like a concrete wall with a metal door on one side. She shoved in the key and the door slammed shut behind her.

Bunny, Carmen, and Peggy were desperately searching the water for their keys. Peggy dove under every few seconds but kept coming up empty-handed. I swam forward until my toes touched the bottom but yelped as my big toe stepped on something jagged. I peered through the water and saw something bright yellow by my feet.

The key.

Finally, things were going my way.

Instead of diving down to pick it up, I wrapped my toes around it and pulled my foot up until my hand could reach. My fingers caught hold of the piece of neon yellow fabric tied to the key. I hopped out of the pool faster than I thought was humanly possible, practically teleported to the door, and yanked it open.

Once I saw what was inside I almost screamed.

I'm not a particularly sporty person. Okay, so the only sport I ever even attempted was baseball and that was only because my brothers made me pitch so they could practice. Once they realized I had no depth perception, hand/eye coordination, patience, motivation, or pretty much any other sports-related quality, they stopped asking. They'd gone back to taking turns pitching and I'd gone back to writing fairy tales in my tiny purple journal.

So you can understand my horror when I walked into this giant box I'd correctly assumed was a torture chamber to find a small, open-ceilinged, basketball court. Amelia was shooting the ball as if she could calculate the exact distance it would need to cross in order for the ball to reach the hoop. I watched as the ball went through the net without even touching the rim. A loud buzz made her smile and her eyes focused on something above my head. I looked up and saw five names on a scoreboard. She smiled smugly as the number three lit up beside her name. A door on the opposite end of the court opened and she ran out. At that second, Carmen and Peggy flew through the door I'd just come through and after a brief look around they ran to grab a basketball. I followed them, my fear temporarily suspended. My still wet feet made a squelching sound as I hurried to grab the nearest ball.

The exit had unlocked when Amelia scored three points. It seemed we each had to score three points before we could leave. I threw my ball at the hoop. It knocked against Peggy's and spun off in a different direction. She gave me a look that made me wonder if she really was going to kill me in my sleep before running after her ball. I ran in the opposite direction to get mine. It wasn't until I reached the corner that I noticed the cameramen. I'd completely forgotten about them, but there they were, two of them in one corner and another running behind Bunny, who'd just arrived.

The scoreboard buzzed and a three appeared next to Carmen's name. The side door opened, and she ran outside. I continued to throw the basketball, or shoot the basketball, or whatever it was called, desperately trying to score. I knocked Peggy's ball in once and she gave me a grateful look. I nodded like I'd meant to do it if only so she'd reconsider my murder. Soon enough, Peggy was through the door. Moments later Bunny was too. I was alone with one camera-man, who looked to me like he was bored out of his mind. I felt kind of bad for him having to watch a journalist – ahem, event planner – shoot baskets with all the finesse of a monkey throwing bananas. Eventually, it must have been too much for him because he left through the entrance.

The second he was gone I ran to the exit and pushed on the door. It wouldn't budge. I roared in frustration. No one said *anything* about having to be good at basketball! If I'd known this was a requirement I wouldn't have even tried to save my job, I would have just gone home like the loser I was.

The entrance banged open and for a second, I thought the pro-ducers had taken pity on me and were letting me leave without making my three baskets. I relaxed and was somewhere between furious and relieved when I saw Andy jogging over to me.

"Finally," I said, irritated. It wasn't his fault I was a crappy bas-ketball player, but it bugged me that they let me struggle for so long. Everyone else was probably already done with the entire course. I threw the ball at him in frustration, which he caught without even blinking. "I've been here so long that even the cameraman got bored and left. I'm tired, I'm wet, and *now* I can't get the door open." I waved my hand angrily at the exit.

"It's locked electronically. You have to make three baskets before it'll open." He pivoted on his heel and threw the ball. It *swooshed* as it fell through the net. He ran forward, grabbed the ball, and did a weird jump thing under the basket and scored another point.

I gritted my teeth. "Point proven. You're good at basketball. I suck. Can we go now?"

He smiled crookedly and even halfway across the court I could see his dimple. He dribbled (ha! at least I knew *one* term) his way back to me. He turned the second he reached me, looked at the bas-ket, then back at me as he threw the ball.

Swoosh!

I blushed. "Fine. You're *great* at basketball. Hurry up and get me out of here."

The ball bounced underneath the basket and another point was added to the number by my name. It was only when I heard a click from the door behind me that I realized what he'd done.

"*Now*," he said, his arrogance coming off him in waves, "we can go."

"Are you sure you can make it through the door with that big head of yours?" I didn't bother keeping teasing voice low as followed him through the now open door.

The door swung shut behind us and once again we stood on the green turf of the football field. Ahead of us were stacks of hay that formed a wall five bales high. In the middle of the wall was an opening. I stared at it, unmoving, before I said to Andy, "Okay, I'm in last place. I lost. Take me home so I can dry off."

I started toward the bleachers, but Andy yanked me back.

"Ow!" I rubbed the shoulder he'd yanked. "What the heck?"

"You haven't lost. Not yet." He looked around us frantically before grabbing my hand and pulling me to the side of the maze. Now we were at the side of the maze I saw a long wall of hay that ran nearly the rest of the field. "Run."

He dragged me behind him at a brisk pace until I wrenched my hand out of his and stopped to catch my breath, hands on my knees. "What are you doing?"

Apparently, he didn't need to catch his breath, because his chest barely rose and fell. "Running. You have to get to the end."

"Why? I'm too far behind. Why does it matter if I finish?"

"The others are still in the maze," he said. "If we hurry, you can be to the exit first and on to the next task."

"Isn't that cheating?"

"If you're not cheating, you're not trying." His eyes lit up and he took my hand again and we ran. We ran and ran. I had a whole new appreciation for football players because even with Andy literally pulling me along it was freaking *hard*. We came to an abrupt stop a few feet from the end of the wall. He peeked around the corner.

"Perfect. They're not here yet." He seemed to relax and almost looked bored as he brushed hay off his striped shirt. Even though he was in dress clothes he didn't seem the least bit sweaty. He didn't even look like he'd been running. Other than a few pieces of hay and some dirt on his shoes, his clothes still looked immaculate. "You should go."

"Why are you helping me?" I was bent over, my hands on my knees, trying to slow my heart rate and being grateful that I'd still been wet when we started running. My clothes were almost dry now, but they'd kept me cool.

"You have to win." He shrugged. "Wanda wants you to have the first date."

"Why?"

He rolled his eyes and gestured for me to go around the corner as if I'd just exited the maze. "Does it matter? The longer you keep questioning this the closer the other girls are going to get and the more likely they'll catch you cheating. Go! You still have two more tasks and those you'll have to get through on your own. Just make sure to choose the table next to me."

He shoved me forward and I scowled at him as I turned the corner. A few yards in front of the maze's exit were five tables with long white tablecloths. Each table had three small boxes on them. The boxes were the size of a shoebox tied with a light green bow like a present. To my surprise, Andy was already at the head of the far-right table. He winked at me, but before I could roll my eyes two cameramen backed out of the maze, their cameras trained on the two girls who'd just exited. Peggy and Carmen.

Andy indicated we should each choose a table. Following his lead, I chose the one he was closest to and Carmen and Peggy chose the two next to me.

"The game is simple. You choose a box and then eat whatever is inside."

"What?!" Peggy asked alarmed.

He went on like he hadn't heard her. "You only have to choose one box. In order for you to move on you have to eat whatever item is inside it."

Amelia arrived then. Carmen chose one of the boxes on her table and tore into it. Amelia took Carmen's cue and was opening a box before Andy had even explained to her what she was supposed to do. Bunny got there just as Carmen squealed, dropping her box and jumped back. A cameraman pushed past her and got so close to it, I couldn't see what was inside. But I guessed Amelia could see it because she let go of her half-open box like it was riddled with Anthrax. Peggy and I looked at our boxes warily and each took a small step back. Bunny still hadn't moved to her table, standing as far away as possible without actually going back in the maze.

Andy casually moved to my side and clasped his hands behind his back. I looked at my three boxes, but just as I reached out to pick one up, Amelia gasped, and my hand jerked back. The cameras were no longer blocking my view and I saw what the problem was. In front of Carmen sat a clear plastic container holding a single beetle. Amelia's hands were over her mouth and I shifted to see a disgusting flesh-colored blob of what looked like someone's brain in front of her.

Something lightly pressed the top of my foot and I almost jumped out of my skin sure it was some deadly creature. Upon looking saw Andy's shoe foot resting on top of my bare foot. I glanced at him, confused, and he looked pointedly at my boxes as if to say *hurry up*.

Bunny had finally gotten to her table and was visibly working up the courage to choose a box. Peggy was unwrapping a box so slowly you'd think she was saving the wrapping to reuse. Andy stepped on my foot again. He was right. I had to hurry.

I reached for the far-right box and was about to pick it up when the pressure on my foot was harder this time. I glared at Andy, but his face was neutral. I reached for it again and Andy squished my toes once again.

What was he doing? I thought he'd said he needed me to win. Why was he slowing me down?

It wasn't until he stepped on my foot a third time and gave me a look that practically screamed, "Hey stupid! At least *try* to understand," that it dawned on me what he was attempting to do.

I reached for the middle box and he stepped on my foot again. Without hesitation, I picked up the third box, briefly waited to make sure I'd gotten the right one and smiled when my foot remained untouched.

A retching noise made me look up and I saw Carmen throwing up several yards away. Amelia swayed where she stood, and her face looked slightly green, but she appeared to be keeping the flesh-colored blob down. Bunny was still staring at her unopened boxes and Peggy was about to eat a fried…something. I ripped open my box, trying to ignore the others, and almost gagged when I saw what was inside – three finger-like brown things.

Crap. Andy was quite literally making me eat crap.

I glowered at him and didn't stop my imaginary self from punching him in the face. He didn't return my dirty look. Instead, his gaze was soft, and he licked his lips.

It didn't seem like he was licking his lips mockingly, but I really couldn't be sure. I gagged as I picked up the first stool, my fingers sticking to its sides. I looked at him desperately, but he gave me the smallest nod. At least I think it was a nod. He barely moved his head. Either way, I decided to trust the man who'd already cheated his way through two tasks for me. I squeezed my eyes shut and before I could change my mind and throw the poop in Andy's face, I shoved it in my mouth. My stomach was already roiling, and I covered my mouth to hold back the puke, but nothing came. Whatever I was eating was definitely not poo. Unless poop was made with chocolate. Actually, it tasted like…a brownie.

Brownies.

I don't think I've ever smiled quite so wide. I shoved the rest of the brownie in my mouth and ran through the curtain, an unsteady Amelia right behind me. Five tables identical to the ones before were in a line, but these tables each had a chair. Farther down, almost to the bleachers, a limo was parked. I debated running straight for the limo but screeched to a stop at one of the tables instead. Amelia practically fell into the chair at the table next to me. A blank piece of paper and pen rested in the middle. At least I wanted it to be blank.

To my chagrin, when I sat down and flipped the paper over there were five short-answer questions.

1. What do you like most about Lincoln?

(His money.) His smile.

I scribbled down my answer, being careful to only write one that *wouldn't* get me kicked off the show.

Just then, Peggy burst through the curtain and although she looked a little pale, she seemed fine overall. She stumbled her way to a table and sat down. I glanced over at Amelia and my anxiety kicked up a notch seeing her furiously answer the questions. Determined not to get distracted again, I went back to my quiz.

2. What color are Lincoln's eyes?

(Uhh…) *Brown*

3. What is Lincoln's favorite activity?

(Seeing what ridiculous things he can get women to do for a date.) *Football*

4. Where was Lincoln's childhood home?

(With his parents.) *With his parents*

5. Where does Lincoln want to get married?

(How the h*** do I know?!) *Somewhere on a beach*

My chair fell over as I pushed away from the table and, in true Paige style, I went with it and landed in a heap. Swearing, I climbed up and ran toward the limo, noticing out of the corner of my eye that Bunny and Carmen had arrived at some point and were busily completing their quizzes. I was feet away from the limo's door when Amelia suddenly cut me off and threw her elbow into my stomach.

I slowed my pace with a ragged breath, clutching my stomach, both annoyed and impressed at her fortitude. Was violence allowed? If only I'd known…

Getting the wind knocked out of me slowed me down enough that Amelia reached the limo door first. Just as she did, Lincoln stepped out of it, his black loafers looking out of place on the raked dirt. The game was over. I put my hands on my knees, trying to catch my breath. I didn't have it in me to feel bad for losing. I was too busy rubbing the now forming bruise on my ribs. Actually, my first thought was of Andy. He said I was supposed to win. Was he going to get in trouble for not trying harder to get me through the course? Then again, what else could he have done? Broken Amelia's legs?

The moment the last of the girls arrived, the five of us were pushed together and Andy and Lincoln stepped in front of the camera. To my surprise, Andy immediately disqualified Amelia for poor sportsmanship. I smiled smugly. It would drive her crazy knowing that she would have won if she didn't cheat. But when I saw the demented look on her face and wondered if Carla would agree to buy me a gun for protection. Between Amelia's overly competitive nature and Peggy's sleep-stalking, I wasn't quite sure I was safe.

"Congratulations, Paige!" Andy clapped a few times to showcase his fake pride, jerking my attention back to him. "You've won the first date with my friend, Lincoln." He put his arm around Lincoln and patted his chest like you would pat a dog you were showing off.

"Thanks," was all I managed to say. What had just happened? I knew Andy helped me cheat, but how did they arrange the rest of it? If Amelia hadn't elbowed me in the stomach, would she have been disqualified, based on her answers to the quiz? Based on Andy's earlier comment and helping me bypass the maze, I was certain I already knew the answer.

"Join us tomorrow night to see Lincoln and Paige on their first date. Get ready by downloading our app so you can rate the date as the night goes on. Should Paige be the one who marries a millionaire? You decide. Have a good night, everyone!" He and Lincoln waved at the camera and I genuinely smiled as another cameraman got close-ups of each of our reactions. But I wasn't smiling about winning the date. No, I'd won the first round because the producer cheated which meant I'd just gotten my first scoop. I was officially one step closer to saving my career.

LOOK! EXCLUSIVE

cheater, cheater, chocolate eater
by an Anonymous Contributor

We've already seen *The Bachelor. American Idol* is so done it's a dry, shriveled piece of chicken. And *Dancing with the Stars*…okay, we still like that one. So who can blame us for thinking *Who Wants to Marry a Millionaire?* would be worth watching? I mean, of course, we'd give it a shot. It's like that nice guy you meet at a bar that technically has nothing wrong with him other than the fact he's not the really hot guy at the other end of the bar. It's just polite to give him a chance. Which is why, when I watched *WWTMAM* last night I was thinking the same thing. Ehh. Nice guy. No spark.

It's true that there weren't any romantic sparks, but there certainly were some dangerous ones. Between Rachel pushing the other contestant into the pool and Amelia elbowing Paige in the stomach, there was more than enough to keep someone entertained for an hour. It was like watching a bad date. Painful, but you knew it'd be a good story.

The juiciest stuff was, as usual, off-screen. Lucky for us, we've got an inside source, and now so do you. According to our anonymous source, the lie detectors that determined who would stay and who would go? Fake. The contestants were chosen long before they arrived. Turns out the winner of the first task was chosen beforehand too. Our source says Paige was in last place for most of the round and still managed to "miraculously" win.

The round ended with a *Survivor*-like challenge of eating something out of a mysterious box. We all swore with Paige as we saw what was in hers. Crap. She was being forced to eat crap. Except it wasn't. Multiple sources report seeing Andy give Paige a signal saying it was alright to eat the… brownies. Yummy, yummy, brownies in rather unfortunate shapes. All the other contestants were forced to eat unmentionable things – seriously, I can't mention them without gagging – and Paige gets off with eating brownies? Really?

What else are the show's producers hiding? It almost makes you want to watch the next episode. Fortunately, you can save yourself the trouble and read all about it – the real story – right here on *Look!*

Chapter $8

"Good work, Paige. I'm pleasantly surprised." Carla rarely said "good work" to anyone and it made me float to cloud nine. About an hour earlier I'd emailed her my first article hastily written in the Notes app on my phone. I was silently congratulating myself when she said, "We're pushing it live tomorrow."

Live? As in *online*? Ready for search engines to find and for people to see?

"Carla, no!"

"Excuse me?"

I backtracked. "I just mean that if you publish this article tomorrow then the cast and crew of the show are going to see it. *Lincoln* will see it."

"I've read the piece multiple times and in it you give no indication of who you are or who your source is. The producers will probably assume it's a fan theory *Look!* published as a puff piece."

"And if they don't?" My breaths were shallow, and I lowered my voice even though I was alone in my room. "I signed a confidentiality agreement. I could go to prison for this."

Carla scoffed. "You'd be fined, not sent to prison. A few thousand dollars at the most. Besides, they'll suspect the show's staff first, not the contestants. The producers won't think any of their contestants are stupid enough to throw away the possibility of marrying into money."

"I can't afford a fine of a few thousand dollars! I can't even afford a fine of a hundred dollars. Besides, how am I supposed to remain undercover if everyone is looking for me?"

She groaned. "Fine. I'll publish whats-her-name's article about James Franco's new goldfish. It's dreadfully boring, but it does have a cute picture of his dog looking through the fishbowl. We'll make sure the picture is bigger than the article."

Relief swelled inside me and I let out a long sigh. "Thank you."

"We'll publish your article in two days. Get me the next installment by then."

She hung up before I could protest again. I flopped onto the bed face-first.

$$$

"That chick should have played professional rugby," I said to Andy, referring to Amelia elbowing me earlier, as we climbed the stairs to the deck. Hours had passed since the first task and dinner tonight was supposed to be a barbeque. My growling stomach was intrigued to see how a millionaire interpreted the word. "Please tell me that was planned."

"Nope," Andy said. "Amelia was a complete surprise to everyone."

"Good to know my bruised ribs weren't premeditated."

"Not this time."

"But there are plans for the future?"

Andy raised his eyebrows. "You never know what a reality show will cook up."

He veered to the right as I took a seat at the ornately decorated wooden picnic table. Not only did it have a tablecloth and placemats, but it also had cloth napkins, charger plates, and tiered candles. A leafy green plant was in the middle of the table on top of a crystal pedestal. The setting sun cast a warm glow on the table and I felt the day start to wash away in the dimming light.

A barbeque indeed.

"Everyone please take a seat. We're about to start." Wanda clapped her hands to get our attention.

The other women took their seats, two of us on one side of the table and three on the other. The head of the table was reserved for Lincoln. Wanda explained what shots the cameras were going to get and where Lincoln would enter. I sat by Bunny and Amelia sat directly across from me. She was doing her best to ignore my existence which I guessed was better than eliminating my existence. Still, the fear of her stabbing me with a steak knife didn't stop me from catching her eye and giving her a bright smile. She looked like a tea kettle about to explode.

After about twenty minutes of the cameras getting shots of all of us, my head began to pound, and my stomach rumbled. I kept fidgeting, wishing I could pull out my phone and check the time. Finally, Lincoln appeared and took his seat at the head of the table. I craned my neck to see if they were carrying the food out now that he was there.

They weren't. Wanda made Lincoln walk out and walk back in again two times before she decided the cameras had gotten the right amount of light. By this time the sun was almost down, and the twinkling lights strung around the patio were lit. After Lincoln greeted us they finally brought out the food. I wanted to make the comment that part of the fun of a barbeque was that the food was cooked outside, but I was so hungry I didn't dare open my mouth. Wanda would probably send me to bed without dinner if I criticized another of her ideas.

Servers in black button-up shirts set platters of fruit skewers and grilled vegetables on the table. Amelia took the tongs in front of her and picked some leaves off the plant in the crystal pedestal. My mouth dropped open, amazed that she could be so rude, but as Bunny copied her I realized what everyone else apparently already knew.

The pedestal didn't hold a plant. It held a salad.

It wasn't until the servers disappeared that I started to panic as I looked around at the table. Fruit. Vegetables. Salad. This couldn't be all the food. Was this just the appetizer? They were going to bring out the steak and burgers next, right?

Everyone began piling their plate with food. I did the same although I wasn't happy about it. A moment later the servers appeared once again and put down a plate in front of each of us. I eagerly awaited my plate, but when I saw what was on it I wanted to throw it across the room in protest.

It was salmon. A salmon so small it could have fit in the palm of my hand. Salmon so itsy-bitsy that even a Grizzly Bear wouldn't think killing it would be worth the effort. I was ready to bet I could finish it in five bites or less. A single lemon wedge adorned the other half of the plate. I stared solemnly at my near-empty plate before realizing Bunny was talking to me.

"I'm sorry, what was that?" I asked politely while stacking multiple fruit skewers on my plate.

Bunny's nose twitched, and her eyes flitted between me and my pyramid shaped collection of fruit skewers. It gave me the overwhelming impression of...well...a bunny. Her pale hair and darting eyes made me feel like she was preparing to steal my food and flee.

"I was just saying how awful this all is," she said.

"Oh," I said, relieved someone else felt the same way. "I know! When they said barbeque, I expected more than just fruit."

She nibbled on a pepper. "It almost makes me want to leave out of principle."

"I'm sure there will be more food later on. Or at least dessert. It's just," I picked up a skewer of honeydew, "they expect me to fill up on fruit? How am I supposed to survive?"

Bunny's eyes locked with mine and her voice took on a hard edge. "They can hear you, you know."

I glanced over my shoulder at Wanda who was talking with a tech. "Good, maybe they'll arrange for some real food next time."

"Not the producers. The fruit."

I'd heard her wrong. "I'm sorry?"

"The fruit can hear you," she spat. "The strawberries and bananas are already writhing in pain because of the skewers. They don't need your negativity too."

I blinked slowly. "What?"

"Ooh," she spoke as if she was talking to a little boy who'd skinned his knee, "here sweeties." To my shock, she picked up a few skewers, pulled off all the fruit, and threw each piece over the railing of the deck into the garden below.

I couldn't remember how to close my mouth.

"They want to touch the Earth," she explained as if it was the most obvious thing in the world.

"The fruit is talking to you?" I could only imagine the fodder this would give my next article.

"Of course. Don't they talk to you?" Bunny bit into a carrot.

"Can't say that they do."

"You need to listen harder."

"That must be it."

Bunny turned away from me to talk to Peggy, sitting across from her, which effectively ended the weirdest conversation I'd had so far. In my life.

"I'm Carmen." Carmen held her hand out across the table. I noticed the cameras pointed in our direction and so I tentatively took it.

"Paige."

"Where are you from, Paige?" she asked.

I stared at her for a moment before turning back to my plate and spending the rest of the meal silently eating salmon, vegetables, and salad. No fruit.

$$$

Two hours later the so-called food was cleared, and I was wishing I'd brought a jacket. And a pizza. I hugged myself and rubbed my arms trying to warm them. It was now completely dark. The only light came from the candles on the table and strands of bistro lights around the deck. I avoided thinking about the cold by praying for dessert. It was the least they could do.

"Thank you for joining us for dinner, ladies." I recognized the deep voice belonging to Andy and I swiveled in my chair to see him standing at the opposite end of the table. "Congratulations on making it into the top five. Over the next few days, you'll each have a chance to get to know Lincoln a little better. Paige, since you won the first task, you'll go out with Lincoln tomorrow evening. Keep in mind America will be watching. It's not just a first date with Lincoln. It's a first date with America."

I debated whether I should roll my eyes about his scripted lines or puke from nerves.

"You next task is the day after tomorrow." The day my second article was due. Andy smiled at each of us in turn. "Thank you again for joining us this evening. We'll see you tomorrow."

The cameras filmed each goodbye to Lincoln as he went around the table giving us hugs goodnight. When his arms wrapped around me he spoke softly in my ear. "Hope you're not afraid of heights." He was hugging Bunny before I could respond.

When the cameras stopped filming, Lincoln left, and Andy and Wanda started a ridiculously mysterious debate about the next day's events: "But what do we do about *the thing*?" "You have to make sure you-know-who gets everything set up at that place before it starts." After Lincoln was out of sight, more servers came out and started gathering the dishes. I leaned toward Carmen and said, "I guess this means there's no dessert?"

Carmen looked at me blankly, smiled and then said, "I'm Carmen. What's your name?"

I shook my head and followed Peggy back to our room.

$$$

"Dinner was delish, wasn't it?" Peggy said from the bathroom. We were still sharing a room, despite Lincoln only having five women left. Apparently, only the final two were given individual rooms.

"Hmm..." A grunt of indifference was the best I could do. I was flat on my bed, staring at the ceiling, painting imaginary pictures of triple-decker hamburgers and Kung Pao Chicken from that one Chinese place near where Jemma and I lived. I could never remember the name of it.

"I was pretty disappointed we didn't get more time with Lincoln," she continued content without a response. "We've been here two days and we've barely had a chance to speak with him."

"Hmm…" Was it called Mr. Wong's? Had I just made that up?

"It's going to be pretty hard to convince him to like us if we never get to talk."

"Hmm…" No, it was something untraditional. A weird name not even remotely associated with Chinese food.

"I think I'll see how breakfast goes and then readjust my strategy."

"Good idea." Jenny's Diner. That was it. Jenny's had the *best* egg rolls.

"What's your strategy?" Peggy came back into the room pulling her hair into a ponytail.

"Strategy?" I sat up. "For what?"

Peggy looked dumbfounded. "You can't win this game without a strategy. Paige, you have the first date. You have to be prepared."

"Isn't that the man's job?" She didn't get the joke, so I moved on. "What's your strategy?"

"Uh-uh." Peggy shook her head. "I'm not giving you any ideas. I like you and everything, but there's only one Lincoln Lockwood."

"Right." I rolled my eyes and laid on my side facing away from Peggy. She sighed loudly and finished getting ready for bed.

I was grateful when she finally turned off the lights, sure I'd fall asleep immediately. I tossed and turned for hours, holding a pillow to my stomach to muffle its growling. My eyes wouldn't stay closed. They kept flitting open without me realizing it until I found myself staring at the clock or the ceiling desperately trying to focus on anything but the wrenching hunger pains in my stomach. I got up and drank a glass of water. I tried chewing gum. I recited the entire Gettysburg Address from memory (thank you, Mrs. Peters, for making me memorize that in eighth grade). I squeezed my eyes shut and tried to remember reading my college math book. It always worked miracles at getting me to sleep in college. Usually during class. But it was useless. I couldn't sleep. Not with the monster clawing at my insides.

I rolled over for the thousandth time and screamed. Once again, Peggy was standing next to my bed, watching me sleep. I hadn't even heard her get up.

I cursed and threw my pillow at her. "Get away from me!"

"Watching you is soothing," she said in the same eerie Dakota Fanning voice she'd used the night before.

Scrambling out of bed, I grabbed my cell phone and stomped to the bedroom door.

"You are out of your *freakin' mind*," I snarled and yanked the door shut behind me.

I stood in the hallway unsure what to do. I missed Jemma. She never watched me sleep. Or if she did, at least she didn't let me know about it. A stabbing pain shot up from my bellybutton to my ribs and made me double over for a second. It was then I decided I'd had enough.

I wanted food and I wanted it now.

Chapter $9

"Everyone here is insane!" I hissed when Jemma picked up the phone.

"Why are you whispering?"

"Because it's 2:00 a.m. Everyone went to bed hours ago." I tiptoed to the doorway to home base and peered inside to see if it was safe to enter.

"And you're awake because...?" I heard her keys rattling and knew she was probably unlocking our apartment door. I opened my mouth to tell her my depressing tale when a sound came from the hallway. I ninja crouched behind the kitchen island and waited.

"Paige?" Jemma said. "You still there?"

I didn't say anything, straining to hear any other sounds.

"Paige, I don't mean to sound grouchy or anything, but you do realize I just got home from an eight-hour shift and feel like dead weight. If you're not going to speak to me I'm going to hang up and go to bed."

"Sorry," I whispered. "I thought I heard someone."

"Where are you?"

"In the kitchen trying to find food."

"Don't they serve you like a seven-course meal or something?"

"Sure." I crawled toward the fridge. "If you like quinoa and basil leaves. Half the girls here are anorexic, and the other half are vegetarian. Dinner drags on for hours because they're filming the whole thing and have to get every angle right, so I never get out of there in time to snag real food."

"Earlier you were including yourself in that 'insane' generalization, right?"

"I'm serious, Jemma. I am honestly fearing for my life. If I don't come back from this I want you to take all $782.43 in my savings account and give it to Reality TV Rehab, LLC in my name."

"Permission to take $20 to buy a pizza?"

"You're such a good friend." I reached the fridge and sat down in front of it. I felt like one of those cats who sat staring at the fridge until it was given milk.

"Why do you think everyone is insane?"

"I woke up in the middle of the night to find my roommate standing over me, watching me sleep."

Silence.

"She's the nicest person during the day, but at night she turns into Mr. Hyde."

"You need to get your own room."

"This other girl, Amelia, is a total brat. A girl named Carmen will be in the middle of talking to you and then just walk off like she realized she's got somewhere to be. And Bunny, I kid you not about the name, thinks fruit can talk. Apparently, at dinner tonight the skewers were hurting the fruit."

"Where did they find these people?"

"The internet."

"I knew Google couldn't be trusted."

"Isn't there at least one sane person on every reality show? Like Randy on American Idol or the cameraman on Teen Mom."

"I hate to say it, but it looks like it's you."

"Yet another qualification to add to my growing resume." I looked around to make sure I was still alone.

"Hey, it's better to be the sane one than the one who can't keep her clothes on," Jemma said.

"I'm not sure the two are comparable." I opened the fridge. "No."

"Okay, you can be the sane *and* slutty one."

"No," I moaned. "No, no, no, no, no!"

"Relax. I was kidding."

"The fridge is empty." I sat down again, letting the fridge doors fall open. The light revealed a perfectly clean, entirely empty fridge.

"What?"

"The fridge is empty," I repeated with dismay. "There aren't even any condiments."

"Were you going to eat mayo out of the jar or something?"

"No, I just… There's no food." My stomach growled as if it heard me.

"What about the cupboards?"

"Yes! Cupboards!" I shot up, barely trying to keep my voice down. I opened the cupboard closest to me. Empty. I opened the next. Empty.

"No, no, no, no, no!" I cried as I opened every cupboard and drawer in the room. All of them were empty.

"There's not even a stray packet of salt." I wanted to cry.

"Isn't that mansion massive?"

"Yeah."

"Shouldn't a home that big have food?"

"Your point?"

"There's got to be another kitchen."

"Well sure, in the private wing of the house. It's probably where they keep all the food."

"Go get some!"

"I'm not supposed to go over there," I said.

"Paige," Jemma said matter-of-factly. "You said yourself that you've barely eaten anything in two days. This is an emergency. If Mr. Millionaire can't feed his guests, then he's not the kind of person you want to marry."

"I'm going to put aside the fact you implied I'm going to marry him and focus on the fact that you basically just gave me permission to steal food."

"Once you're married half of everything he owns will be yours anyway."

"I'm hanging up now."

"Get some food!" I heard her cry as I pressed the end button.

I stashed my phone. I shouldn't go wandering around Lincoln's private rooms. I should just go back to bed. I would have some fruit in the morning. Far away from Bunny.

My stomach grumbled.

I crept down a dark hall without the slightest idea where I was going. Kitchens were usually at the back of the house, right? I didn't know where I'd heard that bit of info or if I'd just made it up, but it sounded good to me. All I had to do was stay by the windows that showed the backyard. I'd eventually run into the private kitchen.

At least that's what I thought until I ran into a dead end. A staircase to my left led upstairs and a staircase to my right led down. I looked back the way I'd come, contemplating bagging the mission. Right as I took a step to retreat a pain stabbed my stomach and I clutched at it.

Upstairs seemed like a good bet. I'd go up.

I turned the corner at the top of the stairs and practically cried out with relief when I saw a giant stainless-steel refrigerator. I flew toward it, my stomach hurt so much I no longer cared about being quiet. Inside I found a Valhalla of food.

Milk.

Eggs.

Turkey.

Chicken.

Bread.

Cheese.

Some amazing pasta salad-looking thing that convinced me my taste buds would explode upon eating it.

Then the motherlode: pie.

I lunged for the pie and tore through the drawers looking for some kind of utensil. I found an extra-large fork I'm sure was most likely meant for serving but used it to shovel the fluffy chocolate filling into my mouth.

I moaned.

Never, in my entire life, had anything tasted so heavenly. Still holding the pie, I rested my back against the fridge's closed doors and slid to the floor.

I was just starting on the second half of the pie (yeah, I know. Get over it.) when the light flipped on. I froze. I was hidden in my spot on the floor. Maybe whoever it was wouldn't come around the counter?

Bare feet padded on the floor and I squeezed my eyes shut using every ounce of willpower to tap into unknown superpowers and make myself disappear.

No such luck.

"Paige?"

I squinted up at Andy, dressed in a plain white t-shirt and Batman pajama pants. Heat blazed through my cheeks. His hair stuck up on one side and he was bleary-eyed as though he was still trying to wake up. He looked remarkably good for someone who'd just woken up. I cringed thinking of how I must look to him: a wild-haired pie-stealing savage holding a giant fork midair.

"Should I even ask what you're doing?" Andy ran a hand through his hair.

I smiled, praying I didn't have chocolate in my teeth. "I was hungry."

"Didn't you like dinner?"

"I'm from Texas. Barbeque is the kind of food you need a bib to eat. What we had tonight was not even close."

Andy shook his head but smiled, his tiny dimple appearing. He held out a hand to help me up. I stuck the fork in my mouth to free one hand and let him pull me to my feet.

"Thanks," I said, setting the pie and fork down on the counter. "How did you know I was here?"

"You're not the only one who needs snacks in the middle of the night. I was just getting out of bed when I heard someone. I thought it must be Lincoln."

"Right," I said looking down. "I'm sorry. I know I shouldn't have come to this part of the house, it's just that there was no food in the kitchen we're usually in and all we had for dinner was the world's smallest salmon on a bed of microscopic green leaves and I've been starving for the past two days and it would be pretty sad if water was the most filling thing in a millionaire's mansion so I knew there had to be other food and I just started wandering until I found this kitchen and then I saw the pie and it looked like a gift from heaven so I ate it."

Andy stared at me for a long moment, taking in my rambling speech, and then stepped past me to the fridge. He rummaged around for a second before pulling out bread and cheese.

"I'm going to make myself a grilled cheese. Do you want one?" His said this matter-of-factly like he did this every night.

"Really?" I raised an eyebrow.

"You can devour an entire pie, but I can't have a grilled cheese?" His tone was mocking, and I blushed.

"It was only half a pie."

"Yeah? You've got a tiny bit of whipped cream right," his thumb wiped the corner of my mouth, "there."

Butterflies flew across my skin, but he didn't appear to notice the way my breath caught, because soon he was heating up a pan on the stove.

"You're not going to turn me in?" I asked as I took a seat at the counter.

"For what?"

"For being in the forbidden wing." I added a spooky edge to my voice.

He laughed and poured me a glass of water. "I think you're safe."

"Really? Because I'm pretty sure if Wanda walked in right now I'd be sent home."

"No danger of that. Wanda isn't staying here."

"What? I thought the whole crew was staying here."

"Just me."

"Wow." I ran my finger around the rim of my glass. "How'd you get the gig?"

"Linc and I grew up together." He shrugged. "We've been best friends forever. I live here."

The journalist in me perked up at hearing this.

"So, was this show his idea or yours?"

He laughed as he put two grilled cheese sandwiches on plates and came to sit by me. "Neither, believe it or not. Wanda approached Linc late last year with the idea and it kind of spiraled from there."

"And Lincoln wanted you to host?"

"Wanda did, actually. I did an internship with KTLR."

"In production?"

He turned to face me, an amused look on his face. "Broadcast journalism."

"Where?"

"UCLA."

"When did you graduate?"

"Am I being interviewed?"

It took me a moment to realize he was joking.

"Oh, sorry." I let out a nervous laugh. "Sometimes my curiosity gets the better of me."

He resumed eating. "Your turn. Tell me about yourself."

"What do you want to know?" I said through a mouthful of cheese.

"Everything."

I raised my eyebrows, but he didn't retract his statement. I swallowed and said, "There's not really that much to tell. I'm an event planner in Manhattan, but I'm originally from a small town outside Austin. I have two older brothers who drive me crazy, but who I still love, and only partially out of family obligation. And I enjoy fashion, writing, and long walks on the beach." I winked at this last statement.

"Long walks on the beach, huh?" He took a drink. "Must be hard living in the city."

"Then I guess it's a good thing I'm here."

"I guess it is."

I finished off the last of my sandwich and was debating how rude it was to ask for a second, but before I could say anything Andy was at the stove making another one. Despite my still-grumbling stomach, I said, "You don't have to do that."

He gave me a skeptical look that said he didn't have a choice in the matter, he'd heard my stomach. Which made me smile because the last thing I wanted him to do was to stop piling cheese onto that slice of bread. Cheese had never looked so sexy.

"So, why'd you help me today?" I'd been wondering since it happened, but I couldn't figure out when I could ask him without anyone else around. Tonight was probably one of the only chances I was going to get.

He kept his back to me as he grilled. "I told you, you needed to win."

"Why me?"

"Wanda wanted you to have the first date." He shrugged. It was exactly what he'd said earlier, but I was hoping to get more.

"And here I thought Wanda didn't like me." Although I didn't particularly like her, the two of us being on friendly terms would make exposing secrets way easier.

Andy snorted. "She doesn't."

Okay…never mind.

He faced me with a grimace – dang! He even looked good frowning! – and flipped the sandwich without watching. "Sorry, I didn't mean it that way."

It was my turn to snort. "There aren't a lot of other ways to say that."

"I just mean that she's stereotypical, you know?"

"No, I don't know," I said pleasantly. I wasn't offended by his comment, so I wasn't sure why he kept looking down and shifting like he was embarrassed. I was even smiling. How could he be misinterpreting? Maybe my smile wasn't smiley. Maybe my exhaustion made my smile look more like a hungry, easily provoked, lion.

"Well… it's just… you know how people are… and… they um … and…" he stammered.

"Spit it out, Rain Man, it's the middle of the night."

My borderline rude encouragement was all he needed because he laughed then shot me a 'Fine. You deserve this' look. "You're a redhead."

"Yeah, so?"

"So I believe her exact words were, 'She's bound to blow up over something stupid and we need an explosive first episode.'"

"Excuse me?" I was taken aback.

Andy shook his head. "She thought she was being punny."

"She assumes I have a temper and that I'll keep things interesting by being rude?"

"Yep." He put the grilled cheese in front of me and sat down again to eat his own.

I threw my head back and laughed. Loudly. I laughed so loudly, in fact, that Andy put his hand over my mouth and *shushed* me.

"Just because I'm awake doesn't mean the rest of the house needs to be! Lincoln can't know you're in here." But my laughter was contagious, and he started chuckling. It was clear he was going to keep his hand over my mouth until I stopped my hysterics. "It's not that funny!"

Unfortunately, all this did was make me laugh harder. I pushed his hand away. He stood and wrapped one arm around my shoulders and pulled me to him, his hand still covering my mouth. The way he held me would have made me think he was going to abduct me if I hadn't known him. As it was I felt his chest rising and falling with silent laughter as he tried to muffle mine. I took several deep breaths through my nose, calming myself as much as possible, and then stuck my tongue out and licked his hand.

He jerked back, as I'd planned, and made a face as he wiped his hand on his shirt. "That's disgusting!"

I let the remainder of my laughter out in a breath and said, "Why do you taste like salt?

Dropping back onto his barstool he said, "I sprinkle a little salt on the cheese before I grill it."

"You put the salt on your hand first?"

"I measure it that way."

I chortled then pursed my lips to stop myself from resuming my involuntary fit. He frowned, but I could tell from the smile in his eyes that he wasn't really upset.

"Just eat your sandwich."

We ate in silence, frequently glancing at one another and smiling, both trying not to laugh. As my hunger subsided, my exhaustion set in.

"You, Andy," I said standing up, unable to stop a huge smile from growing across my face, "are my new favorite person. I will forever be indebted to you and your enviable cheese sandwich grilling skills."

"Anytime," he said with an equally big smile and took our plates to the sink.

"I might have to take you up on that if the rest of the meals you have planned are as delicious as they were today."

"In my defense, Wanda planned the menu." He pointed at me to emphasize this fact. "She said she figured it wouldn't matter what we served because none of the women would eat anything anyway."

"Wanda has clearly never met a Texan."

"Clearly." He took a step toward me. I must have thought he was going in for a hug or something, because without thinking I opened my arms and leaned toward him.

He stepped back with an amused look on his face. "I was going to turn on the stairway light for you." He flipped a switch behind me.

I wrapped my arms around myself trying to cover and rocked back on my heels.

"Right, so," I pointed over my shoulder, grateful the dim light hid my now red face, "I should go."

"Right." He folded his arms and covered his mouth with one hand, hiding his laughter. Torn between wanting to double over with laughter and mortification, I hurried to the staircase.

"Paige." I looked back and saw he was no longer laughing. "Thanks for the company."

I smiled sheepishly and then disappeared down the stairs.

Chapter $10

Bagels and an assortment of cream cheeses were on the kitchen island the next morning at breakfast. I could not stop smiling. Andy must have gone out and gotten them for me earlier. The bagels were on a platter next to the fruit and protein drinks. The other girls did not appreciate it. They all tried to avoid staring (or inhaling) the bagels, but as they played on their phones while sipping their spinach shakes, they kept stealing glances as if they could satiate their hunger with each look.

I was just starting on my second bagel – they were all for me, anyway, let's face it – when Bunny shot off the couch with a loud gasp. Everyone's attention went to her. She started choking on her drink and we all ran over to make sure she was okay. She waved us away, instead pointing vigorously at her phone then shoved it at me while she continued coughing violently. I examined the screen she'd pointed to and gasped aloud.

"What?" Amelia's tone was irritated. She snatched the phone from my hand and read aloud. "'Cheater, Cheater, Chocolate Eater.'"

It was my article. The article Carla said she was going to wait to publish. She was supposed to wait. Why didn't she wait? She was going to publish the goldfish article! Everyone loved goldfish! Except for Jemma. She had a fear of goldfish. She told me was a specific form of ichthyophobia rarely seen and it was nothing to joke about.

Cue eye roll.

Amelia's voice quieted as she continued to read. I watched her carefully, scraping through my memory of the article to see if there were any possible implications of my involvement.

Wanda's shoes *click-clacked* on the floor interrupting us. "Sit! All of you!"

We all sat down where we were. Bunny, who'd been in the middle of the room choking, sat on the floor attempting to control her cough.

Andy entered the room a moment behind her. "Wanda, calm down."

Wanda ignored him. "We have a leak."

"Is it a bad leak?" Carmen asked.

"A very bad leak," Wanda replied grimly. "It seems –"

"Where's the leak? It's not my bathroom, is it? All my stuff is on the floor. Amelia took up all the counter space."

Wanda ignored Carmen like a pro and continued, "I assume you already know, but *Look!* published an article revealing the first task and Paige's win of the first date. The article has accused the studio of rigging the first task to ensure Paige's win."

"Yes!" Amelia yelled and pumped her fist in the air. "I hadn't read that part yet. That means, I won, right?"

She had the decency to look ashamed as Wanda scowled. "No. Andy and I have decided to proceed as planned. The magazine claims it has proof, but the fact is that a legal contract has been broken."

Proof? Now I had to come up with *proof?*

"We will find the mole and make them pay. You have my word." Wanda's determination was unnerving. Like the Godfather on his period.

"What Wanda means," Andy calmly broke in, "is that we're investigating the situation. We believe we have some leads and will be interviewing the staff today."

The staff. I told myself to relax. They didn't suspect the contestants. Not yet.

"Now, if you'll excuse us, we have some business to attend to." Andy gently took Wanda's arm.

"Oh, and Paige," she barked as they went down the hallway. "Your date with Lincoln is at six tonight. Meet in the foyer. And you better be ready to go." Wanda's unspoken threat made the hair on my arms stand up, but she didn't spare us another glance as she let Andy lead her away.

$$$

"I don't understand. You should have published the James Franco article." I ground my teeth not caring if Carla could hear it through the phone. Peggy and the others had gone swimming, but since their hostility toward me about my date with Lincoln was near a boiling point, I'd opted for a mid-morning nap. And an angry call to my boss.

"It was a false article." She sounded distracted as if she were filing her nails. "It wasn't James Franco's goldfish. He doesn't even have a dog. The picture was misleading."

"It had a dog though! Dog pictures perform really, really well! You've seen the stats about the unreasonable number of articles read that feature dog photos. An article could be about how long it takes paint to dry and it'd still be a success if it had a dog photo in it. Everyone loves dogs!"

"I hate dogs."

"Color me surprised," I said blandly.

"Excuse me?"

"Post a picture of a cat." I pressed on, ignoring the implications of my comment. "It's perfect. A cat and a goldfish! It'll be adorable."

"James Franco doesn't have a cat either."

"A dust bunny then. Anything other than that article!"

"It's already published. The studio has already contacted us and threatened to sue. We anticipate the documents will arrive this afternoon. We'll take care of the legal aspect if you take care of the articles."

"You want me to keep writing even while they're threatening to sue?"

"Yes."

"But, Carla –"

"Paige, if you can't handle this you need to tell me. Now. I'll buy your ticket to Austin myself and have your things sent to you." She must have been serious if she remembered I was from Austin.

I took a deep breath. "No. Take care of the legal side and I'll take care of the story."

"Good. That's what I want to hear. Get to work." She hung up.

I threw my phone on the bed and groaned knowing I had to trust her. I had no other choice.

$$$

My heartbeat pounded in my ears. Lincoln and I stood at the railing of a bridge, looking down at the vast valley and river below. The harness tightened around us, forcing us closer together. It occurred to me that most women who were standing this close to a handsome millionaire might take advantage of their proximity. I, however, kept peeking over the edge and scooting as far away as possible, determined to put more than three feet between me and the chasm. Unfortunately, I was considerably smaller than Lincoln and couldn't move him an inch. I felt like a dog desperately trying to run away from a vet, but whose owner kept pulling on the leash, keeping him from escaping his doom.

"Lincoln?" I said, my eyes glued to the extreme drop far too close to my feet. "I'm not sure about this."

He put his hands on my shoulders even as someone behind me tugged on my waistband. I threw my arms around Lincoln to stop the serial killers (who preferred to be called Jump Masters) from pushing me off the bridge. Even though they had repeatedly told me they wouldn't throw me off in a sudden fit of rage, I did not trust them.

"We don't have to do this if you don't want to," Lincoln said.

The other women, even Peggy who'd seemed fine last night, glared at me so long after Wanda reminded me of my date, that I'd spent the day hiding in my room until it was time to meet Lincoln in the foyer. The whole thing was a production that took much longer than it should have. "Picking me up" involved him walking from the forbidden wing of the house to where I waited in the entryway. Not only did the cameras follow us down the halls and out the front door, but so did the other contestants.

I was embarrassingly excited when we reached the steakhouse for dinner - fillet mignon with blue cheese crumbles, I wanted to die - and was having a rather nice time until he helped me into the helicopter. It wasn't until we got to the bridge that Lincoln told me what we were doing.

Bungee jumping at sunset. What could be more romantic?

Anything. Literally *anything else*, including watching Jurassic Park while Lincoln clipped my toenails, would be more romantic than bungee jumping.

The camera crew had no sympathy for me. My eyes scanned their faces, trying to find Andy, certain he would be able to get me out of this somehow. But Andy was nowhere to be seen. I looked back to Lincoln and took a shaky breath.

"Yes," I said. "Let's do it. It'll be fine."

"Can you at least smile?" the cameraman, Paulo, called to me. I'd met him in the helicopter. He was a grimy looking man with black hair he'd slicked back into a ponytail and a Charlie Chaplin mustache.

I shot him a menacing grin. "I'll do my best."

Lincoln took my head in his hands and made me look at him.

"It'll be fine," he repeated. He wrapped me in his arms and I hid my head in his chest.

"Ready?" one of the serial killers said.

I shook my head into Lincoln's chest, but forced myself to take a deep breath and say "yes."

We inched our way forward until the soles of our shoes were a breath away from our imminent deaths.

I looked up, up, up into Lincoln's eyes. He was at least a foot taller than me. His broad shoulders dwarfed mine and I had the horrible thought that I could potentially use him as a cushion before we went *splat*.

"If I die," I said, my body trembling, "I will come back and haunt you at your mansion for the rest of your life."

"Which mansion? I have several."

"All of them." I tried to focus on Lincoln's voice and ignore Paulo's calls to his crew.

"Even abroad?"

My fingers dug into the back of his hundred-dollar shirt and I didn't even care if I ruined it.

"What can I say? I've always wanted to see Italy." And we jumped.

$$$

"I've never truly hated anyone before," I said later as we sat side-by-side roasting marshmallows, "but I think I might actually hate you."

"Ouch," Lincoln said, and I nudged him with my shoulder to let him know I was kidding. Someone had set up a roaring fire at the bottom of the ravine and we sat on a camping chair made for two. I pulled my marshmallow out of the fire and Lincoln helped me sandwich it between two graham crackers. I set down the roasting stick and took the s'more from Lincoln. White fluff oozed out onto my hand as I bit into it.

"Mmm…" I moaned with pleasure. "You should serve this for dessert every night."

He bit into his own and said, with a mouth still full of marshmallow, "Why would I give dessert to someone who hates me?"

I poked him in the ribs. "You forced me to jump off a bridge."

"'Forced' is a strong word."

The marshmallow I threw bounced off his nose and he laughed. We sat in companionable silence while we finished our s'mores. I had to admit that I was having a lot more fun than I thought I would. Yes, I would have nightmares about bungee jumping for the next ten years but being with Lincoln was nice. Comfortable.

"You've got a little chocolate," he used his thumb to wipe the corner of my lip, "right there."

His words instantly reminded me of Andy and the night before, but the air was heavy around us as I watched him lick the chocolate off his thumb. I pushed Andy out of my mind as Lincoln leaned closer and cupped my cheek in his hand. Everything slowed as his mouth touched mine. I don't know how long we sat there kissing, but it was long enough that I jumped a little when a voice interrupted us.

"We need to get the lead-in again. The fire was casting a shadow." It was Paulo.

The cameras. I'd forgotten all about them.

Embarrassment and anger made me flush. I opened my mouth to tell them off but was taken aback when Lincoln nodded and said, "No problem. Tell me when you're ready."

"Sorry?" I must have misheard.

"They just need to capture the beginning again. No big deal." Lincoln shrugged and stretched.

I gaped at him until Paulo said "Okay!" and suddenly Lincoln's hand was caressing my cheek. I pulled away, and his brow furrowed.

"What's wrong?"

"The camera." I waved my hand in its direction. "That was kind of private."

"This is reality TV, Paige. Nothing is private."

"Not even our first kiss?"

"Especially not your first kiss!" Paulo called. I liked him less and less by the second. I didn't think he'd be able to hear us, but apparently, I was wrong. My cheeks grew hot.

"Paige," Lincoln said, taking my hand, "I know it's not ideal, but it's part of the contract. They can film whatever and whenever they want. I would love to be alone with you right now, but I can't."

The dancing fire cast shadows on his face and his eyes pleaded for me to understand. I immediately felt empathetic. This wasn't his fault. He didn't plan on kissing me.

Did he?

"With that article published this morning we have no idea if our viewership will increase or decrease," he said. "Wanda wants us to keep things interesting. They just need another shot. Is that okay?"

Keep things interesting.

"I guess..." I trailed off. Supposedly I should be grateful he was asking for my permission in the first place. He was right; according to the contract they pretty much owned me. Besides, I hadn't noticed the cameras filming earlier. Now that I was aware of them, did it really make it so different?

"It's fine," I said and forced a smile trying to convince myself. "Of course it is."

"Just forget the cameras are there," he said. "Like before."

I nodded and took a shaky breath. He didn't caress my cheek like before, but instead just held my hand and looked at me for a minute. His thumb stroked the back of my hand. I thought about the way he'd wiped the chocolate off my lip, but my memory flashed to the way Andy wiped off the whipped cream in the same way. There weren't any cameras last night.

Lincoln moved closer. "Your hair is gorgeous in this light," he said softly and tucked a piece behind my ear. His fingers traced my jawline and his eyes focused on my lips. He met my eyes once, asking permission before he put his lips to mine.

It was soft at first. Sweet. I wanted to enjoy it, but I was painfully aware of the cameras taking in my every movement. I was scared to move too much in case we lost the light again. Lincoln's hands wrapped around my waist and tugged me toward him. He deepened the kiss and I kissed him back, but it was half-hearted, like how I'd kiss guys in college the night before an exam. I'd desperately wanted a distraction, but the equations and facts kept running through my mind. Lincoln must have sensed my hesitation because he abruptly stopped kissing me.

"How was that?" he asked Paulo.

"Good, but I'd love it if we could get a few more seconds –"

"No." Lincoln stood and held out his hand to help me up. "We're done for tonight."

I could hear the disappointment in Paulo's answering assent, but I couldn't bring myself to care. I was grateful to Lincoln for ending the...whatever it is that was. Moment? Rerun? I had no idea, but I was glad it was over. We hiked a little while to a place the helicopter could land and as we took off into the night, I took squeezed Lincoln's hand in a "thank you."

Chapter $11

That night I went back to Lincoln's private kitchen for food. I wasn't particularly hungry, but I couldn't fall asleep until I was certain Peggy wasn't watching me. And she'd decided that tonight would be a good night to work on her memoir. Her handwritten memoir. I thought about offering to transcribe them for her at fifty cents per word but decided it wouldn't be worth it to have to read through her life's history. I told her I was going to sit by the pool and pull a Henry David Thoreau.

So there I was at one a.m., sitting on a barstool in the dark, in a millionaire's off-limits kitchen, eating a bowl of Lucky Charms I'd found by unceremoniously going through all the cupboards. I'd been there – eating cereal so slowly the marshmallows were twice their original size – for almost twenty minutes and Andy still hadn't appeared. I put my now empty bowl in the sink, leaned against the counter, and wondered why I was so disappointed. It wasn't like we'd planned to meet here or anything. We weren't really even friends. Even as I thought it, I could almost feel his quiet laughter as he held me trying to muffle mine.

Maybe if I'd turned on the oven light he would have come in to see if something was wrong. He'd think it was a burglar or some other devious criminal wandering around the mansion. It wasn't like anyone would even hear an intruder in a place this big.

It occurred to me then that I could go deeper into Lincoln's house, find his office, and steal whatever sensitive information he had on his computer, or his silver briefcase full of money, or his priceless ceramic monkey from India… Yeah, that sounded like a lot of work. I sighed and turned to leave.

And ran smack dab into someone's chest.

I jumped and let out a yelp. I would have fallen over backward if Andy hadn't caught me.

"I'm sorry to frighten you. It's just me," he hurriedly explained, and then as an afterthought, he added, "Andy."

I heard the flip of a switch and dim lights underneath the cupboards lit up. Heat rushed to my face and I put one hand on my hip trying to look casual. "Oh hey, Andy. What's up?"

He smiled a lopsided smile and said, "Oh, you know, just stealing food from my generous hosts."

Guilt crashed over me and I hid my face in my hands. "You're right, I'm so sorry. This is totally rude. I should not…"

"Paige," Andy said and put his hands on my shoulders. I peeked at him through my fingers. "I'm kidding. It's fine. I'm happy to see you."

"You are?" I asked sheepishly, heat spreading across my cheeks for an entirely different reason.

He quickly let go of me and moved past me to the fridge. "Sure. I mean, I wanted to hear about your date with Linc."

Oh.

Right.

I squashed whatever stupid emotion I felt back to the bottom of my stomach. Andy was the producer. He'd probably seen the footage already. Of course, he wanted to know how I felt about the whole thing. Why else would he want to see me? I pushed the feeling down until I convinced myself I'd never felt anything at all.

"Well," I faced him, "I didn't yell at Lincoln so I'm afraid Wanda's going to be disappointed."

Andy pulled an ice cream carton out of the freezer and held it up in question. And who am I to say no to ice cream?

"I believe I heard some footage of you telling Lincoln you hated him." He reached into a cupboard to get bowls and his blue t-shirt lifted above the waistband of his superman sweats exposing a thin line of skin. No tan lines. If I didn't know better, I'd say he mowed the lawn shirtless. I looked away.

"'Hate' is a strong word," I replied, reusing Lincoln's earlier phrase.

"It's also a four-letter word, which if I remember correctly, you seemed to use a lot of after you two jumped." His voice was full of mockery.

"Hey," I playfully argued, "you try jumping off a cliff and not screaming every swear word you've learned since Kindergarten."

"I've already done that."

"Really? You've bungee jumped off that cliff?"

"Twice." Finished scooping out ice cream, he replaced the container and put our bowls and spoons on the counter. We sat on the same stools we had the night before – right next to each other.

"Now I know why you and Lincoln are friends. You're both insane."

"That and our devastatingly good looks."

"It's cute that you two have a club."

"A club of millionaires."

"You'rrree a miyonaire?" I slurred. He raised his eyebrows, clearly amused, and I gulped the ice cream in my mouth and repeated, "You're a millionaire?"

He chuckled and shook his head. "No, I'm not a millionaire."

"Crap. I was hoping to have a backup." I winked at him.

"What about you? Are you a millionaire?"

I let out a single laugh. "What kind of question is that?"

"You can ask me, but I can't ask you?" he teased.

"Fair point." I downed another spoonful before answering. "No, I'm not a millionaire."

"Dang. I was thinking if the whole thing with you and Lincoln didn't work out then maybe I could be the one to marry a millionaire."

"Ha ha." I nudged him with my elbow. "You're hilarious."

My spoon made a *clink* and I looked down to see that my bowl was empty. A second later Andy's spoon mimicked mine and we both just stared at our bowls for a moment unsure what to do.

"I guess I should –" but before I could finish, Andy interrupted saying, "Do you want some more ice cream?"

Oddly relieved, I nodded and waited patiently while he got us more. After he'd sat down again I broke the silence as though we hadn't stopped talking at all. "Assuming you aren't going to marry a millionaire. What would you do instead? I know a sugar mama is hard to beat, but everyone's got to have a Plan B."

"Hmm…" Andy put his finger to his chin as if deep in thought, before sighing deeply and saying, "I imagine I'd live in a tiny one-room house with my wife and a handful of kids. I'd have a horrible job that paid next to nothing, have my boss constantly yell at me, and be forced to try and scrape up just enough money to bring home a Christmas turkey for my son, Tim, who isn't expected to live past the new year."

"How touching." I wiped away a fake tear. "But I said you weren't going to marry a millionaire, not that you'd be transported into a Charles Dickens' novel."

"You should have been more specific," he said with mock astonishment. "I only know what you tell me."

"Then I should tell you something," I said seriously. He furrowed his brow, but relaxed when he saw my teasing smile. Anxiety fluttered in my stomach warning me to stop speaking, but I plowed on. "I didn't really want any more ice cream."

"I should tell you something too." He frowned and fingered the ice cream container. He sounded so serious my internal freak-out-o-meter almost hit the red zone, but then he grinned. "I didn't really want any more ice cream either."

$$$

Why, why, why, why would anyone be awake this early? Andy and I had talked until the ice cream turned liquid, which was about four hours earlier. An hour ago, Peggy yanked me out of bed insisting I had to get ready or I was going to be late.

"Get ready" apparently meant putting on your cutest pajamas and doing your hair and makeup just enough so it seemed like you woke up looking like a natural beauty. I grumbled the whole time I put on my makeup, but I was too self-conscious to go au naturel on camera.

We gathered in the grand theater, a multi-level room that was decorated as if we were in 1950. Black and white movie posters hung on the wall, hand-drawn posters with a painted color overlay, and of course, countless framed autographs from Oscar winners like Julia Roberts. I stopped to read one of them:

To Linc,
    Don't forget that you're my freebie. ♥
                    Love, Jen L.

Lincoln was Jennifer Lawrence's freebie?! I rolled my eyes not positive why I was surprised. Wanda shooed us to our seats in the dimly lit theater head and made my way to the fifth row of leather recliners. We were about halfway back from the screen and my eyes fluttered shut when I sat down. This recliner was softer than my bed. I wondered if Peggy would follow me in here if I disappeared in the night. All I needed was a blanket and I'd be out. I put up the footrest and settled in for whatever it was we were watching at this forsaken hour.

My head jerked up a second later when I heard Wanda's voice. I don't know why she gave me a dirty look. I was awake. I was. But no matter how many times told myself that I *could not fall asleep* my vision kept going cross-eyed as I tried to keep my eyes open and focus.

"Remember that you signed an agreement," she was saying, "You agreed that we could showcase everything we filmed, and we could present it in any way we chose. You do not have a say. The episode is…."

I jerked awake again, unsuccessful at my original task, and sat up straight to get my blood flowing. I focused on looking at random things around the room. A poster of Casablanca. A popcorn machine in the corner. Andy walking up the stairs. A creepy life-sized replica of Jimmy Stewart.

Andy.

The theater was too dark for me to tell for sure, but by the way he was dragging his feet I assumed his exhaustion matched my own. He took a swig from the coke bottle he was holding, caught my eye and held it up to me in salute. I stuck my tongue out at him, but he just smiled and sat in a seat behind me.

"...family and friends about the premiere tonight," Wanda finished and took a seat on the front row.

I didn't understand what she had said, but I was proud of myself for staying awake for the rest of it. However, that didn't stop me from yawning as the low lights went dark and the screen lit up.

Andy's face lit up the screen and he introduced the show. A story about a man on an epic search for love who just so happened to be a millionaire and wanted nothing more than to marry a gorgeous blonde trophy wife who would stand next to him in pictures and never say a word to anyone.

Or something like that.

Andy narrated the first few minutes as the cameras focused on a driveway with a familiar set-up of desks and lie detectors.

"I will ask you a series of questions to which you will respond with a simple 'yes' or 'no.' At no time during this test..." On-screen Andy repeated the words he'd said to us during the beginning round's lie-detector test. Oh man, his voice was soothing.

I slipped back into the memory of watching his eyes sparkle with amusement as he handed me the broken tablet. Only instead of taking it from him, I grabbed his hand and we laughed as we ran toward the back of the house. We jumped the fence and were running to the pool when someone kicked me in the back.

My eyes flew open and I gasped so loudly everyone in the theater turned to look at me. It only took half a second to remember what was going on. "I was just really into the show," I said lamely. I could hear Andy snickering behind me. "It surprised me."

"It's just dinner…" Carmen said with confusion. "You were there." Now she remembered me?

"Of course. I'm just imagining how everyone watching will react."

"To what?" Amelia scoffed. "The salmon?"

I had an urge to tell Amelia that the size of the salmon was, in fact, appalling and I'm surprised we all didn't gasp in horror that night, but Wanda *shhhhed* us and we fell quiet. Relaxing in the recliner once again, I turned and glared at Andy for kicking my chair. Although, I'm not sure he saw my mean face because he just kept grinning at me. I was about to turn back to the screen when he leaned forward and extended his Coke.

I looked between him and the Coke so many times it was borderline embarrassing. It wasn't until he sighed and whispered, "Just take it," that I did just that. It kept me awake enough that I was able to criticize myself throughout the rest of the episode. I was so white I practically glowed on camera. For the first time in my life I wish I'd gotten a spray tan.

I would have turned orange, but at least I would have shown up on camera.

"Next time on *Who Wants to Marry a Millionaire?*" The hour ended with a teaser of the following episode that would be aired the next evening. The screen changed to a shot of Amelia grinning and then switched to an aerial view of the obstacle course. "Who will win the first date with a millionaire bachelor?" Shots rotated through Carmen scoring a basket, Peggy throwing up (which made me feel another wave of gratitude toward Andy), and the five of us sprinting toward the blow-up obstacle course.

"Tune in for an explosive episode that follows Lincoln's first date, first kiss, and first fight." I tilted the Coke bottle back as the screen filled with a close-up of my face. Through the bottle, I watched my screen-self say to Lincoln, "I might actually hate you."

I spit out the coke and started coughing. Bunny patted me on the back, but I was in too much shock to acknowledge the kind gesture.

The crew edited it wrong. It was totally out of context! They made it seem like I was a *beyotch* who hated Lincoln! HATED! I could just imagine how Carla would react. Lincoln was probably going to kick me off the show based on perception alone.

"Who wants to marry a millionaire? You decide." Andy's voice faded, the lights brightened, and everyone in the theater stared at me for the second time in an hour. Wanda had a look of pure glee on her face and I couldn't believe it when she pulled her phone from her pocket and aimed it at me, ready to record my reaction.

Replaying every youth acting camp memory, I unleashed what measly skills I could recall and started to laugh. The other girls looked at me like I'd lost my mind, Wanda looked sorely disappointed, and I heard Andy snort.

"That looked hilarious! Everyone is going to be so surprised when they hear the other half of that sentence." I covered my mouth to stifle my fake giggles and stood up. "Good work, you guys!" I turned to Andy and knowing no one else could see, I gave him a deadly look. I continued fake chuckling as I left, everyone still shocked into silence.

$$$

"I'm going to *kill him*!" I growled when Jemma answered. An hour had passed since the episode's preview and I was sprawled out on a chaise in a tiny den-like room with dark wood paneling on the walls. I'd found the room by accident – well, by snooping, but I *accidentally* stumbled upon it while snooping. At least that's the version I was going with to keep me out of Hell. Really, I was searching the house for a meat locker certain I'd find something in there to use as a murder weapon, but I found this room instead.

"You can't kill him yet," Jemma replied sleepily. "You're not married. If you kill him now you won't get any life insurance money."

"Not Lincoln. Andy. I'm going to kill Andy."

"Who?"

"The producer and host of the show. Keep up."

"Is Andy his full name?

I paused, confused and irritated. "I don't know. Why?"

"Andy just seems like too nice of a name to belong to someone you're going to kill."

"So?"

"His name is probably Andrew. What's his last name?"

"Warner."

"Andrew Jonathan Warner. Now *that's* the name of someone you could kill," she said perkily, now fully awake.

"I didn't say his middle name was Jonathan."

"I know. I made it up."

"Are you going to continue to rename everyone on the show or can I continue?" I asked impatiently.

"Sorry," she said, not at all sorry. "Please explain what Andrew Jonathan Warner did that has driven you to murder."

"He edited the footage of my date with Lincoln."

"You went on a date with Lincoln?!"

"Yes, but that's not –"

"What did you do?"

"We went bungee jumping, but –"

"You went bungee jumping?" Her incredulity was clear and slightly offensive.

"Hey," I said hotly, "I do stuff."

"Sure, like reading an entire book in three hours or staying up all night watching *Stranger Things* or eating a whole pizza in one sitting or –"

"Yes, Jemma," I interrupted, launching one of the chaise's pillows across the room in frustration, "I went bungee jumping."

"Okay, and?"

"And afterward I told Lincoln I hated him for making me go."

"Duh."

"Only it came out as, 'I think I might actually hate you.'"

"People will know it's a joke."

"They might, except they edited the next episode so in the preview the only thing you hear me saying is, 'I might actually hate you.'"

"Uh-oh."

"Yeah."

"It's probably not as bad as you think."

"It is."

"You're being dramatic. I'll watch the premiere tonight and text you what I think of the teaser."

"Even if I am, I'm still killing Andy."

She paused so long I looked at my phone to make sure we were still connected. "Jemma?"

"I hate to play devil's advocate here, but isn't making things appear more complicated than they actually are Andrew Jonathan Warner's job? It's reality TV. He's supposed to make it dramatic."

"I'm going to get sent home!"

"Not necessarily. They probably put the whole conversation in the actual episode, just shortened it for the teaser."

"I don't care. Either way, he shouldn't have done it."

"I don't understand why you're so upset about this. Isn't this just more fodder for your article? It's why you're there – to expose reality TV for what it really is."

She was right. My anger was subsiding, but some part of me was still upset. "I guess you're right."

"Why are you so mad at Andrew Jonathan Warner in particular? Doesn't that show have multiple producers? Shouldn't you be mad at all of them?"

"I guess so…I just thought Andy and I were kind of friends."

"Why would you think that?"

"Well, we stayed up all night. Talking."

"YOU'RE HAVING AN AFFAIR WITH ONE OF THE PRODUCERS?!?" I jerked the phone away from my ear.

"*Shhh*!" I hissed as though the walls could hear us. "Of course not. We just talked. Remember the night I went looking for food? Well, I found Lincoln's private kitchen and then Andy walked in on me. Instead of kicking me out he made me a grilled cheese."

"Is that a euphemism?"

"Get your mind out of the gutter."

"I want your life so bad."

"Yeah, it's super fun," I said drily. "By the way, why are you awake?"

"Because some slut called and woke me up."

"I mean, why are you *sooo* awake? You're usually asleep right now."

She squealed. "The studio catered lunch today – yesterday – and it gave everyone food poisoning. It was all gone by the time I arrived so thankfully I didn't get any. And then the bar's new assistant manager forgot to submit the food order, so we ran out of everything."

"Oh my gosh, that's great!" I squealed along with her.

"My boss sent all the waitresses home promising to pay us for the full shift. It's the first time I've slept all night in months."

"Good! I'm so happy for you!" And I genuinely was. Jemma worked ridiculous hours and deserved a full night's sleep. I checked the time on my phone and groaned. "I better go. I'm supposed to be downstairs by ten and I still have to get ready."

"Okay, and listen, if you're that worried about the teaser trailer, just make sure you do something that will prove to everyone that you like him."

"Like what?"

"Jump his bones on camera."

"That's not exactly the kind of job I'm trying to keep, but I'll give it a try."

"Think of all the pretty money! Green looks great on redheads!"

Tears pricked my eyes as a sudden wave of homesickness came over me. "I miss you."

"Same," she replied.

I couldn't be certain, but I was pretty sure she was on the verge of tears too.

Chapter $12

Lincoln spun a key ring around one finger. We were in the driveway once again, the five of us standing in a line facing the street where five SUVs were parked facing the driveway. Each was a different color: red, yellow, blue, black, and white. It was obvious each contestant was going to be assigned a car, but I didn't have any idea why. Maybe we'd reenact that scene from *Footloose* and play Chicken. That could be fun.

I squinted at Lincoln, praying my eyes wouldn't water enough to ruin my makeup. The last thing I needed was for people to think I was crying before we'd even started a challenge. For some reason, all the other girls wore sunglasses and clutched their purses, but I didn't know we were even going to be outside. Then again, I did leave the theater early.

"This challenge is a little different from what you'd expect." Andy was standing next to the blue SUV and the camera followed him as he went to stand beside Lincoln. "Married couples need to be able to understand one another and empathize with each other. So today, instead of having our contestants race for Lincoln's heart, they are going to take a walk through his past."

Yay.

Andy slapped Lincoln on the back. "And this guy has quite the colorful past." He gave Lincoln and then the camera a toothy grin. My heart sped up a little, but I was certain it was just nerves from the upcoming task.

"Each contestant is assigned a car and inside each car is an envelope with a task in it. Each contestant's task is different but of equal difficulty. This will ensure that none of you will follow one other. Upon each task's completion, you will be given another envelope. There are four envelopes. The final envelope gives a meeting place. All contestants must be finished with their tasks and at the final location by 4:00 this afternoon. A cameraman is inside each car and will film your progress throughout the day. Lincoln will now hand out the keys."

Lincoln pulled several more keychains out of his pocket and handed one to each of us in turn. Every keychain had a colored square attached and imprinted with Who Wants to Be a Millionaire? Mine was red. Amelia's – who stood next to me – was yellow.

As soon as Lincoln was once again standing by Andy, Andy held out his hands as if to say, "what are you waiting for?" and then yelled, "Go!"

We bolted toward the SUVs and I hopped into the red one. I quickly nodded in greeting to Paulo who was in the backseat already busy filming. A red envelope was taped to the steering wheel and I tore it open:

Lincoln was integral in the construction of this building:

_____

You'll find Steve there. Tell him Lincoln's birthday and you'll get your next clue.

Building, building, building. My mind raced as I tried to remember everything I'd read about Lincoln's business. He designed a fashion app at nineteen but switched directions a couple years later after meeting a homeless child playing soccer in the street. He'd never mentioned the child again but said the experience had changed his life. Sometime after that, he'd developed the video game app to help kids learn to code and even started a charity for foster children. He'd ended up going into low-income communities and building youth centers.

Youth centers.

It hit me like a lightning bolt. I threw the SUV in reverse and screeched to a halt when I almost hit Amelia's yellow SUV. She was backing up…slooooowwwly. I would have thought she was doing it on purpose to delay me if Carmen, Bunny, and Peggy hadn't already zoomed away. I learned how to drive in my dad's truck, so the SUV's size wasn't anything new to me, but it was obvious Amelia had never driven a larger car because she was executing an overly cautious twenty-two-point turn. The street leading to the driveway wasn't even small. Or busy. It was a private road.

Five minutes later – I'm not exaggerating, I even turned on the radio at Paulo's request – I was ready to push Amelia out of her car's driver's seat and back it up myself. She finally succeeded, and I heaved a sigh of relief. A moment later I was speeding down the road after her. The property gate was already open, and I followed her all the way out of Beverley Glen to the freeway.

"Hey Siri," I said to my phone which buzzed to life, "Give me directions to the Colorado Center."

"Getting directions," said a robotic voice in a British man's accent (I love a British accent). "You will arrive in approximately twenty minutes."

I arrived in eighteen. Except I had to spend *another* twenty minutes driving around the parking lot trying to find a parking place. The third time I drove turtle-slow behind a lady in a wide-brimmed sun hat walking to her car. She didn't seem at all concerned that a giant red SUV was three feet away, following her down two rows of cars. When she finally arrived at her silver Prius she spent another two minutes digging through her purse for her keys. I tried telling Paulo how exasperating this was, but every time I opened my mouth he started filming. It was apparent the two of us were not going to have many conversations on our journey. I was about to lay on my horn when the lady finally backed up and drove off. I expertly maneuvered into the vacant spot and barely remembered to lock the doors as I ran toward the Colorado Center's entrance.

The Colorado Center was named after the street that Lincoln had said: "changed his life." He was pretty tight-lipped about what exactly happened on that street and only said that he met someone who opened his eyes to the crime against children occurring in downtown LA. He'd partnered with several homeless shelters to create the center with the purpose of keeping kids off the streets. In the years since the center had opened, allowing kids ages eight-to-eighteen the opportunity for athletic and artistic pursuits at no charge, crime had significantly gone down in the area.

It was a large rectangular building that looked just like every other building downtown. It wasn't until I was inside that I noticed its true size. I felt like I'd entered a showroom at a museum, not the lobby of a community center. Pure white walls stood two stories tall, leading up to a ceiling made entirely of glass. The glass was tinted, but the light streaming through it was still bright. It reminded me of the roof of my family's greenhouse back home. On the far side of the room, there was a reception desk with girl sitting behind it. I was surprised to see someone her age manning the desk since it was a school day. My flip-flops made embarrassingly loud smacks against the polished floor as I ran to her.

"Hi." Out of breath from running, I slapped my hands against the desk. "Can you tell me where Steve is?"

"Who?" The girl, seemingly about sixteen-years-old, stared at Paulo a few feet away holding the camera. She wore a name tag pinned above her pocket that said, "Alice." Her large round glasses gave her bug eyes and slipped to the end of her nose. She pushed them back up.

"Steve."

"Steve who?"

"I don't know his last name."

Alice wouldn't stop looking at the camera. "How am I supposed to help you find someone when you don't know his name?"

"I do know his name," I explained. "I just don't know his last name. Do you know anyone named Steve? He's supposed to have something for me."

She finally turned to me and said, "I don't know anyone named Steve."

My shoulders slumped, and I ran a hand through my hair. A square metal clock on the wall above the reception desk said that it'd been just over an hour since I'd left Lincoln's house.

"Is there anyone else here that might be able to help me?" I refrained from saying "anyone older" because I thought it might make her less likely to help me.

"It's just me. My manager went out to lunch, but she'll be back in an hour or so." She shook her head, let out a small gasp, and put her hand over her mouth. "Oh, please forget I said that. I'm not supposed to tell anyone I'm here alone – except I'm not, not really. Stephen comes around every once-in-a-while to –"

"Stephen?" My voice was sharp. "You said you didn't know anyone named Steve!"

"His name is Stephen. Not Steve." Her voice shook at my tone and I immediately felt guilty.

"I'm sorry," I said gently. "I'm on a…quest, yeah, a quest, for love. One of the things I need to do is find this guy named Steve – sorry, Stephen – and get something from him." Alice still looked skeptical and kept shooting glances at the camera.

"Why is he filming you?"

"Because my quest is going to be on TV," I explained. "Can you take me to Stephen now? Please?"

"I guess…" She hesitated for one more moment and then gestured for us to follow her down the hall.

I expected the halls to be similar to the lobby, but instead of pristine white walls, the walls were glass. You could see inside every room and from the looks of it the complex had every sport and exercise imaginable. We passed rooms with tennis courts, rooms with ballet bars, rooms with thick cloths hanging from the ceiling. In one room a boy was twisting the cloth around his body, pulling himself up somehow and doing flips mid-air. Another room we passed was full of punching bags and a lot of really angry-looking tattooed teenagers with boxing gloves.

Near the end of the hall was a man around my age, wearing jeans and a blue cotton t-shirt cleaning a section of the glass wall. His brown hair was long enough that it was curling around his ears and he had at least ten piercings in one ear and a gage in the other. He looked up when we got close and tossed a bottle of cleaner onto the ground, wiping his hands with a rag.

"These two were looking for you, Steve," Alice said as she folded her arms and strode away.

Steve's narrowed eyes studied my body, but not in an appreciative way. No, it was in more of a 'does she have any weapons hidden under that yellow sundress' kind of way.

"No way you're a cop. Too pretty." He didn't say it like a compliment. He looked at the camera but continued to address me. "And what's with Scorsese?"

"Listen, Steve," I clasped my hands together ready to plead for this janitor to give me my next clue, "I know –"

"Nobody calls me Steve." His expression hardened, and his fist clenched the rag he held. Scorsese, as Steve had affectionately called Paulo, had the nerve to back up several steps. I glared at him before turning back to Steve.

"Right, Stephen, then," I began. "Lincoln Lockwood sent me here and said that you had something to give me."

"Lincoln Lockwood?" His shoulders relaxed, and he threw the rag aside. "Funny guy. He knows I hate being called Steve. He mentioned a lady might stop by to see me. I guess I just thought he meant an old lady." He chuckled and pulled a folded envelope out of his back pocket. I reached out to take it, but he snatched it back. "Oh, right. I'm supposed to ask you when Lincoln's birthday is?"

"It's…um…" Lincoln's birthday, Lincoln's birthday…May 6? May 12? September 22? I had no idea. Why couldn't I remember? I'd stared at the date on his Wikipedia page before I'd come and repeated it over and over and over. I'd already forgotten?

Steve folded his arms and flipped the envelope back and forth impatiently.

Impatient to a fault, I snatched it out of his hands.

"Hey!"

I gave him the look my mom gave my brothers when they threatened to call CPS because she took away their Nintendo. He stepped back and held up his hands in surrender.

"I was just trying to do what I promised. No reason to get hostile."

Ignoring him, I tore open the second envelope.

"Well, Prince, Genoa and Lucca are now no more than private estates of the Bonaparte family."

Find your next clue inside Lincoln's favorite book at his favorite spot.

"What does that mean?" I jumped, just then realizing that Steve had moved to read over my shoulder. "I've known him forever and he never said anything about Bonaparte."

"It's a quote from a book. Lincoln's favorite one, apparently." I chewed on my lower lip.

Steve shrugged. "At least the second part's easy."

"You know his favorite spot?" I swatted away the camera that kept getting far too close to my face. "Where is it?"

"I'm not helping you." He picked up his rag and started walking away.

I grabbed his arm to stop him. "Yes, you are. I only have a few more hours and I don't know how long it's going to take to get to Lincoln's 'favorite place.' I need your help."

Steve's eyes roamed up and down my body in an entirely different way. "What do I get out of this?"

I scowled. "What do you want?"

He looked at the camera and then back at me before he grinned so wide like a kid on the first day of summer. "I want a kiss."

"Excuse me?" My jaw dropped.

"You heard me."

I looked back and forth between Steve and Paulo, but Paulo was not coming to my rescue. On the contrary, I could see his shoulders shaking with barely contained laughter as (I'm sure) he zoomed in on us.

Folding my arms, I turned back to Steve. "This could be considered extortion."

"I don't know about extortion, I just know that you have to plant a big wet one on these two lips or I'm not telling you where to go."

"'A big wet one?'" I rolled my eyes. "You sound like Alfalfa."

Confusion clouded his face. "Who?"

"Never mind." I steeled myself, mentally and physically, and then gave Steve a quick kiss right on the mouth.

I must have caught him by surprise, despite it coming at his request because he stepped back so quickly he almost fell over. I caught his arm as he steadied himself. His eyes were wide and bright, but I think it was more in shock than anything. "His favorite spot is where he met me."

"What?" Anger flared inside me. "I can't believe I believed that you knew!"

"I'm serious, Red." He nodded, still smiling like an idiot. "We met on the steps outside St. Joseph Church."

"Why on earth would that be his favorite spot?"

"Beats me. He said the day he met me is when his life changed."

It hit me all at once. "You're the one," I said in awe.

He looked alarmed. "Hey now, just 'cause I wanted you to kiss me doesn't mean –"

"Shut up." I held up a hand. "You're the one that inspired him to start the community youth center. You must have been…what…" It was my turn to look him up and down. "Fourteen when you two met?"

"Fifteen." Steve's chin jutted up slightly.

"Fifteen," I said in awe. "Thank you, Stephen, for your help."

I walked away, still shaking my head, and pulled out my phone to find directions to St. Joseph Church. An angry red battery glared at me from the screen, informing me that my phone only had 20% life left. I made a face before disregarding it and pulling up directions. I was about to turn the corner when Steve called out, "Are you at least going to tell me what that quote is from?"

I halted and put the palm of my hand to my head. I launched Google and typed in the quote. "*War and Peace*," I yelled back to him. "It's the first line of *War and Peace*."

Once Paulo and I were back on the road, I thought more about what I'd learned about Lincoln. I didn't have to be a detective to know that Steve must have been the victim of child violence when he and Lincoln had crossed paths. It made me hurt in a way I couldn't quite explain to know that the problem had been so widespread, Lincoln had felt the need to create a massive complex to help combat it. It'd taken a few years, but he'd done it. He'd built the community youth center and, not only that, but he'd given Stephen a job there.

What kind of man did that?

Lost in thought, it wasn't until I turned into a public parking garage that I noticed the time. It was almost 2:00. Any new revelations about Lincoln wouldn't matter if I didn't make it back to the house first. But then again, after everyone saw the trailer for the next episode, I might as well pack my bags.

Unless I finished first.

The church loomed high above us

"That's a church." Paulo shook his head. "I can't film in there."

"Fine," I said. "Wait here. I'll be fast."

I spied a handicap parking space right next to the entrance and squealed into it. Hearing the illegal parking warning bells go off in my mind, I parked and ran to the church. I threw the doors open with such force, I'm pretty sure it awoke the gargoyles on the roof.

Okay, so there weren't any gargoyles up there, but the bang was still really loud.

I would have outright run, but I could practically hear my mother berating me for being disrespectful in a church so, like any occasional church-goer, I compromised my morals.

"May I help you?" I screeched to a stop and turned to a man dressed in a simple black suit standing between two pews.

"Hi," I said struggling to breathe. "I'm looking for a book."

The man nodded. "I know exactly what you're talking about." He bent behind one of the pews and came up holding a thick black book.

A bible.

I almost laughed out loud. "I like you! You're funny. I didn't know Priests were allowed to be funny."

"I'm a Bishop," he said seriously.

"Oh, well, then," I coughed feeling incredibly ignorant. "Anyway, I need the book *War and Peace*. I was told you had it here. Lincoln Lockwood sent me."

"Ahh," he nodded again. I followed him through a side door into a small room with plastic toys spilled across the floor. The Bishop went and opened a corner cupboard. He motioned for me to come see and I looked inside to find a handful of picture books, several DVDs, and one very large, thick book. I pulled out *War and Peace* and looked at him incredulously.

"You thought you should have a bit of light reading in case the kids got bored?"

He didn't smile.

I was starting to think the Bible thing hadn't been a joke.

Embarrassment colored my cheeks and I flipped through the pages until I found what I was looking for. I tossed the book back into the cupboard, noticing the Bishop wincing at my apparent disrespect of literature, and tore open the envelope.

The paper was blank except for an address.

Was this the final meeting place? I couldn't stop smiling.

"Thanks, Bishop!" I bowed and ran out of there. It wasn't until I was to the church's doors that I realized I probably shouldn't have bowed to a Bishop. I prayed for forgiveness as I pushed my way outside. I halted on the church steps and looked frantically for the red SUV. I'd parked it right there…didn't I? I jogged down the street but didn't see it. Did Paulo move it? I pulled out my phone. I didn't have any missed texts or calls from unknown numbers. If he had, he'd park and come find me, wouldn't he?

My phone vibrated, an angry red outline of the battery flashed, and the screen went black.

Oh good. No car, a missing cameraman, and a dead phone. If it was dark this would be the perfect time to get murdered.

I paced the sidewalk scanning the streets for the red SUV, but all I saw were yellow taxis and gray Priuses. I tried to turn my phone on again, but it showed no signs of life. I grumbled and waited what felt like another fifteen minutes before I turned back to the church.

The Bishop should have a phone, right?

I flew up the steps and yanked on the church's doors, but they didn't budge. It was only after yanking a second time that I saw a black sign to the right of the doors:

CLOSED

That stupid Bishop had locked me out!

Apparently, God was not as forgiving as I would have hoped.

And calling his servant "stupid" probably didn't help matters.

I let out a frustrated scream causing a family of tourists to hurry their children to the other side of the street. I grimaced and waved in an attempt to show them I was harmless. They gave me wary looks and practically shoved their children into the nearest parked cab.

Reaching the sidewalk, I raised my arm and after a minute a cab stopped in front of me.

"Where to?" The driver, an old man with an Irish accent, asked once I was inside.

"Oh...I..." Should I go to the address on the paper? Or back to the mansion? My eyes found the dashboard clock and I gasped. "Is it really 3:15?"

The man nodded, ignoring my obvious dismay. "Address?"

I shoved the paper with the address at him. "How fast can you get here? Can you get there by 4:00?"

He started laughing and pointed at the paper. "That is on the other side of Los Angeles. We will be in traffic for over an hour."

Groaning, I hid my face in my hands. "Fine. Just take me to Beverley Glen."

"There's an extra fee for locations more than 15 miles away."

"Fine, whatever." It wasn't until he squeezed the cab into traffic that I realized I didn't actually have any money, but I kept that fact to myself. I did not want to be kicked out of the cab before we'd even gone one block. Besides, Lincoln was a millionaire. I'm sure he wouldn't have a problem paying for my cab.

It wasn't long before we were at a dead stop on the freeway on-ramp.

"Is this going to take very long?" Even though I knew I was going to lose, I wanted to get there at least close to 4:00.

He nodded seriously. "A very long time."

I groaned again and let my head fall back against the seat. Maybe I should have stayed at the church. Maybe if I'd become a nun or something, then I wouldn't have to face the humiliation of being sent back to New York to get fired.

If only.

Chapter $13

"Address?"

I jerked awake at the driver's voice. It was dark out and the cab was parked on the side of the road in front of the giant gate that led into Lincoln's "neighborhood."

"Oh, um…I'm not sure of the number. Just go up to the gate – the guard will let me in."

The driver grumbled but pulled up to the guard. I rolled down my window to speak with the tall, lanky middle-aged man who looked like he was somewhere between dozing off and preparing for an attack.

"Hi!" I said in an overly chipper voice. "We're going to Lincoln Lockwood's house?"

"Name and ID." He held out his hand.

"Oh, silly me." I pretended to search the back of the cab for a minute before I turned back to the guard. "I'm so sorry, but it looks like I left my purse at the house."

"What?!" The cab driver yelled from the front seat, but the guard didn't convey any emotion.

"I'm sorry, miss, but I can't let you inside."

"But I should be on the list." I crossed my fingers and leaned out the window. "Paige Michaels?"

He glanced at a paper I couldn't see and then shook his head. "No. I'm going to need you to turn around." He motioned for the cab driver to go take the small road circling the guardhouse.

"Please, if you could just call Lincoln." At this point, about half my body was outside the window. "I'm one of the contestants on the show."

"I must be paid!" the driver interrupted.

"I don't know what you're talking about," the guard said.

"The show, the reality show," I rushed to explain. "Please just call him."

He sighed, picked up an office-style phone and pressed a single button. He hung up a moment later.

"No answer. He's clearly not expecting anyone. Please, sir, turn the car around."

The driver let out a string of curse words but shifted the car into drive. With me still hanging out the window, he spun the car around the guard house and screeched to a stop at the curb.

"Out!" he barked.

I struggled to return to my seat. "What do you mean?"

"Outside. I will wait for payment here. You will wait outside." Apparently, the driver didn't like how long I stared at him in disbelief because he got out of the driver's seat and opened my door.

"Hey!" I yelped as he grabbed my arm and pulled me out of the cab. He slammed the driver's door behind him and I heard the locks click.

"I can't pay you if I can't get back to the house!" I yelled.

He rolled down his window and glared at me. "I do not care if you get to the house. I care about getting paid. I suggest you figure out a way to get the money. I will wait here, with the meter running, of course."

"Of course!" I resisted the urge to kick one of his tires as I stalked back to the guard.

"Will you call him again please?" I tapped my foot while I waited, but once again Lincoln didn't answer the guard's call. I slumped my

WHO WANTS TO MARRY A MILLIONAIRE?

way over to the curb opposite the cab and plopped down. On the verge of tears, I pulled out my phone to call Jemma but was brutally reminded it was dead. I longed to throw it across the street and if I'd had more than $800 in my bank account, I would have.

Just then the guard called out, "He's on his way."

When a black Mercedes came through the gate a little while later and parked next to the guard's hut, I ran over to greet it. To my surprise, Andy, not Lincoln, was the one to step out of the driver's side.

"Andy!" I threw myself at him, tears of relief forming in my eyes. "Thank –"

"Where have you been, Paige?!" Andy's voice scared me. I stopped short of flinging my arms around him. He held me at arm's length, gripping my shoulders tightly. "You've been missing for hours! Paulo showed up and said that you took off when you got to the church."

Instantly, my eyes were dry. "Oh, please! He *abandoned* me! He left while I was inside getting the clue. I came out and couldn't find him. I waited for him forever and had to get a cab to get back here, which took *five hours* because of traffic, and then the stupid guard wouldn't let me in and Lincoln wasn't answering –"

"Why didn't you just call?" Andy threw his hands in the air. "I've called you a hundred times in the past four hours, but you kept sending me to voicemail!"

A loud horn broke through our fight and we both looked over to the angry cab driver who was holding his hand out the window impatiently. Andy looked at me and I gave him my best "you've got to be kidding me" look.

He stalked over to the cab, swore when he saw the price on the display, pulled out his wallet and handed the driver several hundred-dollar bills.

Hundred. Dollar. Bills.

Bills. As in, more than one.

I pointed in disbelief at the cab driving away as Andy returned to my side, pocketing his wallet. "Why do you have so much cash? And in *hundreds*?"

He grabbed my pointed finger with one hand, pulled me toward the Mercedes and opened the passenger-side door for me. When I didn't make a move to get in, he sighed and said, "I don't like credit cards, okay?"

I didn't say anything as I got in the car.

The two of us were quiet as Andy drove us back to the estate. After we pulled into the garage, Andy led me out a side door and through the back gate. Crickets chirped obnoxiously as we walked down the path to the pool. We turned past a giant bush and I stopped in my tracks.

"Where is everyone?" Lincoln and a couple of cameramen were the only ones around. One man was taking down the giant lights they'd use for filming.

"Inside," Andy said without waiting. "We finished filming over an hour ago."

"But what about me?" I rushed to catch up.

"Paulo said you left. We couldn't wait around forever." Andy left me alone and over to one of the cameramen and clapped him on the shoulder. "Take some shots of Paige arriving and then call it a night."

"Paige!" Lincoln called, clearly surprised. I guessed Andy hadn't told him when the guard called. "Where have you been?"

It was amazing how quickly the cameras were focused on us. I couldn't stop looking between them and Andy, but Lincoln came toward me and took my hands. I tore my gaze away from Andy's tired face and faced him.

"I'm sorry we finished filming without you," Lincoln said without glancing at the camera. "We thought you'd left."

I furrowed my brow. "Without my wallet? I left my purse in the car."

It was his turn to look confused. "Paulo didn't say anything about your wallet."

"Lincoln!" Wanda, having just come out of the house, called to him and just like that he was gone.

I sighed and didn't bother looking away when the camera got right in my face. I rolled my eyes and walked over to Andy, pleased to see the cameraman stay behind, apparently disappointed with my lack of tears.

"Thanks," I said when I reached Andy. "For picking me up. And the cab. And…everything."

"You're welcome," he said flatly.

"I guess I lost the race." I forced a laugh.

Andy searched my face before he said, "Lost? Paige, you didn't even finish. You're most likely off the show."

"Wait, what?"

"We'll have to see what the vote is tonight, but you're probably in last place."

"What do you mean tonight? The first episode isn't even supposed to premiere until tomorrow!" I had to have more time. I needed more time.

"We're doing a double-feature tonight because of the magazine article that came out this morning. They've already edited the footage from today. I'll make sure they get the footage of you arriving in there, but we decided to do a live elimination. It's America's choice, but it's likely you'll be on a plane by midnight."

It hit me then. An audience polled elimination. The lowest score was sent home.

"No." I clutched my stomach as if I'd been sucker punched.

"I'm sorry, Paige." He looked like he meant it, too. My mind was reeling. If I was off the show I was fired.

I was fired.

Andy looked around and took a step closer. His voice was a distant whisper when he said, "But maybe when the show's over in a couple weeks, I could come to New York and –"

I couldn't get fired.

It didn't even occur to me that I was interrupting him when I said, "I can't lose."

He took a step back. Running a hand over his exhausted face, he mumbled something about needing coke – or, more likely, a Coke – and wandered off leaving me to revel in my miserable failure.

I lost. I REALLY lost. Not only did I come in last place, I didn't even finish!

No. I could not get sent home. The only way America would keep me around is if they thought I was the best one for Lincoln. I had to prove to everyone that I wanted him – even if I didn't. But what should I do? The only advice Jemma had given me was to jump his bones. And that wasn't happening. But come to think of it, Jemma did have one other trick…

"Hey, Lincoln." He was standing with Wanda several yards away. I strode over to him like I was Gigi Hadid on a runway. Except I was short with red hair and absolutely nothing like Gigi Hadid on a runway. Lincoln turned around and raised his eyebrows in question. Out of my periphery, I noticed the cameras closing in on us.

Good.

I stopped when my shoes touched his and put my hands on his chest. Praying for Jemma's spirit to take over my body so I could have a chance of pulling this off, I prepared to mimic a move I'd seen her pull a thousand times.

Step 1: Flip hair over shoulder.

Step 2: Finger collar of his shirt.

Step 3: Look up through thick lashes.

I followed the steps like a pro, or like Jemma, and tried to put on a sexy pout. "Don't you think the loser should at least get a consolation prize?"

Without waiting for a response and fully conscious of both cameras zoomed in on us, I covered his mouth with mine. I kissed him like Allie kisses Noah in *The Notebook*. At least, that's what I intended it to look like. It probably looked more like Toby kissing Eunice in *She's the Man*, but whatever. It got the point across. I hope.

After kissing him, I slowly pulled away, my hands still on his face. A cry of outrage came from behind me. I looked over my shoulder at the other girls who'd just appeared. They stood on the deck looking down at us, all four pairs of eyes boring into me. Carmen's mouth hung open. Peggy blushed and covered her mouth with one hand. Bunny's nose kept twitching as if she were about to cry. But Amelia was the worst. Amelia had a smile on her lips and hatred in her eyes. I wouldn't have been surprised if she turned into the Hulk and smashed me into the pavement.

I turned back to Lincoln whose eyes were still shut and let my hands slip to his shoulders. He kept his eyes shut for another second and took a deep breath. I couldn't believe it. I'd left him breathless. The last man I'd left breathless was Alan Squires in 10th grade and that was only because he'd forgotten his inhaler.

I focused on smoothing the collar of Lincoln's shirt as his bright eyes stared down at me. Why was he looking at me like that? The kiss was nice, but it wasn't that nice. Was it? Maybe I was too focused on everything else to really pay attention.

"I feel like that was more of a prize for me than for you," he said quietly.

"Winning isn't everything," I said. Before I could talk myself out of it, I touched my lips to his one more time and then turned to walk away. I almost tripped when I saw Andy. He'd already come back from getting a Coke and had seen the whole thing.

And he didn't look happy.

$$$

The premiere was almost two hours later, but we didn't get a chance to watch it. The end of the second episode we were rushing around getting prepared. Andy had gone and checked the SUV for my purse and had someone drop it off in my room. I plugged my phone in to charge while I dressed in a fitted tea-length rose-colored gown with flowers sewn onto sheer sleeves. Peggy, elegantly adorned in a mid-thigh LBD, tried to stream the premiere on her phone but was unable to get it without a subscription. We were both silent as we finished getting ready for the night, calmly putting our makeup on, and even helping one another zip up our dresses.

I knew the second episode started at 9:00 tonight and I assumed my date would be the first part. Remembering that Jemma said she'd text me while she watched the episode, I rushed to turn on my now fully-charged phone. Instead of texts from Jemma, I saw that I'd missed one call from Carla and six calls from a number I didn't recognize. I checked my voicemail and heard Andy's voice asking where I was. Each message became more and more urgent. I saved Andy's number before deleting all of them, including the one from Carla.

I was still angry at her for releasing the first article early. She could wait.

I checked the clock what seemed like every hour but was really only every thirty seconds. I couldn't stop wondering which part they were showing and knowing the audience would rate my second task as they watched. Maybe if I got enough points I'd be allowed to stay. I didn't even know if it was possible, but I wrung my hands as I waited.

"Paige, it's time to go," Peggy said. Not looking up from my phone, I followed her out back to stand by the pool.

"Congratulations, Paige!" Andy's announcer voice clued me in that we were already on air.

Andy pulled me aside as a tech directed the other contestants to a white couch in front of the pool. "From what you and Lincoln told me, you had a good date, and America thinks so too."

It was clearly my turn to speak, and for once I wasn't tongue-tied. "We did," I said happily. "It was one of the best dates of my life. Even if he did practically throw me off a cliff." I winked at the camera. Andy laughed, though I couldn't tell whether or not it was faked and gestured for me to sit on the couch by the others.

"The group's second task was to complete a scavenger hunt." Andy addressed the cameras. "Each contestant had separate, but equally difficult clues to help them through their hunt. When we get back we'll see how each contestant tackled each situation and which one of them was unable to finish at all."

Rude.

The cameras turned off for the commercial break and Andy explained we'd be able to watch the scavenger hunt. One tech put up a large white screen in front of the couch while another tech set up a hand-held projector. Several minutes later commercials started playing on the screen in surprisingly high quality.

After a commercial involving an elephant and a beer, music echoed around us as a bar graph appeared on the screen. It was the perfect combination to build suspense and anticipation. The bars above each of our names moved up and down depending on the scores we'd received from voters. Carmen and Peggy were about the same score, but Amelia's bar climbed upward with every passing second. Mine moved up and down, up and down, reminding me of a yoga class Jemma and I had taken where neither of us could contort ourselves into the right pose and spent the evening falling to the ground and clambering back up.

The bars' movement slowed and soon the tallest one was flashing gold and a number above everyone else's bar. Amelia had the highest score at 93. The number two floated over Peggy's bar which had reached 87. Bunny was fourth at 83. My fingernails dug into my palms as my eyes zoomed in on my score.

86. 86? 86?

I was a hot mess! Who in the world would vote for me? Only then did I see the number three floating above my bar.

"Carmen," Andy put a consolidating hand on her shoulder, "I'm so sorry, but it looks like marrying a millionaire is just not in the cards for you."

Was Carmen going home? Instead of me? My head swiveled to see her score and I grimaced. Dang. That had to hurt. A 46. I didn't particularly like Carmen, but I didn't hate her either. In fact, other than making fun of her memory, I didn't really think about her at all. Maybe no one else did either, and maybe that was the problem.

Lincoln had appeared at some point during the scoring and held his arms out to Carmen. To her eternal credit, she didn't wail with grief like the previously eliminated contestants. She gave Lincoln a watery smile, a hug and left with a quiet, "Good luck."

Once she was off-camera, but long before she was out of earshot, Andy practically shouted, "Amelia! Congratulations on finishing the scavenger hunt first and winning the approval of all of America. You're awarded the second date with Lincoln."

Peggy looked forlorn, but Bunny huffed and stamped her foot. Yes, she actually *stamped her foot*. I couldn't totally blame her, but at the same time, I couldn't believe she would act like such a child. She'd get her turn. Maybe.

The second they finished filming, Amelia cornered Lincoln to talk. Bunny marched off with her arms folded and Peggy unsuccessfully tried to get Lincoln's attention by walking back-and-forth past him and Amelia. I just kind of stood there awkwardly, wondering how long it would be before I could get something to eat.

"How is our most relatable contestant doing?" I turned at the sound of Andy's voice.

"What are you talking about?"

He gave me his phone in response. It was his Twitter feed. Tweets were rapidly coming through with the hashtag #RelatableRed.

> Can't say how many times I've locked my keys in my car. #relatablered #wwtmam

> Is it just me or is Paige the only one worth watching on this show? Cracks me up! #relatablered #wwtmam

> So glad someone on this show is #keepingitreal. #relatablered #wwtmam

I handed him his phone and after saying goodnight, I disappeared to go write my next article.

LOOK! EXCLUSIVE

the most likable future mrs. millionaire
(and the least)
by an Anonymous Contributor

The best part of reality TV, besides girls' nights filled with copious amounts of wine and chocolate, is trash talking the contestants. Not only is it better than watching a RomCom, it encourages social interaction and serious debate. That, and it's fun to gossip. ☺ In the true spirit of Hollywood, we've taken the contestants' latest scores and compiled a detailed (and judgmental) list of their rankings, from least to most liked.

#5: Carmen Something: Carmen might not be the most disliked contestant, but she certainly is the most forgettable. Both for fans and in-person. Which is probably why she was voted off. As all true die-hard reality fans will remember, she's comparable to Taylor Hicks, the winner of American Idol's 5th season. After the season ended Hicks went on to perform on Broadway and (unfortunately for him and American Idol's PR department) no one's really kept track of him since. Wait…who was I supposed to be talking about?

#4: Bunny (no joke) Hopkins: Although she's been cursed with an ill-fated name, she's been blessed with good looks. Unfortunately, that's all she's got going for her. The blonde bombshell spends her time fighting for fruit rights. Yes, you did read that correctly. In case you weren't aware, fruit not only contains nutrition, but also human emotions. In her eyes, eating fruit classifies you as a cold-hearted killer. If that's not enough to put her in fourth place, her obnoxious, bunny-like mannerisms are. Every time she gnaws on carrots, twitches her nose, or munches on peanuts it's loud enough to make someone wish they were locked in a dark room with the drip, drip, drip, of a leaky faucet. Even that would be preferable to the torture of Bunny's idiosyncrasies.

#3: Peggy Cochran: Disney is currently recruiting Peggy to become their next Disney princess. Her luscious blonde locks and bright blue eyes make it easy to imagine her chipper voice singing woodland animals to sleep. With an Instagram feed full of impossible yoga poses (who does the Crow pose on a rock in the middle of the ocean??) and cat videos she should be the most likable. But maybe the reason Princess is stuck in third place is that no one is buying this. Not even Disney princesses are perfect. What deep, dark, highly-embarrassing secret is she trying to hide? Until we find out, Namaste away from this chick.

#2: Paige Michaels: Paige might be WWTMAM's walking disaster, but something about her cringe-inducing moments makes her near and dear to our hearts. Her Jennifer Lawrence-esque attitude has the inter-webs clambering to be her best friend. Could the reason she's still a contestant have more to do with the fact that she's relatable? If you need further evidence think about the last time you were stranded with no money and a dead phone. It induces the "poor thing" emotion which entices viewers to give her the sympathy vote. Still, Paige is just the kind of person who would gladly commiserate with us over a bad day providing cookie dough and a Hallmark movie. That, at least, makes her perfect for us, if not for Lincoln.

#1: Amelia Gregory: Remember that cheerleader in high school who all the guys wanted and every girl wanted to be? Meet Amelia, your routine New York fashion model whose stunning face has been splashed across the web in ads for Marc Jacobs and Calvin Klein. A stereotypical candidate, her confident personality might be best suited for Mr. Lincoln Lockwood. She's got trophy-wife/future divorcee written all over her.

Chapter $14

"I understand you're upset, but it's not that big of a deal. Especially tonight's article."

I halted on the top stair. I couldn't tell if Andy was on the phone or not. And, if not, then I was going to be in big trouble if someone else saw me. In the middle of the night. While everyone was on the lookout for a mole.

Meaning me. I was the mole. Not that they were looking for a *mole* mole. It was more likely they'd have raccoons in this neighborhood than moles. Just thought I'd clarify.

It was quiet for a moment before Andy spoke again. He was on the phone. Good. "It's just a puff piece, it's nothing to worry about. Any blogger could have posted the exact same thing."

Andy thought my article was a puff piece? Gee, thanks. I mean, yeah, it wasn't on its way to a Pulitzer or anything, but Carla needed the article to be tame in order to calm down the lawyers. I'd written the whole thing on my phone in less than an hour and texted it to her. I'd slept for a while, waking automatically at 2:00 a.m. even though I wasn't hungry. It was as if my body needed to see Andy. (That sounds really dirty, but trust me, it was unintentional. Mostly.) I'd wandered the halls to Lincoln's kitchen anyway and was now eavesdropping on Andy's phone call.

"Wanda, it's going to be alright. No one will care that we fudged Carmen's points. It's like the article said: she was forgettable." I could hear the shrug in his voice even as my heart skipped a beat. "And weird. She asked me who I was like twenty times."

They changed Carmen's score?

Another pause and he sighed. "We'll figure out who it was. We'll fire them and, if we have to, we'll sue *Look!* Besides, I think I might know who it is."

He did?? I leaned forward on the steps and lost my balance. I tumbled forward and caught myself on the tile floor with one hand. Andy appeared at the staircase, his phone to his ear and his brow furrowed.

"Wanda, go to bed. We'll talk about this tomorrow." He hung up and held out a hand to help me up.

"Thanks." I brushed my hands off and chewed my lower lip before deciding there was no use pretending I hadn't overheard. "It sounds like this whole leak thing is going to give Wanda a nervous breakdown."

He let out a harsh laugh and ran a hand through his hair. His sexy middle-of-the-night hair. "Or something." He went to the fridge and started pulling out food. I followed him, but stood a few feet away, unsure if I should leave.

"I can go," I finally said, pointing behind me. "I'm not that hungry anyway."

"It's no big deal." Andy put a gallon of milk on the counter. "I won't be able to sleep for a while."

I let out a breath I didn't realize I was holding. "You sure?"

"Yeah." He leaned against the island and folded his arms. "Besides, if you go I'll miss my chance to practice my cooking."

I narrowed my eyes and he smirked. "Fine, Mr. Fieri, what will you be dishing up tonight?"

"I was thinking Chicken Cordon Bleu and linguini," he said elegantly.

"At two in the morning?"

"Too much?"

I wrinkled my nose. "How about cookie dough instead?"

"We have cookie dough in the fridge. That won't allow me to show off."

"Uh-uh, no way. Pre-made cookie dough is fine when you're with your girlfriends lamenting a bad date, but homemade cookie dough? That's good all the time. Especially in the middle of the night."

He laughed. "Okay, I'll find a recipe." He pulled his phone out of his pocket.

I *tsked*. "Oh, you poor, poor man. Only an amateur has to use a recipe to make cookie dough. Why doesn't the Master Chef take a night off and let me show him how it's really done?"

He held his arms out as if to say, "be my guest." I playfully pushed past him and after putting away the ingredients I didn't need, I started going through the cupboards to find what I did. I found everything except one vital ingredient.

"How can a millionaire not have chocolate chips?" I was aghast. I honestly couldn't see how a gourmet kitchen could be missing this staple.

Andy, now sitting on a barstool, shrugged. "I guess Lincoln never eats Chocolate Chip Cookies."

I whirled around. "What do you mean 'never eats Chocolate Chip Cookies'? That's ludicrous!"

"Uh-oh. Is it a deal breaker? Are you leaving the show over this?"

"I might as well. I could never be with a man who doesn't like Chocolate Chip Cookies."

"Wow, this is serious. I guess it's a good thing then that I love Chocolate Chip Cookies." He winked and I blushed, pursing my lips to suppress a smile, then turning back to the cupboards to find something else we could substitute. I hit pay dirt on the top shelf of the pantry.

"Aha!" I whirled around a manic grin on my face. I held up the Hershey's bar. "This will work beautifully!"

"A Hershey's bar?"

"Yes," I said. I took a knife from the knife block and placed it and the chocolate in front of him. "Grab a cutting board and start chopping."

"You're an awfully demanding chef."

"Hurry now! Chop, chop!" I clapped my hands together. He laughed and after finding a cutting board he got to work chopping the bar into tiny cubes.

As he chopped chocolate and I mixed ingredients we talked about college and the stupid things we'd done. He told me how he and his roommates used to take cafeteria trays and use them as sleds. They'd race down hills of snow and then freeze their glove-less hands as they threw snowballs at girls' windows. I told him about my family and how my mom wanted me to marry a guy I'd gone to high school with and how she brought it up every time I called. I told him it was one of the many reasons I was determined to make it in Manhattan. I wanted to prove I could take care of myself.

"I've got to say," I said during a lull in the conversation. "Cooking in Lincoln's kitchen is ten times better than cooking in mine. My roommate Jemma and I are practically on top of each other any time we try to use the sink. I'd gladly switch to this kitchen any day of the week."

"Why don't you? Switch apartments, I mean."

I snorted and poured flour into the bowl. "We're in the only place we can afford. It might be a crappy studio, but it's a miracle we found it and we're not giving it up to save our lives."

"But you work for one of the top event planning companies in New York," he said, surprised. "I would have thought you had plenty of money."

Crap. I'd gotten too comfortable. Had I said anything else that might incriminate me?

"In your application, it said something about how you loved to shop at designer stores in your spare time."

Crap, crap, crap, crappity, crap, crap. I turned away and started opening and closing drawers to keep him from seeing my panicked face.

"Oh yeah," I stammered. "I do...but um...you know New York. One of the most expensive places in the world."

"Do you spend all your money on clothes or something?"

"Something like that?" Oops. That wasn't supposed to come out sounding like a question.

"I –"

"Oh!" I grabbed a spatula out of one of the open drawers and held it up as if it were the holy grail. "Found one!" The flour dusted the dough as I used it to scrape the sides of the bowl. I engrossed myself in mixing it in until all traces were gone. I didn't look at Andy again until it was done and then motioned he should bring the chocolate.

His arm brushed mine as he stirred in the makeshift chocolate chips. I stared at his arm, strong and tan under his standard white t-shirt. His muscles were tight against the sleeves and the veins in his forearm stood out against his skin. We were quiet as he continued stirring, even after everything was mixed together. The chocolate chunks gave the dough a deliciously rough quality, shavings of chocolate breaking off and dotting the caramel-colored mixture. I was hypnotized by the movement of the dough and the way Andy's hand gripped the spoon.

Closing my eyes, I cleared my throat. "I'll get us some spoons."

"No." Andy put a hand on my back to stop me. "Let me get them."

I took a staggered breath and smiled when he handed me my spoon. My tension eased and I giggled when he stuffed a big spoonful in his mouth all at once. Upon tasting it, he beamed.

"What if it wasn't any good? You would have been stuck with a mouthful of gross cookie dough."

He swallowed with some difficulty and said, "I trust you."

If his words were said to make me laugh, it didn't work. I considered his statement as we each ate another spoonful in silence. How could he trust me? Even with something as small as cookie dough? He didn't even know me. He went to put his spoon in the sink and I licked mine clean, ready to do the same. I'd just finished cleaning it off, still thinking about the words "I trust you" when I felt him behind me. Hands rested on my shoulders, soft and gentle. His mouth was at my ear and his breath hot on my cheek. All thoughts of trust flew from my mind.

"I'm sorry for asking you about money," he said. "It's none of my business."

Money? What money? I struggled to make sense of his words. And then I remembered. He was talking about all the money I supposedly earned and then wasted on clothes. Had I been worried about that? I couldn't recall. He was standing so close. I told myself to get it together. It was getting late and I was tired. That was the only reason my vision was blurring and my skin singing.

And then his lips were on my neck and his hands slid down my sides, resting on my hips. My eyes fluttered closed as his lips moved down the length of my neck, feather-soft kisses leaving a trail of sparks in their wake. I leaned back into him and he brushed my hair over one shoulder. Kisses traced their way around my collar but slowed as they reached my spine, eventually stopping altogether.

Well, that just wouldn't do.

The spoon I still held clattered to the counter and I twisted in his arms so we stood face-to-face. Wrapping my arms around his neck, I pulled him down to meet me, but before our mouths could meet he lifted me onto the counter. My legs locked around his back and I gave him a cheeky grin as I tossed my hair back. Our smiles were almost touching when we heard a noise.

"Andy?" Lincoln's voice came from the hallway. "Is that you?"

We leaped apart, and in my haste to get off the counter I fell onto my hands and knees like a cat. I could hear the soft slap of bare feet against tile seconds away. I scrambled to stand so I could run to the stairs, but Andy's hand pushed down on my head to keep me hidden. The footsteps stopped.

"Hey." Lincoln's voice was only a few feet away. "I thought I heard you up. Everything okay?"

"Oh sure," Andy said, overly casual in my opinion. "Couldn't sleep, that's all."

"Was it because you had a craving for Chocolate Chip Cookies?"

"What? Oh, you mean all this. No, I, uh…wanted to um…yeah, I had a craving."

Oh man. I hid my face in my hands trying not to groan. For someone who could turn the charm off and on like a stereo, Andy sucked at lying. If he couldn't pull this off, we were going to get caught and I'd be on the next flight to New York. I'd probably arrive just in time for Carla to fire me on her way to a lunch meeting.

"Okay…" It was clear Lincoln either thought Andy was lying or had lost his mind and decided to start sleep-baking.

"I'll clean all this up. You can go back to bed."

"Actually, now that you're up," one of the barstools scraped against the floor as it was pulled out, "I've been wanting to talk to you."

"It can wait, can't it?"

"I guess," he said. "But it's about the whole Paige thing and I wondered if you –"

The Paige thing? My head shot up.

"Aww man," Andy yawned. Loudly. "I'm sorry, but I'm wiped. Can we do this tomorrow?"

My brow furrowed. What did Lincoln have to say that Andy didn't want me to hear?

"Uh, sure, I guess." The stool scraped against the tile again and Lincoln's bare feet slapped against the floor as he headed for the hallway. He stopped. "You sure you don't want help cleaning up?"

"Nah," Andy said. "If I don't do it how is my sleep self ever going to learn?"

"Ha. Sure. 'Night."

"'Night," Andy called. I didn't move until Andy helped me up.

"What 'Paige thing' was he talking about?" I asked quietly.

"Don't worry about it." Andy rubbed my shoulders and glanced over at the way Lincoln had gone. "It's nothing."

"It doesn't seem like nothing."

"Whatever it is, I'll take care of it." I narrowed my eyes, but he changed the subject. "You should go back to bed. I'll clean this up."

"Okay," I conceded. I was exhausted and knew if I pushed the matter of "the Paige thing" my sass might get the better of me. Better to wait until tomorrow. Unsure of how to say goodnight – we'd just been on the verge of kissing – I squeezed his hand and gave him a quick peck on the cheek before I left.

As I made my way back to the contestants' part of the house, the reality of what had just happened hit me. Lincoln had almost caught me making out – kind of – with Andy. I wasn't even engaged to the guy and I was already cheating. Although, now that I thought about it, Lincoln and I didn't have any commitment other than the legal contract. Right? So was I cheating on him or not? He was dating three other girls… I groaned, deciding to take a quick pit stop. I went inside the small movie theater and made sure its sound-proofed door was closed before I pulled out my phone.

"I'm having an affair with the producer," I announced when Jemma picked up.

She shrieked. "I knew it!"

"I need your help."

"Paige, I know we're close, but there are some things I don't feel comfortable talking about."

"Give me a reality check. Remind me exactly why I'm here and what I need to accomplish because all I can think about right now is that five minutes ago there was a totally hot guy kissing my neck and I'm about two seconds away from figuring out a way to justify going back there."

"He *is* pretty hot."

"*Right*?!" I squealed like a high school girl who just got asked to homecoming. "He's got muscles that rival Zac Efron's."

"And his *eyes*?! I mean, I would happily drown in an ocean that blue."

"And he's so, so sweet. I majorly messed up with the scavenger hunt thing and he was so worried he called me like ten times."

"Awww!"

"It's like he gets me, you know? Like I don't have to be anyone else but myself."

"Oh my gosh, Paige. You are so smitten!"

I twirled in a circle with a laugh before realizing what I was doing. I stopped mid-twirl and slapped my forehead. "Ugh! No! This is exactly what I need you to stop me from doing. I don't have time for this. I have to find a story and I have to find it now before I'm kicked off the show."

"You have a story. If the first task was rigged, the others have to be too."

"I did overhear Andy saying something about how they fudged Carmen's scores so she's the one who got kicked off. But how can I prove that?"

"I don't know. You're the reporter. How'd you prove the sorority was bribing professors with sexual favors in order to pass their classes?"

I shrugged even though she couldn't see me. "I went through the president's lingerie drawer and found a roster of which professors were their 'clients.' The lingerie drawer is most cliché hiding place, but pretty girls do it all the time."

The line was quiet.

"Jem? You there?"

"Yep."

"What're you...? Oohhhh."

"I knew you'd get there."

"I just have to find a time to go through their drawers."

"Ding, ding, ding! We have a winner!"

"Thanks, Jem. I'd be lost without you."

The second I reached my room I wanted to go through Peggy's drawers but knew that with her unpredictable sleep cycle it wouldn't be safe. It would have to wait until morning. I climbed under the covers, and as I closed my eyes I told myself that one night of dreaming about Andy really wouldn't hurt anything.

It was, after all, only one night.

Chapter $15

"I'm disappointed, Paige," CARLA said sharply. "I should have the second installment by now. Another five-hundred words at the very least."

"I got you the second installment – the likability piece."

I eased the door shut behind me as she ranted about my lack of a story and waited for my eyes to adjust to the darkness. Amelia was on her one-on-one date which meant the rest of us had "free time." My free time consisted of wandering aimlessly around the halls, tired of sitting in the small(er) theater watching Friends with the others when I pulled out my phone and saw three missed phone calls from Carla. Panicked, I hurried to find a place I could talk. The only place I could find where I wouldn't be overheard was a steam room. A room that even though it wasn't currently being used still felt like a closet.

"I need a second in-depth installment. The likability piece was fine to satiate people after the second task aired, but I want the dirt."

"What dirt?" I asked, my voice low. I'd gone through Peggy's things that morning while she was in the shower but didn't find anything news-worthy. There wasn't a person in the world who wanted to read about her menstrual cycle – which, it turned out, was the overall theme of her memoir. "Nothing even remotely interesting has happened since last night's episode aired."

Except for my middle of the night rendezvous with Andy.

And invading my roommate's privacy.

But other than that, it had been cucumber water and rattling off Friends quotes with Peggy and Bunny while debating how Amelia's date was going. We would have to wait though. Her date wouldn't air until tomorrow night after our third task had taken place.

"You've made it through two tasks – one of which you've claimed was rigged. Figure out if the second one was too. Write about that. Just write me something! I'm not publishing a story about you sitting around watching *Gilmore Girls* with three other women unless one of those women murders the rest of the contestants while Lorelai is prattling on in the background."

"We've been watching *Friends*."

"Get me a story, Paige. I want one by tomorrow."

"But the next elimination is tomorrow. Give me through the weekend. I guarantee something will have happened by then."

"You're a reporter, Paige. If nothing's happening, *make* something happen."

"But –"

"Tomorrow!" she barked and hung up.

I groaned and banged my head against one of the steam room's walls. I was tired. I was hungry. Again. And was it getting hot in here?

The overhead lights buzzed to life and I squeezed my eyes shut at the sudden light. The air felt heavy and humid and when I opened my eyes the air was starting to fog. Someone had turned on the sauna.

I hurried to the door and yanked on the handle. It wouldn't budge. I banged on the door hoping someone would hear me. My clothes stuck to my body and I felt my hair getting frizzier by the second. A minute or so later the door creaked open and I stumbled out, pushing past someone wrapped in a towel. I took a deep breath of fresh air before I turned around and saw Bunny staring at me like I was a ghost haunting a spa. I didn't bother giving an explanation. I just nodded and said, "Don't stay in too long."

Then I escaped down the hall as fast as I could.

Once I turned the corner I ran my fingers through my hair trying to ensure it didn't get too frizzy. It seemed to have the opposite effect because I passed a hallway mirror on the way back to my room and it was like a toy troll was looking back at me. I was too busy manhandling my hair to notice that I'd taken a wrong turn. Soon I was wandering around, completely lost in a maze of Philippe Starck furniture and Picasso prints (at least I think they were prints). I climbed some stairs only to end up in a loft-type area with only two doors in sight. One door was slightly open and, pushing it open further, I saw it was a bedroom with a view of the community golf course in the distance.

Being the stellar investigative reporter that I am, I felt it was my duty to go inside and take a quick look around. Just to make sure everything was in order, of course. A couple of necklaces were flat on the dresser and a nude slip was on top of the bed covers. It had to be another contestant's room. A phone charger rested on the nightstand next to a paperback copy of *The Girl with the Dragon Tattoo* and a pink leather booklet. *The Girl with the Dragon Tattoo*… Other than myself, there was only one person here who could read and understand, that book. I glanced at the bedroom door to make sure I was still alone, before opening the pink leather booklet. The passport inside confirmed my suspicions. It was Amelia's.

My eyes lit up, delighted at my lucky break. Amelia was the first room I'd wanted to check, but I'd had no idea where she slept. Until now. I stopped myself from letting loose an evil laugh.

I returned the passport to its place and went to the closet. An empty suitcase was pushed up against the side wall and a dozen gowns and blouses hung from a rod. I combed through her gowns one-by-one – not because I thought I'd find anything of interest, but because I just really like clothes and man, alive, did Amelia have some *nice* clothes. I closed the closet doors feeling jealous that she was tall enough to make those dresses look stunning. They'd look like curtains on me.

Amelia was far too clean for my taste. Hardly anything was left out. She clearly had a blatant disregard for casual snooping.

Remembering what I'd told Jemma, I eased open the top dresser drawer. There, underneath a blush-inducing red bra, was a manila envelope. (See? Predictable.) Once again, I checked that I was alone and then pulled out the papers.

The papers contained a bunch of legal mumbo-jumbo. My first thought was that she was getting a divorce or buying a house or something else that required hundreds of words that only lawyers understood. I browsed each page worried she would come back and catch me and I wouldn't have found anything of interest. But then two words caught my eye: sexual harassment. Intrigued, I sped-read paragraph after paragraph. From what I could gather someone was sexually harassing Amelia and she threatened to sue unless there was an agreed upon settlement. I turned the page and read a statement Amelia had made.

> "I did not harass Mr. Blackwell, sexually or otherwise. He approached me and said if I wanted to survive in the modeling industry I was expected to show my commitment by going "above and beyond." I deny any and all allegations asserting that I repeatedly propositioned him in order to appear in high-end ads."

Wait…

I reread the statement.

Oh. My. Gosh. *Amelia* was the one being sued for sexually harassing her boss? I skimmed past the Dismissal of Pending Litigation and flipped the document's pages until I found what I was looking for. Settlement amount. My jaw dropped.

$700,000.

Seven-hundred-thousand dollars? This was too good. I snapped a picture with my phone. I took several more pictures of the documents before carefully placing the file back underneath her bras and closing the drawer. Doubting I would find anything nearly as juicy, I left. I'd only taken one step outside her room before being caught.

Cross "spy" off my list of potential career choices in case the whole reporter thing didn't work out.

"Paige?" Amelia stood at the opposite end of the landing, one hand on the stair railing. "What are you doing? I've never seen you in this part of the house before. I almost didn't recognize you with your hair that tall."

"Oh," I ignored her dig and waved a hand, "I was just wandering."

"In my bedroom?" She came to stand in front of me and folded her arms.

"Is that your bedroom?" I pointed over my shoulder. "It's beautiful. I'm sorry I went inside. I could just see the golf course from your window and wanted a closer look. It's incredible." That statement, at least, was sincere. "Do you have your own room?"

She nodded slowly, still suspicious.

"I share with Peggy," I lamented, then was quick to add, "not that she's difficult to share with or anything! I would just love a room like yours. Quiet. Maybe even a view." My voice sounded wistful and my story was almost convincing to my own ears.

"Hmm…" Amelia looked me up and down, frowned, and then brushed past me. "Admire the view from another room next time."

"Of course, again, I'm sorry, I didn't mean to intrude."

"I'm sure you didn't." Her sarcasm deserved an award. In other circumstances, we might have been friends.

"How was your date?" I asked, continuing to play nice.

"Everything a first date should be," she smirked, "and so, so much more."

I tried to smile nonchalantly, but even I couldn't ignore her implications as she shut her bedroom door in my face.

$$$

The second I walked into my room Peggy greeted me at the door reminding me of an overjoyed puppy. She announced Amelia was back from her date (knew that) and Lincoln was throwing a pool party tonight (did not know that). I managed to extricate myself and escape to the bathroom where I showered off the steam-induced sweat and tamed my hair. Peggy was still bouncing up and down – already in her bikini, I might add – with excitement, too eager to wait for me to finish getting ready before she burst into the bathroom.

"Come on, Paige, it's time to go!" She clasped her hands together under her chin.

"You don't have to wait for me." In fact, I really, really wanted her to leave just so I could have a minute of peace and quiet.

"We're roommates. We're supposed to do everything together."

"It's been three days."

"So?"

"So…" How did one say 'You creep me out and the second you get kicked off this show we're never speaking again' without sounding rude? I sighed in resignation. "I'll hurry."

She squealed satisfied and bounced out of the bathroom leaving me to finish meticulously applying my makeup. I picked up my black kohl eyeliner and was about to apply it when I decided to screw it. I was supposed to have some sort of strategy, right? A way to stand out?

I quickly brushed on some waterproof mascara and braided my hair in pigtails. After dressing in bright yellow retro swim shorts and a polka dot pink top, I slapped on an excessive amount of sunscreen (SPF 70 to be sure) and grabbed a towel.

"Ready?" I asked a no longer hyper Peggy.

"You're going like that?"

I considered my outfit. "Yes."

"You're going to be on camera you know."

"Wait, what? Is this whole thing *filmed*?"

Her eyes widened.

I smirked, loving the fact she didn't recognize my sarcasm. "What's wrong with my outfit?"

"Nothing's wrong with the swimsuit, but you're barely wearing any makeup and your hair isn't done."

"Sure it is. I have pigtails." I wiggled one at her.

She threw up her hands and grabbed her towel. "Fine. Let's go."

Grinning, I grabbed my own towel and trailed after her. When we arrived at home base she held out a hand to stop me.

"Let me go first. I can't be seen with you looking like that."

"Really? We're going to the pool. We're all just going to get wet anyway."

She let out a harsh laugh. "Right. Just let me go first. Count to one hundred and then you can come out."

She sashayed her way out the back door and, after dutifully counting to one hundred (I only made it to twenty-two), I followed her. Wanda could be heard cheerfully bossing someone around. I paused when I reached the open doors. Sure enough, cameramen and set hands were turning the backyard from what was normally Better Homes & Gardens beautiful into a chaotic obstacle course. I'd never seen so many cameras so close to water. It was like they were asking for new equipment.

I skipped over thick cords and wires before making it to the lounge chairs where I chose one to hold my towel. Amelia was sprawled out on a chair a few away from mine in a white string bikini, posture suggesting she was asleep, but I doubted it. On the opposite side of the pool, Bunny was slathering suntan lotion on her long legs. Peggy, on the other hand, was sipping a pink drink while posing provocatively at a picnic table. I opted for watching the chaos from the comfort of a tiny spot of shade. Wanda was not happy about this and tried several times to get me to move into the light. I insisted I would once we began filming. Satisfied with this answer she went inside and called out for Lincoln. At least one camera was trained on each of us ready for go time.

When Lincoln came outside it was like an electric current ran through the air - backs straightened, hair was tossed, coy smiles were given - until he headed straight for me and I stood to greet him. I brushed off my hands and prayed I didn't stink of sunblock.

"Paige!" Lincoln seemed far too happy to see me than the occasion warranted, but I returned his hug unable to help noticing the daggered stares from the other girls. He'd passed them all without so much as a glance. I probably would have been hurt too. But I wasn't about to apologize for his attention. I needed it to stay on this show. I had to get the real story.

"I'm happy to see you," he confessed. "I feel like I haven't seen you in forever."

I wanted to point out that it had only been a day, but I swallowed the words.

"Have you had fun with the other women?"

"Um, yeah. We watched *Friends* earlier."

"Sounds fun. I want to take you out again. Tomorrow morning? Before the third task?"

"I'd love to."

"Great!"

I didn't know how to respond so I just smiled.

"Well, I guess we should get this party started, yeah?" He dropped my hands and hollered for everyone to get in the pool.

I soon found out why Peggy laughed at my comment about swimming. No one was swimming. It turned out that a pool party consisted of dipping your feet in the water, lying on a floating chair, or drinking who-knows-what out of glasses with tiny umbrellas (which, I admit, were way cute), and basically working on your tan. The contestants were wearing so much makeup one stray drop of water would probably make them melt. I was the only person actually in the water, immersed up to my head. My braids were even wet. Lincoln was at the edge of the pool, swinging his feet in the water, while Peggy, Amelia, and Bunny fawned over him. They were all so giggly I half expected them to offer to peel him grapes and feed them to him.

I felt stupid joining their clique, so I floated on my back and dog-paddled around. After about fifteen minutes – that felt like an hour – I pulled myself out of the pool and went to get a drink.

"Having fun?"

My martini glass halfway to my lips, I turned to find Andy standing before me.

Shirtless.

My skin was burning up. Was I getting sunburned? I fought the urge to fan myself.

I took a swig of my drink, grateful for the ice-cold flavor. "I didn't expect you to join us."

"Disappointed?"

"Not if means you'll keep me company."

"What kind of man would I be if I left a beautiful woman to drink alone?"

"Ever the gentleman." I figured must be getting burned. My cheeks were flushed, and I was feeling a little light-headed. Maybe I was dehydrated too. The sun was setting so I hadn't brought sunblock down with me. An unexpected image of Andy rubbing sunblock on my back while I sipped a Pina Colada sprang to mind.

"Paige, darling?" Amelia called startling me out of my daydream. I'd never been so grateful to hear her voice.

"Yes, Amelia, darling?" I called back, my voice dripping with sarcasm.

"Can you bring me an Evian pretty please?"

I rolled my eyes and gave Andy a "she's demanding, but I'm a good person and am not going to judge her for it" look and grabbed a water out of the ice chest.

"Oh my," she said with alarm as she took it from my hands, her other hand already holding a margarita.

"What?"

"Nothing." She shook her head, her blonde curls bouncing with the movement. She gave me a dazzlingly fake smile. "Thank you for the water."

"Come on, Amelia. Just tell me."

Amelia glanced at the cameras moving toward us and then at the two other girls sitting close by, now listening intently, and then leaned toward me as if to whisper a secret. Unfortunately, she didn't whisper. Even Wanda, who was reclining herself under a shade tree heard her.

"It's just…well…when you came over you seemed a little bloated and I worried it was because you'd been drinking too much. I was going to tell you to slow down. But as you came closer I realized it's just the way you're built." She took a drink of her deep red strawberry margarita and waved a dismissive hand. "It's no big deal, though. You're obviously comfortable in your own body. I mean, it takes a lot of confidence to wear a suit like that."

Shocked at her words, I was speechless. And I'm *never* speechless. Ask Jemma. I talk so much I can be really obnoxious.

Really, *really* obnoxious.

It seemed everyone else was speechless as well and the camera-men shifted uncomfortably. Lincoln actually got up to go "use the restroom" and one cameraman decided to follow him.

Unable to do anything but blink, I walked away from them, trying not to suck in my stomach and cry. I would not let them get to me. In an effort to calm my embarrassment, I imagined my mom saying the comforting words she'd repeated throughout my life. Amelia's words meant nothing. I should let it go. I barely knew her. She'd probably had too much to drink. Maybe she was only acting that way because she didn't know any other way. She might have grown up in a hor-rible environment. She probably didn't know kindness. Maybe she was anorexic as a teenager. Maybe – I shut my mother's voice up as soon as I saw the diving board. I darted toward it. My brothers would have given me advice too. And it would have been so much better. I knew exactly what to do. It was childish and could, especially in this circumstance, be considered rude.

I was going to do it anyway.

"Cannonball!" I shouted and jumped off the diving board. My skin stung as I plummeted into the pool, my arms wrapped tight around my knees. I pushed off the bottom and broke the surface of the water overjoyed to see I'd had perfect aim.

Amelia was soaked. Her mascara was running down her cheeks and her perfect bouncy curls were now stringy snakes. Even better was that her red margarita had spilled all over her legs and her *white* bikini bottoms.

"Oh my gosh!" I put a hand to my mouth in mock horror while trying not to laugh. Lincoln picked that moment to return and his gaze immediately went to Amelia's now bright red bikini bottoms. He turned red and looked away, once again looking like he wanted to be anywhere but here. This whole thing was turning out ten times better than expected.

If Amelia were crying, I couldn't tell because her makeup was already ruined. She looked back-and-forth between Lincoln and me before she screamed and ran away. It wasn't until she was running away that I truly felt bad. I could just imagine my mom's disapprov-ing look.

Sometimes I hated my mom for raising me to be a good person. I huffed angrily as I hopped out of the pool and ran after her. "Amelia!"

I didn't have to go far.

"Amelia," I slowed as I caught up to her near the staircase, my wet feet squeaking on the tile, "I'm so sorry."

"Sorry? Are you kidding me? You made it, so I can't even run away without further embarrassing myself," she snarled. She pointed to the edge where the tile met the carpet. I went over to inspect the world's smallest pink spot. "I was heading upstairs, but then I dripped on the carpet. I dripped red water on to a millionaire's carpet!"

I squinted. "It's really more of a pink color."

I moved out of range as she rose a hand that I'm sure was meant to slap me. "Amelia, take a breath. First off, he's a millionaire. He can replace all the carpet in the entire neighborhood without blinking an eye." I tentatively stepped closer and put my hand on her shoulder. "Secondly, the cameras caught everything" she let out a sob "which *means* that they'll have caught the margarita spilling. No one will think it's anything but an unfortunate accident."

She let loose a harsh laugh and swatted my hands away. "Accident? It wasn't an accident."

"Well, no, drenching you with water was not an accident. The margarita *was* an accident. It was also a bonus, I'll admit, but an accident nonetheless."

Her gaze focused on something over my shoulder and she flung her arms around me. I braced myself to fight back in case she decided to strangle me.

"Oh, Paige!" Amelia cried and squeezed me tighter. "Even though what you did was horribly cruel I forgive you."

"I'll grab a towel for you, Amelia," I heard Andy say from the doorway.

Ahh. The cameras must have finally made it inside. We had company.

I returned the hug, but before she released me she put her lips to my ear.

"Watch your back," she hissed. She dug her nails into my shoulders for good measure, smiled sweetly, and wrapped the towel Andy had brought her around her waist and headed upstairs.

If only she knew.

"Let's go, Andy, we've got to make sure we got the footage we need," Wanda said.

Andy ignored her and said to me, "That was quite a stunt you pulled."

"I'm auditioning for a *Heavy Weights'* remake."

"You've definitely got it in the bag."

"Andy!" Wanda barked and put her hands on her hips.

Andy rolled his eyes, but lowered his voice and said, "See you later?"

I met his eyes for the briefest second and nodded, a smile tugging at the corner of my mouth. Even as he walked away I could tell he was grinning.

Chapter $16

Andy sat on the countertop waiting for me. I bit my lip to stop my smile from getting too big for my face. I was already on an adrenaline high from submitting my article about Amelia's lawsuit to Carla, but seeing Andy just put me over the top.

"Hey," I said coming into view.

He jumped off the counter with a grin. His usual sweatpants and white t-shirt were gone, replaced by jeans, a dark green sweater, and...shoes. I raised an eyebrow.

"Going somewhere?"

"We both are."

"Where are we going at 1:00 a.m.?"

Instead of responding he frowned and motioned for me to follow him. We went down a hallway and turned right a couple times before stopping at a door. He held up a finger for me to wait. A moment later he came out and handed me a wad of fabric.

"Hopefully that one will work."

"Why do I need a sweater?"

"Just put it on."

I did as he said. I'd never thought of Andy's lean form as substantially bigger than mine, but as I pulled the blue hoodie over my head

I felt like a child. It almost reached my knees and the sleeves were long enough to hide my fingers. The fabric inside was worn down to its threads and there was a bleach stain on the collar. It smelled vaguely of campfire and I was sure it looked horrible on me.

I never wanted to take it off.

Andy grimaced. "Sorry, I grabbed my older one thinking it'd be smaller. Guess I was wrong." He pulled at one of the sleeves trying to find my hand. "I can find you another."

"No," I said firmly. "It's perfect."

He didn't look convinced.

"Really, I love it. It's warm and it makes me feel safe." This received a look that was somewhere between disbelief and pride. "Where are we going?" I asked again.

"It's a surprise," he said. "I hope you're up for a walk."

"I'm barefoot."

We turned a corner and he pointed at a door a few feet away. "There should be thongs in there."

My mouth fell open in mock surprise. "Andy, a thong is not necessary for a walk."

"Oh...uh...no...I..." Andy held up his hands and tried to find the right words. "I didn't mean – I just – there should be..."

"Calm down," I laughed and went over to the closet. "I knew what you meant. I'm just saying you should really reevaluate your vocabulary."

I sorted through a surprising number of flip-flops until I found a pair in my size. Andy and I didn't speak again until we reached the sidewalk in front of Lincoln's mansion.

"Now will you tell me where we're going?"

"We're going for a walk."

"Thanks, Sherlock, where are we walking?"

Andy smiled mischievously and walked backward in front of me. "Have you ever seen a lunar eclipse?"

"No..."

"There's a park a few streets away that has the most amazing view. It's the perfect place to see a lunar eclipse."

$$$

"I didn't even know there was a lunar eclipse tonight," I said. The short walk led us to a park a few blocks from Lincoln's mansion. We lay in a clearing surrounded by trees and a lush garden allowing an unobstructed view of the sky. All streetlights were blocked by the trees and the only light came from a full moon, giving everything a romantic glow. We were lying side-by-side but, much to my irritation, not quite touching.

"There's not."

I pushed myself onto my elbows and stared at him as understanding washed over me. "You little liar."

"I didn't lie."

"You said there was a lunar eclipse!"

"No, I said that this would be the perfect place to see a lunar eclipse." He put his hands behind his head, using them as a pillow. "And it would be. There just doesn't happen to be an eclipse tonight."

"I believe that's called lying by omission."

His responding smile asked me what I was going to do about it.

"Why did we come here if there was never an eclipse?"

"Because I wanted to spend time with you." His voice was serious now. "Just you. No mansion or cameras. No obstacle courses or scavenger hunts. No sneaking around. I wanted to get to know you, Paige. The real you."

The real me. My smile faltered. How could he ever come to know the real me? Not everything I'd told him was a lie, but I was lying about a major part of my life.

His brow furrowed, and he opened his mouth to say something, but I didn't want to hear it. I didn't want him to ask me what was wrong. I didn't want to tell him another lie. I wanted to forget everything and just enjoy the night. In a sudden rush of bravery, I broke down the invisible barrier that kept us from touching and kissed his cheek. I laid my head on his shoulder, my hand resting on his chest and whatever he'd been about to say faded away. His arm slipped around me as if by habit and I nestled closer.

"And?" I asked. "What do you think?"

His fingers intertwined with mine and he stared into my eyes. "I think..." His thumb began tracing the lines on my palm sending electric currents up my arm. "I think I want to keep getting to know you."

We must have dozed off at some point because the next thing I knew is that the top of my body was a heavenly kind of warm and my legs were chilly. I hesitantly opened my eyes to see the sky was a gradient of blues, the kind you'd see in a painting of the sun rising to block out the stars. The world came back to me in pieces as I woke and once I was fully awake I had no desire to ever move again. Andy's arms were wrapped tightly around me, his face buried in my hair. My legs, on the other hand, were still on the cold grass. Even with the chill, I snuggled closer, inhaling his musky scent along with the smell of fresh-cut grass.

I couldn't believe how comfortable I was with him. I honestly couldn't remember the last time I'd felt so peaceful. I considered myself a pretty confident person – I mean, I had my moments when I was as insecure as a Chihuahua next to a Great Dane – and I prided myself on being able to talk to anyone and make anyone feel at ease. It was a quality that helped make me a good journalist. But even if I was confident talking to people, it was always because we were talking about them. You just asked questions and listened when you interviewed someone. You never had to reveal any information about yourself. And I was okay with that.

Until now. He said he wanted to get to know me. The real me.

The real me that he could never know.

No, I decided. I was never moving again.

That decision lasted about a minute. My toes soon felt like they were in buckets of ice and I nudged Andy to wake him up.

"Hey," he said sleepily. One hand rubbed his eyes. "We fell asleep."

"We should get back to the mansion."

As soon as Andy didn't look like he was about to fall asleep on his feet, we started walking back hand-in-hand. When we reached the path leading back to the mansion, I stopped.

"What's wrong?" he asked, his eyebrows furrowed.

"I just…" I didn't know if I should say this aloud, but I plowed on. "I know we need to get back, but…"

Andy took both my hands in his and brought them to his lips for a kiss. He rubbed them with his own to try and get them warm.

"My toes are cold too," I joked. "You should give me a foot rub."

Instead of laughing like I'd expected, he looked at me with excitement, like a child who knew where the secret cookie jar was kept. "Let's take the scenic route," he said and dragged me down a different path.

"I was kidding about a foot rub."

He didn't answer.

"What's gotten into you?" I huffed as we continued running. In the distance, I could make out a small playground with monkey bars and a swing set. No one was there this early and we made our way to the swings. Andy tried to cross the monkey bars but couldn't since he was at least a foot too tall and his feet kept hitting the ground.

I put my hands on my hips and tried to slow my breathing as I watched him.

"Not a runner, huh?"

"I'm more of a yoga girl. At least I would be if I had the money to go to a yoga studio, but I'm warm now which is what matters." It was true. Running had increased my body temperature to the point I almost wanted to take my sweater off. I mean, I couldn't breathe, and my thighs felt like they were in a blood pressure cuff, but I wasn't cold anymore. I struggled to take another breath. I couldn't be that out of shape. I mean, I lived in New York. The only thing New Yorkers do is walk. And walk. And yell at people walking.

"I pictured you more of a synchronized swimming kind of girl."

"You got me," I said sarcastically, my breath evening out.

"How do you feel about swing sets?"

"My feelings toward them tend to be positive."

He held his hands out to one of the black seats, presenting it like a throne. I expected him to take the spot next to me, but instead, he stood behind me and pushed. We didn't speak, I just let him push me higher and higher until I was swinging too high for him to reach. He leaned against one of the poles watching me laugh and pump my legs to keep going. My fingers gripped the cold metal chain tighter as I sliced through the calm morning air, chasing the rising sun. I was a bird flying away from my responsibilities and fears. I was totally and completely free.

Glancing down, I saw Andy, still leaning against one of the poles still watching me, looking for all the world like there was nothing he'd rather do that continue to watch me soar.

I allowed the swing to come to a gradual stop.

"I've never known anyone who loved swinging that much." He held out his hands to help me out of the swing.

I shrugged a shoulder and looked up at him. "It's the closest I've ever gotten to flying."

"Just when I think I've got you figured out, you go and surprise me."

We stood face-to-face and I stepped closer to him, the tips of my flip-flops bumping his shoes.

"Is that a bad thing?"

"No. It's impressive." He swallowed.

I shouldn't be doing this. I should back away. Andy didn't know who I was. Not really, anyway. My mind chanted "stop, stop, stop," but my body kept moving closer as if my brain had given up control entirely. It was like that time in college when I found the homemade Christmas cookies my roommate had made for her boyfriend. I told myself to only steal one, just one, and then another until I kept telling myself to stop but they were *sooooo* good. Once I'd tasted them I couldn't get enough. I ate them all.

I wondered if once I tasted Andy I'd ever get enough.

My lips parted, and I was breathing his air. He was close. So close. Too close. We were the closest two people could be without actually touching. And then suddenly we were. One of his hands moved to my waist and my arms made their way around his neck. He brushed my hair behind one ear and his chest rose and fell in tandem with mine. Somewhere in the back of my mind, something was telling me to hit the brakes, that for some reason this wasn't a good idea, but my brain was foggy, and this seemed like the best idea in the world.

Our lips brushed, but it was so light it could have been my imagination. They touched again and I knew an actual kiss was coming and I should be patient, but patience has never been my best quality and, man, why did he have to torment me like this? I had a crush on a terrorist. Or one of those really big Russian men who tortured Scarlett Johansson in that one Avengers movie. She could handle torture just fine if it meant she'd get the information she needed, but she was Scarlett Johansson and I was just Paige Michaels and I didn't need to save the world, I needed this gorgeous man to put his freakin' lips on mine. I mean, really, it wouldn't be difficult. They were *rightthere* – a breath apart but impossibly far away. His lips hovered just over mine, enjoying my eagerness-soon-to-be-irritation far too much. He was about to get slapped for it. Or kissed senseless.

But then I was the one getting kissed senseless and all my thoughts of Christmas cookies and Scarlett Johansson instantly disappeared as if they'd never been there in the first place.

$$$

We held hands as we silently strode up Lincoln's driveway. The sun was peeking over the mansions in the distance telling me we'd stayed out far too long. Once inside, Andy led me to the staircase to my room. I slipped out of his sweater, rolled it into a ball and gave it to him.

"Thanks for this," I said. "I had a lot of fun."

"I'm glad you agreed to come. I like spending time with you."

"Back at you."

Tucking the sweater under one arm, he put a hand on each side of my face and kissed my forehead. I gave him a look that clearly told him that wasn't good enough and he leaned closer to kiss me.

"Oh!" A squeak of alarm made Andy and I snap apart like a rubber band. Amelia stood several stairs above us in gym shorts and a baggy t-shirt with headphones draped around her neck.

She's a runner. I knew there was a reason I didn't trust her.

I tried to look nonchalant, but the look on her face told me we looked guiltier than a dog caught with a chewed-up pair of shoes.

Which was ridiculous. We had no reason to feel guilty about any-thing – right? I mean, it's not like Lincoln wasn't dating (and kissing) other women. Couldn't I date other men? Except if we weren't break-ing any rules, why was my face so warm?

Guilty or not, Amelia was clearly thrilled at this new development.

"Paige," she said with a sly grin, her eyes darting back and forth between us, "how nice to see you up so early."

"Amelia." I smiled, unsure what else I could say.

"Mr. Warner, I didn't realize you and Paige were so close."

"Paige and I were just talking about what insomniacs we both are. It's nice to get to know all of the contestants, especially since one of them will be marrying my best friend."

"Hopefully it'll be the one you want." Her gaze locked with his, her eyes flashing with the thrill of new secrets. "Or, I should say, don't want."

"You should go before it gets too hot." I gave her a tight smile and motioned across the room to the back door. "It's been a pleasure."

"Yes, things are definitely starting to heat up, aren't they?" She waggled her fingers at us making me want to break each perfectly manicured nail and then disappeared out the door.

"How much do you think she saw?" Andy asked once we were sure she was gone.

I groaned. "I don't think she saw you kiss my forehead, but I don't think she saw anything good."

I leaned my head against his chest. He started to gather me in his arms, but I jerked away when I heard footsteps padding across the floor.

"Paige? What is it?"

"Did you hear that?" I whispered.

"No. What did you hear?"

I took a few steps in the direction the footsteps came from, but the only thing I saw were shadows forming from the light of the ris-ing sun.

"Paige?"

A whooshing sound made me jump, only for me to realize it was the sound of the fridge filling up the ice. I groaned again, louder this time. "I'm losing my mind."

"What?"

"I thought I heard footsteps and then the fridge and I'm just paranoid all of a sudden and we're not even doing anything wrong." I turned to face him. "Right?"

Andy cast his eyes down. "I guess I'm not sure."

"You're the producer," I said playfully. "Don't you make the rules?"

It was silent for a beat too long.

"I should go to bed." He only nodded in response.

When I reached the first staircase landing I turned back to say one more goodnight, but Andy was already gone.

LOOK! EXCLUSIVE

scandal in the spotlight
by an Anonymous Contributor

Delightfully crazy contestants, million-dollar eye candy, and insane tasks, how could WWTMAM get any better? Oh, I know! A sex scandal.

Amelia Gregory is being sued by her former boss at Elite Talent Management (ETM), Mr. Tyler Blackwell, for sexual harassment. Public records quoted Gregory's statement about the allegations:

"I did not harass Mr. Blackwell, sexually or otherwise. He approached me and said if I wanted to survive in the modeling industry I was expected to show my commitment by going 'above and beyond.' I deny any and all allegations asserting that I repeatedly propositioned him in order to appear in high-end ads."

Blackwell is suing our friend, Amelia, for $1.2 million dollars in damages. He states that he has lost significant business and "perceived excellence" in the talent acquisition industry. The public record states that he claims Amelia has been destroying his reputation by accusing him of sexual harassment. Supposedly her frequent "visits" have caused his clients to drop him as an agent due to his "poor character" and "lack of integrity."

Looks like America's number one pick for the millionaire bride is in need of some cash – fast. What better way to get it – and national support – than by garnering the affections of a gorgeous millionaire? Then again, maybe she's trying to forget about the lawsuit by pursuing the love of a normal, hard-working man who just so happens to be filthy rich. And if you believe that, I'd like to introduce you to Bunny Hopkins, because it seems reality is something you both have trouble accepting.

The rest of us aren't surprised.

Chapter $17

"They're not filming this?" I asked Lincoln later that morning as he drove us to a restaurant. Supposedly, Kirby's Waffle and Bacon House had the world's best scones. Don't ask me why it's named after waffles and bacon.

"It's not really official..."

"Officially what?"

"A date date. Like an official part of the game."

"Oh." I took a moment to process this. "Then why...?"

"I'd just like to really know the person I'm going to end up with, you know?"

"Okay," I said. He looked at me expectantly, waiting for more of an answer, but when I didn't give him one he smiled.

"Okay," he said. We drove the rest of the way in companionable silence.

Kirby's Waffle and Bacon House was exactly what you'd expect a place called Kirby's Waffle and Bacon House to be. It was a small building just off the highway on an empty lot of gravel and dirt across the street from a run-down strip mall. A single palm tree stood in front of the entrance and a sign with the diner's name hung from one of its branches. The area seemed so run down that I wondered if it was really such a good idea to leave Lincoln's Tesla in the parking lot. But when he pulled around the back of the building, I noticed at least two other Teslas, a yellow Porsche, and an assortment of other high-end vehicles mixed in with plenty of Hondas and Toyotas. Kirby's, it seemed, was the place to be.

"Wow," I said in awe when we walked inside. The inside matched the outside with torn vinyl booths and a counter surrounded by 60s-style barstools. Despite the humble décor, people were every-where. It was even more packed than the parking lot suggested. Every single table was full, and another ten people were crowded just inside the entrance next to a sign telling customers to wait to be seated. Lincoln and I made our way to the front.

"Lincoln!" A jovial man, Kirby, I assumed, in a used-to-be-white apron and red wisps of hair appeared behind the counter. He made his way to us and clapped Lincoln on the shoulder. "Glad to have you here. It's been a while."

"Yes, sir, it certainly has."

"You still working hard?" He said, wiping his hands on his apron.

"Oh, not nearly as much lately." Lincoln joked.

"Well, good." The man leaned toward me. "This boy's been work-ing hard his whole life. Seems to me he doesn't know how to stop. You make sure he has some fun once in a while. The wait is about twenty minutes this morning. You two get comfy and we'll get you seated as soon as we can."

Lincoln pointed at a bench against one wall and we moved to occupy the seats that had just opened up.

"I didn't realize millionaires did things like wait in line," I teased.

"Kirby's doesn't give anyone special treatment."

"The owner seems to really like you." I took a spot next to him.

"Yeah, Michael's a good man."

"Michael?"

"You probably thought his name was Kirby, right?"

"Well, yeah."

"Kirby was his pet turtle."

"I'm sorry, did you say turtle?"

"Yep." Lincoln nodded seriously. "He fed that turtle waffles and bacon every morning its whole life. It was the only thing it would eat."

"You're kidding."

"Nope."

"And how long did Kirby live?"

"Almost thirty years."

"He did not."

"True story."

"Dang. Who knew waffles and bacon could extend a turtle's life like that?"

"It's a miracle, that's for sure."

We were seated exactly twenty minutes later and when our scones arrived I thought I was going to die. The crispy golden-brown dough was bigger than the plate it was on. It was piled high with honey butter that melted in a pool of goodness in the middle. It smelled like sugar, cinnamon, and heaven and I couldn't stop staring.

"If you don't start eating that soon, I will," Lincoln said with a twinkle in his eye. I realized with a start that his scone was already halfway gone. I grinned and, copying him, I ripped a piece off and shoved it in my mouth. It was so good I didn't even care that butter was dripping down my chin. In my defense, it was dripping down Lincoln's as well.

After we were through licking our plates, Lincoln said, "I've never met a girl who could finish a whole scone."

"Glad to make your acquaintance."

"I should have taken a picture and sent it to Andy."

The mention of Andy's name made my heart skip a beat. "Andy? Why?"

"He likes girls who can eat. I need his blessing if I'm going to marry you." His smile was all teeth and even though I knew he was kidding, my smile faltered. Why did the idea of marrying Lincoln fill my stomach with lead? He was kind, funny, a hard worker, handsome, smart, and a freaking millionaire. Jemma would check me into a mental hospital if she knew.

He must have realized he said something wrong because he chose that moment to look at his phone. "Oh man, we should probably get back home. They're going to start the third task in a few hours and they'll need me soon."

It was weird to hear someone call the mansion "home" but I guessed when you were used to it like that you didn't know any different. Could I be the kind of person who called a mansion her home? I was being stupid. I wasn't going to marry Lincoln. He was a means to an end, that was all. The scone must have had some weird potion mixed inside that made people reevaluate their love lives. Lincoln threw some cash on the table and, after making sure I was following him, he headed toward the door.

I was only a couple steps behind him when I realized I'd left my purse. I needed to put an alarm on that thing to let me know when it was more than a few feet away from me. I turned back to our booth and saw a waiter leading a tall blonde woman to a table. The way she moved seemed familiar, almost as if a skip was added to every step. A skip...or a hop.

Bunny?

The waiter led her to a table by the window. The woman scoffed as they passed an elderly couple sharing a waffle piled high with strawberries and whipped cream.

That was Bunny alright.

She sat at a table for two and scooted her chair closer to the table. A waiter came to get her order but didn't take the other place setting away.

Was she meeting someone?

I grabbed my purse and followed Lincoln to the parking lot. Just as he reached for my hand I stopped short and hit my forehead with the palm of my hand.

"Dang it," I said. "I forgot my sweater."

"Oh, I can grab it for you." Lincoln turned back to the diner.

I stepped in front of him to block his path. "No, that's okay, I'll get it. The extra steps will help me work off that scone. Meet you at the car?" I dashed off before he could say anything.

I crossed my fingers that Bunny wasn't there just to protest putting strawberries on top of waffles. I ducked behind the lone palm tree and through the diner window, I searched each face. Glimpsing her profile, I took out my phone, not sure what I was hoping would happen. She took a sip from her mug and then her face lit up as someone took the seat across from her.

Paulo?

Thank the fruit trees this was getting good.

I snapped several pictures before deciding to go inside. I weaved through the crowds of people, careful to keep my head down so they wouldn't notice me, but I shouldn't have worried. Both of them were bent over something in the middle of the table. I casually took a seat at an empty table that hadn't been cleared yet and snapped a few pictures.

"About time," I heard Paulo say.

"All the money is there. Promise."

"If they'd thought I left Paige there on purpose..."

"You'd be fired, I know. Everything went according to plan. She came in last. I got what I wanted and now you're getting what you wanted."

"Finally."

Bunny bribed Paulo to leave me behind. She wanted me to be last. I could practically hear Carla's praise as the story formed in my mind.

"Where's your sweater?" Lincoln asked when I got back to the car. He opened the passenger-side door and put his hand on my back.

"Oh," I forced a giggle, "silly me. I didn't bring a sweater."

"Okaaayy..." It was clear he was questioning my sanity, so I slid into the front seat without another word.

He got inside, but before he started the car he looked me up and down.

"What?" I asked.

"You just seem really happy about something. I mean, I'm used to it. Women can't help but be happy whenever I'm around."

I hit his arm playfully. "I think I'm just hyper. All that sugar, you know."

"Sure." He smiled knowingly (man, his teeth were white!) and leaned over. I hesitated only a moment before I kissed him.

"Thanks for breakfast." I tucked my hair behind one ear.

"Anytime," he replied and then kissed me again. It was sweet. Nice even.

I wished it was Andy.

A sound from the front of the car made us break apart and when I looked to see what it was a flash clouded my vision with spots.

The flash was followed by Lincoln releasing a string of curses. He leaned on his horn and started slowly driving through the crowd of people now forming around the car. Even though the paparazzi were surrounding us, I couldn't help but admire the fact I hadn't even heard the Tesla start. It was like you couldn't even tell it was running!

Several more flashes and a constant horn made me momentarily forget the Tesla and focus on the reporters yelling at us. They were all yelling at once and I couldn't understand a word they were saying. I wanted to believe they were saying things like, "We love your hair, Paige!" and "We hate Amelia too!" but their expressions of scorn proved otherwise. Honestly, I was kind of grateful I didn't know what they were saying.

The car would move forward an inch and then Lincoln would slam on the brakes. Despite threatening to hit them with a car, they wouldn't move. Finally, with a growl, Lincoln threw the car in reverse.

"Uhh…Lincoln?" I looked warily at the crowd behind us. "You know there's a bunch of reporters behind us too, right?"

He just looked at me instead of answering.

"I mean, I know reporters suck," myself excluded, "but they are human and you can't just hit—"

He shoved his mouth against mine.

I had to admit, he had a pretty good way of shutting me up. But was now really the time?

"Uh, Linc—" I tried to speak, but he was more aggressive than he'd ever been before. He was practically out of his seat.

He continued to kiss me, making me question his sanity, when he broke away and looked out the rear-view window. Suddenly the car flew backward. Confused, I frantically looked behind us to witness

JESSIE J. HOLMES

the slaughter and saw that all the reporters had moved to the front of the car. No one was behind us.

Lincoln reversed all the way out of the parking lot onto the street. Before I could blink we were racing forward away from the paparazzi and chaos. We didn't speak until we were safely on the freeway.

"Sorry," he said. "I didn't know how else to get us out of there. I knew they'd all push their way to the front to get a better view if we gave them something good."

Something good. Okay then.

"That was...clever." I wasn't sure how to describe it, but "clever" seemed about as descriptive as I could get without offending him.

A ringing echoed through the car and the dashboard's screen lit up with a picture of Andy at the beach. Lincoln swore and, after briefly hesitating, he pressed a button on the steering wheel and the screen went blank.

"You kiss your momma with that mouth?" I said trying to ease the tension. He opened his mouth to reply but the phone rang again. Once again, Andy's face showed up on the screen. Lincoln declined it.

"How many times are you going to ignore his call?"

Lincoln swore again and finally answered it sounding surprisingly nonchalant for someone who'd just ignored three phone calls. "Hey man, what's up?"

Andy didn't bother with a greeting. "Would you like to tell me why we're suddenly trending on social media?"

Trending? It couldn't be – it'd happened less than ten minutes ago!

"Oh, yeah, about that... See...uh...Paige and I went out for scones, you know Kirby's, right? Well, yeah, and..."

"And why did you go out for scones?"

"We just wanted to spend some time together before—"

"Lincoln!" Andy interrupted. It sounded like a warning.

"Look, I don't know how they found out, okay?"

"Lincoln."

"Andy."

"Take me off speaker."

171

"I'm driving."

"*Take me off speaker.*" Andy's voice was hard and I cringed. He sounded like Carla when someone asked for a deadline extension.

Lincoln sighed, pressed a button on his phone and put it to his ear. I couldn't hear what Andy was saying, but based on Lincoln's grimace, it wasn't good. His expression got darker with each passing word and I shifted so I was staring out the window, doing that thing where you're pretending the situation isn't awkward because you can't get out of it.

"*Fine!*" Lincoln's sudden outburst made me jump and I winced when he furiously threw his phone into the back seat.

We didn't speak the entire rest of the drive which gave me plenty of time to ponder what had just happened. Wasn't it normal for the paparazzi to be all over this kind of thing? What was the big deal? I didn't think we were breaking the rules or that this could become a problem.

If Teslas could screech, we would have screeched into Lincoln's garage. As it was, he drove in smoothly and parked in a way that didn't fit his mood at all. Lincoln seemed to have calmed down a bit, but when we saw Andy waiting for us at the garage door we both started to squirm. He was dressed in a dark blue suit with a striped collared shirt and as usual, he looked amazing. Except he didn't look happy to see us. He didn't even look at me at all. No one spoke as we followed him down a few hallways to a set of double doors. Andy opened one of them and motioned us inside.

"After you." Andy's voice was dangerously quiet and neither of us hesitated as we hurried into the room. It was a modern office, with blank walls, simple black chairs, and a view overlooking the golf course. The only thing on the desk was a tiny box of sand, you know the ones that have that mini fork in it and you're supposed to rake the sand in order to calm down? Something told me Andy hadn't done that.

"What were you two thinking?" Andy asked heatedly as soon as the door was closed. "You're supposed to stay in the mansion."

"We just wanted to spend some time together," Lincoln argued.

"Well, your 'time together' could have just cost us a whole lot more than your time is worth."

"We ate scones. That's it."

"That's it?" Andy pulled something up on his phone and then showed us the screen. "You ate scones and that's it. Are you sure that's the story you want to go with?"

On his screen was a picture of Lincoln and I kissing. And "kissing" was putting it mildly. Our faces were smashed together and my hand was mid-air as though I was reaching up to pull him closer. That must have been when I was trying to push him away.

"I needed to get us out of there." Lincoln looked around the room as if seeking confirmation from a non-existent audience that his actions were perfectly logical.

"The worst part is that you dragged her into this!" Andy pointed at me and I immediately felt like curling up into a ball and hiding under the desk. Except the desk was the glass kind without a back so you could see the person's feet and the computer cords and...you get the point.

"How is that the worst part?" Lincoln threw his hands in the air.

"They all want her gone!"

They wanted me kicked off the show? I couldn't be kicked off the show!

"So?"

So?!

"What is wrong with you?" Andy was practically yelling now. "Do you even hear yourself? Listen to these Tweets:

Gurl got probs if she cant play fair. #kissredgoodbye #wwtmam

Linc's got a fav. Why even watch? #kissredgoodbye #wwtmam

Was looking forward to something better than The Bachelor. But at least The Bachelor doesn't allow cheating. #kissredgoodbye #wwtmam

"#wwtmam is trending in the worst way possible."

"Andy, I'm sorry." All the defense was gone from Lincoln's voice.

"You better believe you're sorry. This is going to be a PR nightmare. Between this and the new article this morning about Amelia we've got to work hard to get things back on track."

"Article about Amelia? What article?" Lincoln asked.

I tried to look surprised.

"*Look!* published another anonymous article. It's claiming that Amelia is in the midst of a lawsuit for sexual harassment."

Had Carla already published the article? It'd been less than ten hours. She must have been desperate for a scoop.

"She was sexually harassed?" Lincoln's expression hardened.

"No," Andy shook his head, "she was the one doing the harassment. Wanda's working with the lawyers right now to authenticate the story."

"No, the article got it wrong. She must have been harassed. How is she? Is she okay?"

"She's upset, but she'll be fine. If there's one thing good about this mess you made is that it's taken the heat off of her."

"What can I do?" Lincoln asked earnestly. He cared about Amelia. Why I'd never know, but he really did care.

Andy ran a hand over his face. "Just get out of here."

Like a little boy having just been reprimanded by his father, Lincoln left the office, shutting the door behind him.

I stood, silently, waiting for Andy to acknowledge me, but he was too busy looking at his phone. A minute or so later he looked up from his phone, eyebrows raised. "You're still here?"

I glared at him. "Shut up, you knew I was still here."

"What do you want, Paige?"

"Why were you so mean to him?"

"I wasn't mean to him."

"Yeah, you were." I folded my arms. Part of me couldn't believe I was defending Lincoln after he basically just admitted he didn't care if I got kicked off the show.

"He's got to be more responsible." Andy pointed at the door Lincoln had just exited. "This is his *job*."

"And you're his *friend*."

"I'm always cleaning up his messes."

"It was an accident."

"Taking you out for breakfast wasn't an accident. Kissing you wasn't an accident."

"So that's what this is all about? Lincoln kissing me?" I threw my hands up.

"How many guys do you kiss in one day anyway? We both know it's got to be more than two."

"Ouch."

"Do you even think about it or is it like water to you? Whenever you're thirsty you just get a drink."

My hand tingled with the urge to slap him, but the rational part of me kept it by my side. "You're upset that I'm kissing both of you, I get it. Get mad at me all you want, but don't take your jealousy out on Lincoln."

"He doesn't even—" Andy stopped himself and clenched his jaw.

"He doesn't even what?"

"We're done talking about this."

"We can't just be done talking about this."

"Why not?"

"Because I'm still talking." I pointed at my mouth. "See? Mouth still moving, words still coming out."

His lips twitched and his dimple appeared.

I softened my words. "Lincoln is a good man."

"Yeah," he agreed quietly and turned to stare out the window. "He is."

"You know why I kissed him. He was distracting the reporters."

"It certainly was a distraction."

"I don't know what to do," I said. "I have to stay on this show."

It felt like a hundred years passed in the time it took him to respond. I honestly wasn't sure he was going to respond at all.

"Amelia's right, Paige," he finally said.

It was not at all what I expected. "Amelia? About what?"

"About who I want to win and who I just want." He turned away from the window to look at me. "I can't have you and even if I could, you don't want me."

"What do you mean I don't want you?"

"You're here for Lincoln, not me. You said yourself you have to stay on this show."

"I…" but I didn't know what to say.

He smiled sadly. "That's what I thought."

"Andy, this isn't what I want." How could I make him understand?

"Then what do you want, Paige?"

"I…" but once again, I was at a loss.

"Well, let me know when you figure it out." He went to the door.

"Andy."

He opened the door, but turned back to me and said, "You were out when we made the announcement this morning. The task tonight is at 8:00 p.m. The contestants are gathering at 3:00 to hear the details. Don't be late. Again."

He gave me a dark look and then left me alone.

$$$

I felt like Lincoln ignoring Andy's call with as many times as I ignored Carla's. Instead, I went back to my room (Peggy was MIA, thank heavens) and called Jemma, knowing full well she was most likely asleep and not caring even a little.

"Andy's right," I moaned to Jemma after she called me several rude names for waking her up. "I'm a kissing slut."

"Are you just figuring this out?"

"Hey!"

"Paige, I am too tired to sugarcoat it today. Either suck it up or hang up."

"Jeeze, someone's cranky."

"I got fired."

"What? No, you didn't!"

"Okay, so I got laid off. Same thing practically."

"Oh my gosh, Jem, I'm so sorry! What happened?"

"The owner was caught selling weed to some minors in the alley behind the restaurant. They shut the whole place down."

"Wow."

"You better marry that millionaire or you're not the only one that's going to be moving home."

"I know that's supposed to motivate me, but honestly it just makes me feel a whole lot better knowing I won't be a failure alone."

"Same old Paige, always looking on the bright side."

"You know me."

"Distract me. Tell me about the producer. He thinks you're a kissing slut?"

"Yeah, pictures are all over the internet of me and Lincoln kissing. We went to breakfast this morning which I guess is kind of against the rules because it means I've gotten more time with him than the other girls. Anyway, some photographers saw us and now we're trending."

"Just a sec. I'm looking it up."

A moment later she let out a low whistle. "I didn't even have to search for it. It was in my news notifications. You're right there, in all your lip gloss-less glory making out with a millionaire."

"It's not what it looks like."

"Really? Because it looks like his tongue is down your throat."

"The paparazzi wouldn't get out of the way of the car and he had to get them to move so he kissed me in order to bring the photographers at the back of the car to the front."

"That's one way to do it, I guess."

"Now everyone wants me off the show and Andy thinks I'm a horrible person."

"#KissRedGoodbye is trending. You have your own hashtag!"

I rolled my eyes as she squealed. "That is not a good thing."

"Publicity is publicity. I don't know what Andy's deal is, it's not like you're making out with him too."

Guilty silence.

"Okay…" I could tell she was trying not to freak out. "When was the last time you kissed him?"

"Last night," I admitted. "Well, it was like 5:00 a.m. so really this morning."

"Oh my gosh, Paige! You are such a kissing slut! No wonder Andy's upset. You kissed him and Lincoln within hours of each other!"

"It sounds really bad when you put it like that."

"You apologized, right?"

"What would I even say? 'Hey Andy, I'm sorry I kissed Lincoln, I didn't really want to, but I had to kiss him so I can stay on the show because if I get kicked off then I'll lose my job and have to move back home with my parents.'"

"How about a simple 'I'm sorry'?"

"Jem," I whined, "He asked me what I wanted and I couldn't give him an answer."

"Oh, Paige."

My phone beeped and I groaned after looking at the caller ID. "Carla's calling on the other line and I've already sent her to voice-mail five times. Call you tomorrow?"

"Sure."

"Okay, love ya."

"You too."

"And Jem?" I said quickly before she could hang up.

"You were too good for that place."

"Thanks, Paige."

I'd barely said hello to Carla when she started screaming.

"WHY DIDN'T YOU GET ME THIS STORY FIRST? YOU'RE THE ONE WHO WAS CAUGHT CHEATING! YOU COULDN'T HAVE WRITTEN THE STORY AND THEN GOTTEN CAUGHT?"

"Carla," I said calmly and opened the curtains to get a better view. I could see the pool from here and saw Peggy lounging on one of the chairs, apparently asleep. Bunny rounded a corner and walked past Peggy over to a bunch of camera equipment. So Bunny got back already. (Can anyone else imagine 'Bunny got back' as the title of a hit song? Just me then.)

"I SWEAR, PAIGE, IT'S LIKE YOU'RE TRYING TO KILL ME! YOU COULDN'T HAVE DONE THIS AT A WORSE TIME! WE WERE JUST BARELY GAINING TRACTION ON THE SEXUAL HARASSMENT ARTICLE AND THEN #KISSREDGOODBYE STARTS TRENDING AND NOW BARELY ANYONE WILL KNOW ABOUT AMELIA. YOU SHOULD HAVE TOLD ME!"

Paulo came into view and the pair started chatting. I switched from the call to the camera and took another picture of the two. Having pictures of them talking in two different locations would add credibility to the article.

"Carla."

"THE WORST PART IS I HAD TO HEAR ABOUT IT FROM JUSTIN THE NEW HIPPIE INTERN WHOSE PANTS HANG SO LOW IT'S A MIRACLE HE CAN EVEN WALK!"

"Carla," I repeated.

"AND THEN MARK COMES IN AND ASKS IF WE'RE STILL DOING THAT ONE STORY ON REALITY TV AND WHY WEREN'T WE POSTING ANYTHING ABOUT IT AND I HAD TO EXPLAIN TO THE EDITOR-IN-CHIEF WHY, IF WE HAVE SOMEONE UNDERCOVER, HE HAD TO READ IT ON *PEOPLE*!"

"CARLA!" I yelled into the phone and, much to my surprise, she stopped yelling. "Before we started reenacting *Anger Management*, I was about to tell you that I have a story I guarantee *People* doesn't."

The other line was blissfully silent for a moment.

"You better not be talking about the sexual harassment one."

"Promise."

"Go on."

"I don't have time to give a full recap, but suffice it to say, between these three articles, the press will be hoppin'." I laughed at my own joke. Carla didn't.

"You'll have it to me by noon?"

"I'm working on it as we speak," I lied.

"I swear, Paige, if you let me down–"

"Have I ever?"

"Consistently."

"Well, okay, then," I relented. "You'll have it by noon."

But she'd already hung up.

Chapter $18

I looked down the line at Bunny and wondered how long it would take for her to be sent home. I'd sent my article to Carla almost thirty minutes ago (I blamed the time change for not having it to her in an hour – "Oh, sorry! You meant your noon?"), which meant after edits it would be ready to go live almost immediately. Few people had actually read the sexual harassment article because of #kissred-goodbye. I was hoping the article on Bunny would get them focused on something else. If I were Carla I would wait to publish it until the broadcast tomorrow night to make the biggest impact since everyone would be tweeting during the show.

Bunny didn't look the least bit guilty or nervous about her nefarious plot. She was a good liar.

Maybe we should form a club.

"We've fired Paulo," Wanda announced as she arrived at the pool where we were standing. Andy was not with her.

"What?" I blurted. My article hadn't even come out yet. Had it?

"He was in breach of contract and leaking confidential information to the press."

"Wait," Amelia said with a confused glance in my direction. I pretended not to see it. "He was the one who wrote the article about me?"

"He didn't admit anything, but it's obvious it was him. *Look!* has pulled the article."

Guilt ate at my stomach. Paulo wasn't exactly innocent, but he didn't deserve to get fired for something I had done. We were all quiet.

"Let this be a lesson to you," Wanda continued with a dangerous look. "If you even think about breaking your contract you will be held liable and we *will* press charges."

We stared at her with reverence.

"Now," she said in only a slightly more cheerful tone. "Tonight your attendance is requested at a celebration. One of Lincoln's board members, Harold Walker, recently received a national humanitarian award and Lincoln has chosen to host a celebration in his honor. A limo will arrive at 9:00 p.m. to pick you up. It is a black-tie event so be sure to look your best. We've hired a hair and makeup artist if you choose to use her. First come, first served."

"Is this the third task?" Peggy asked.

"It is. No one at this event will be aware the show is being filmed. They have been told it's for a video montage for Harold. After your arrival, you will be given instructions that will help you to find the next clue and so forth. Three clues will be given. The last one to receive the third and final clue will be eliminated. No one except for the clue givers will know who you are, and you are not to tell anyone. Anyone who breaks the rules will be immediately disqualified and receive no points." Wanda looked at me pointedly. I smiled innocently even as I continued to beat myself up for getting Paulo fired.

What if he was just trying to make it in this business and I'd permanently ruined his chances? Did he have a family? What if he had kids and now couldn't afford to feed them? It would be my fault. What if he had a terminally ill wife and was only filming this show to help provide her with entertainment as she slowly faded away? Okay, probably not that last scenario, but I was still going to Hell.

Wanda dismissed us to go get ready for tonight, but I rushed to catch up with her as she strode away.

"Wanda," I touched her shoulder to get her attention, "was it really necessary to fire Paulo? I mean, the press wasn't that bad. Don't they say that all publicity is good publicity?"

"There's no such thing as bad publicity."

"Exactly," I sighed in relief.

"No, I'm telling you that's the saying. You said it incorrectly."

"Oh, right." I cleared my throat. "But you said it yourself. Maybe you should give Paulo another chance."

"Paulo was a lying, manipulative sub-par cameraman who deserved what he got." She narrowed her eyes. "Why do you care anyway?"

I struggled to think quickly. "I've just…um…been unemployed before and know how difficult it can be."

Wanda *harrumphed*. "Well if I hadn't fired Paulo then this show would most likely have been canceled which means more than just Paulo would be unemployed."

She turned her back on me, ending the conversation.

$$\$\$\$$$

I tried to move past Paulo being fired. He probably would have been fired anyway after my next article was published. Paulo was accepting bribes from a contestant in an effort to rig the show. What was that Godfather saying? "It's personal, not business." No. "It's not personal, it's business." That was it. I had to keep my job. I had to make a living. If he didn't want to get caught, then he shouldn't have done it. I squashed the guilt down into a tiny ball and tucked it away for another day.

The dress helped. It was from Alexander McQueen's new collection, a black off-the-shoulder gown with long lace sleeves. A slit in the dress that went up to my thigh was covered with black lace. It was by far the most beautiful gown I'd ever worn. And the most expensive. I couldn't believe Carla was letting me wear it. The hairdresser the show had hired tied my hair in a loose chignon and I was pleased to see the smoky eye makeup she'd done did not make my eyes look sunken and dull.

Peggy fawned over the dress and kept telling me how beautiful I was. She too looked amazing in a strapless gold dress that made her look more like Belle than ever. Sometimes, especially when she was so nice, it was difficult for me to believe she was a night-stalker. Then I'd remember the crazed look in her eyes.

I met the other girls on the sidewalk right at 9:00 p.m. I was actually ready about 15 minutes earlier, but after Wanda's comment, I wanted to make her sweat a little. I was glad I did. Seeing the pained look on her face as I lazily strolled down the driveway made my day just a little bit brighter.

The limo took us to an event hall about an hour away. I was surprised to see several reporters on the steps leading up to the entrance and tried to hurry through the crowd to get inside. Amelia took every opportunity to pose for the cameras. And, I was sorry to admit, she looked fantastic doing it. Her flawless skin combined with her sunshine locks only made brighter by the flashes of light, made her look every bit the angel she pretended to be.

I felt bad for wishing my article about her had gone viral.

Peggy and Bunny hovered near her hoping to catch some of the spotlight. I used this as a reason to break away from the group and push my way through the doors. Once through security, I continued into the grand hall, passing a large display with a detailed biography and timeline of the honoree's life.

I took in my surroundings and lost my breath.

It was beyond gorgeous.

Crystal chandeliers hung from the ceiling reflecting sparkling light onto every surface. Black and white portraits hung on the walls depicting famous movie stars and musicians. More than a hundred people were milling about the hall, women in designer dresses and men in tuxes milled about the floor occasionally taking an appetizer or drink off a waiter's tray.

I was only a few feet into the hall when a Chinese waiter about my age offered me a tray of the best-looking fortune cookies I'd ever seen. There were only four left.

"Oh, they look delicious," I said. "Thank you, but I wouldn't care for one right now."

"Please," the waiter said with a slight accent.

Maybe he didn't understand English?

"No." I shook my head. "Thank you."

"Perhaps it is the fortune and not the cookie that would spark your hunger."

So English wasn't the problem.

"No, thank you," I repeated.

The waiter rolled his eyes and dropped his shoulders. "Will you please just take one, lady?" His sudden casual demeanor and excellent English made me pause. "It's for whatever stupid game you're playing, and I can't leave until each player gets a cookie."

I was in such shock that I took a cookie without a word.

"Thank you," he said in such an exaggerated voice that I knew he wasn't grateful at all. Once he'd gone, I broke open the cookie only to find two words written on the tiny paper:

The Nutcracker

I turned the paper over, but that was all that was written.

Super helpful.

Almost an hour passed without any luck. I searched every statue so thoroughly that I was starting to get odd looks. I'd even chatted up the musicians while trying to get a look at their instruments. I grabbed a drink from the bar and stood to the side, scanning the crowd. *The Nutcracker*. That was the only clue I got?

"Quite the crowd, isn't it?" I turned toward the voice, only then realizing I needed to look down in order to see its owner.

The question had come from an oily old man who appeared to be in his early 80s. It was apparent he'd decided not to accept his age because he wore an open-collared black silk shirt, purple velvet jacket, and a gold chain around his neck. He looked like a cheap Hugh Hefner. That is if Hugh Hefner didn't already look cheap. My skin crawled.

"All these people, all this money floating around and no one knows what to do with it." The man looked me up and down. "What would you do with all that gold?"

Hire a bodyguard.

I would have walked away, but I needed a good vantage point to search the crowd and every inch of the hall was packed. I took another sip from my glass, choosing to ignore him.

"I have money, you know," he said. "Lots."

Oh good. I've always wanted to marry a man who described his salary as "lots."

"We could fly to Paris. Tonight. You wouldn't even need to pack a thing." He gave a low laugh that generated a coughing fit.

My, he was quite the charmer. I tried not to grimace and continued to scan the crowd.

"May I?" I didn't notice Andy until he was right next to me, holding out his hand and completely ignoring my future sugar daddy.

I nodded at Andy before turning back to the man. "If you'll excuse me."

The man grumbled as I left, but I barely heard him, choosing to focus on Andy. He'd taken my hand and led me several yards away toward the dance floor before I dug in my heels forcing him to face me, one eyebrow raised.

"You're talking to me now?" I said sourly.

"I thought you needed rescuing."

"You thought wrong, kind sir," I said with a tilt of my head. "I can rescue myself."

"Of that, I have no doubt." The look he gave me made my breath hitch.

He started to pull me toward the dance floor, but I resisted. "Andy, I don't dance."

"Of course you do." He resumed pulling me toward the dance floor.

"Sure," I agreed. "In the privacy of my own kitchen with a broom as my dance partner. Not in front of hundreds of people."

We'd reached the edge of the dance floor when he turned back to me. He casually placed one of my hands on his shoulder and took my other hand in his. His arm wound its way behind my back and pulled me closer, reminding me of the night before. Had it only been one day?

"Dancing with me is not at all different from dancing with a broom."

I anxiously looked over his shoulder. "Andy," I whimpered. "They're waltzing."

"Don't you trust me?" he said with a lopsided smile.

"Yes." I was so sure of my answer that I didn't even hesitate.

He put his head next to mine and whispered, "Step on my toes."

I looked down at Andy's shoes. Hugo Boss.

"Are you crazy?" I hissed. "Your shoes must have cost more than five hundred dollars. I'll ruin them."

I felt rather than heard him chuckle. "Just step on my toes."

I did as he said, stepping on his toes as lightly as humanly possible. Suddenly we were whirling around the dance floor and I couldn't spare a thought for his feet. We locked eyes and I couldn't fathom how he could dance like that without even looking at where he was going. But still, those blue eyes were locked on mine as he held me tight, perfectly content to let me squish his toes as we – he – danced.

Dancing with Andy was like a dream.

I felt like I was in a palace dancing with a prince. I could just imagine myself the poor servant, who'd never really lived a day in her life, and then finally getting to go to a grand ball where she met the prince. If this was a dream, then I never wanted to wake up.

The song ended but Andy didn't let me go. He continued to hold me, never breaking eye contact, never loosening his hold. It wasn't until the next song started that I realized I was still standing on his toes.

"Oh!" I stepped off. "I'm sorry. Your feet are probably permanently bruised by now."

"I didn't notice." He cleared his throat before pulling me close once again and whispering in my ear. "The man with the Charlie Chapman mustache and goatee, wearing the red suit coat has your final clue. You'd better hurry. Amelia's already found him."

I looked up at him, my mouth open. "Why help me?"

He stepped away, dropping my hand. "You look beautiful tonight, Paige."

Shaking my head, I started examining the crowd to find the man who held the last clue. I spied him across the room sitting on a floral couch holding a glass of what I hoped was just water and not vodka. He was a rotund man in a double-breasted red coat with large gold buttons and white pants. He did, indeed, look like a Nutcracker. I rushed toward him.

"Excuse me, sir." I sat down beside him. "I've been looking for you."

"Ahh," he swayed slightly as he leaned toward me, "and I have been looking for you."

"Uh-huh," I agreed to placate him. He was obviously drunk. "I mean that I've been looking for the person who can give me the next clue."

"And what might that be?" He hiccupped.

I furrowed my brow. "I don't know. That's why I've been looking for you. You're supposed to give it to me."

"Give w-what to you, my dear?" He hiccupped again.

"The clue."

"What clue?"

I let out a frustrated breath. "The clue that's part of the game. The *Who Wants to Marry a Millionaire?* clue."

"Ahh, that clue! Why didn't you say so in the first place?" I rolled my eyes, but instead of continuing he closed his eyes.

"Sir? Sir!" I poked him hard in the chest.

He jerked awake and puffed out his chest. "What's the password?"

"Give me the clue?" I said sarcastically.

The Nutcracker man started to giggle hysterically at this. "Oh, all right," he said and then blinked several times. "Uh-oh."

"Uh-oh? No uh-oh. What is it?"

"I don't remember the riddle."

I groaned. "Then just give me the answer to the riddle."

"You're no fun." He *harrumphed* but relented. "They're meeting in the kitchen."

"Finally. Thank you."

"Mr. Walker!" An older woman made her way excitedly to the man next to me who was suddenly very lucid as he stood and gave her a hug.

"Miss Eva, how are you?"

"Very well, thank you. I'm so surprised to find you alone in a corner. I thought the crowds would be falling all over themselves to speak with you tonight. This is your party, after all!"

Wait…*his* party? Was this Mr. *Harold* Walker?

Miss Eva turned to me. "This man is by far the most impressive person I have ever met. We met years ago when we were both performing in *The Nutcracker*. It was only his first year, but Harold was –"

"Did you say *The Nutcracker*?"

"Of course, dear!" She said, appalled I didn't already know the story. "Didn't you read his biography on your way inside?"

Done talking to me, she led a perfectly sober Mr. Walker away. I broke my own rules of propriety and sniffed his now empty glass.

No scent.

Water.

He'd been acting. Of course.

It didn't take long at all to find the kitchen. Buildings that hosted events usually had the kitchen as close as possible – right next to the ballroom kind of close. I poked my head through the door to see Andy and Wanda waiting in a far corner next to a cameraman I didn't recognize. It took some maneuvering to make it to where they stood, chefs and salad makers and vegetable choppers (a real title, I'm sure) standing in my way. I was forced to squeeze, duck, and – in one man's case – jump my way over to them.

"Am I really the first one to finish?" I asked a tiny bit out of breath. The second that I'd gotten near enough for a clear shot, the camera focused on me.

"Amelia was," Wanda said, "But she and Lincoln have already gone back to the house."

"Together?" I asked stupidly.

Wanda raised her eyebrows as if I was dense. "Yes. Together."

"Right, I just," I shifted closer to Andy, "I just thought it was against the rules."

"Says the rule-breaker," Andy muttered. Despite our dance, it was clear he was still mad at me. He folded his arms and leaned against the counter looking positively bored.

I stood awkwardly next to them, unable to get out my phone to distract myself, and desperately trying not to stare at Andy. I tried to pass the time by watching the kitchen staff prepare the meals but was distracted by the tapping noise coming from Wanda's direction. She was pressing hard as she scrolled through her phone and I could hear her finger hit the screen each time she swiped. I was just about to make a snarky comment about the power of silence when without warning she gasped, startling me out of my annoyance and Andy from his boredom. Her eyes grew as they read whatever message was on her phone.

"What is it?" Andy asked.

She looked at him as though she'd just gotten news of a tiger loose at the party.

"Another article."

LOOK! EXCLUSIVE

liar, liar, Bunny on fire
by an Anonymous Contributor

In the midst of this morning's buzz caused by our favorite tall, dark, handsome millionaire, and would-be fan favorite, Paige Michaels, another scandal leaped to the top of the rumor mill. Bunny Hopkins, Patron Saint of Fruit, was spotted dining with none other than Paulo Moretti, head cameraman on *Who Wants to Marry a Millionaire?* Only an hour later they were caught exchanging what looked like cash – or rectangular green drugs – at breakfast.

Although it's unlikely the two were having an affair (liar or not, that girl is way too hot for him), their tête-à-tête and exchange of monetary goods would at least imply bribery. Lucky for us, we've got more than implications. Sources say that Bunny paid Paulo so he would leave Paige stranded at the church forcing her to lose the scavenger hunt.

Considering the stakes, can anyone really blame her? I mean, Lincoln is hot, rich, funny, and under 30. Unless you're looking to introduce your parents to your sorority sister's grandpa, those kinds of guys don't come along every day. Lincoln is the type of guy you can take home to Mom one day and then jet off to Paris the next. Personally, I'm kind of surprised this show hasn't taken a twist *Game of Thrones* style.

Could she have also manipulated the last round's points pushing Carmen Something to last place? Signs point to probably. Will this be enough to kick Bunny off the show for good? Then again, I might vote to keep her on. She's got more spunk than anyone expected. Who would have thought fruit's personal Braveheart had it in her?

Chapter $19

We read the article in silence. Well, Andy did. I pretended to read while actually admiring my iPhone photography skills. My article had pictures this time. Remarkably good ones if I said so myself. Which I didn't. It would have been a dead giveaway if I bragged about the photography.

Wanda was about to speak when the clanging of pots and pans crashing to the floor made her fall silent. We all looked at the noise, expecting to see some poor waiter who'd knocked over a tower of pans. Instead, we saw Peggy and Bunny, pushing their way through the kitchen staff, elbowing anyone in their way. Several staff members yelped as they were forced to jump out of the line of fire, accidentally touching a scorching pan or hot burner. Eager, the cameraman stepped in front of me and knelt down to get the full effect of two crazed women hurtling toward us.

I pushed myself as far back against the wall as I could get, bracing myself for impact as it didn't appear either of them would slow down. Then, in a miraculous show of true sportsmanship, Bunny managed to trip Peggy and send her sprawling to the floor, paving her own way to safely reach Andy.

"Congratulations," Wanda said hurriedly. "You're in third place." She grabbed Andy's sleeve and yanked him toward the door.

"Which one of us is in third?" Peggy asked.

"Lars will give you a ride back," Wanda said over her shoulder, ignoring Peggy's question as she continued to pull Andy to the door.

The cameraman looked both confused and alarmed at Wanda's announcement.

"Your name isn't Lars, is it?" I asked, and he shook his head.

"It's Larry."

I glanced between a disheveled Bunny, a fuming Peggy, and a nondescript cameraman and decided the last thing I wanted was to ride back to the mansion with them. So, like the good reporter I was, I ran after Andy and Wanda.

I caught up with them in the parking lot. They'd just gotten into Andy's car. I'd never run so fast in heels before. Andy shifted the car into reverse right as I opened the rear door and slid in.

"What the –" Andy slammed on the breaks, and even though the car was barely moving it was enough to rock the car forward. "Are you trying to get yourself killed?"

"You're the one who was going to drive off without me." I deflected his question, out of breath.

"You were supposed to go with Lars."

"I believe you mean Larry, and I thought you were only talking to Bunny and Peggy."

"Who's Larry?" Wanda asked seemingly unsurprised by my sudden appearance.

I put on my seatbelt. "I'm here now so I might as well just ride with you."

Andy looked at Wanda as if asking for permission and she rolled her eyes but nodded. He backed his car out of his parking spot ridiculously slowly and it was my turn to roll my eyes.

"About the article," Wanda started to tap on her phone again.

"Maybe we should talk about it later." He glanced at me in the rearview mirror.

She ignored him and started to read something on her phone. I recognized the words of my article immediately. "'Although it's unlikely the two were having an affair...'"

"And I guess we're talking about it," he said under his breath.

She finished reading aloud and turned to him excitedly. "This is the perfect twist. We already fired that sell-out, Paulo, and when we eliminate Bunny, Peggy will be bumped to third place."

"Of course, we'll have to make sure Bunny's elimination is as dramatic as possible. It's a good thing she tripped Peggy in order to win tonight. Otherwise, she would already have to be eliminated and what good would that do?"

"Don't you find it strange that once again Peggy is miraculously saved from elimination?"

"Who cares?" Wanda was practically out of her seat in excitement. "This is good for us. Finally, some positive press!"

"Positive press? Who wrote this one?"

"It was published by *Look!* again, but the article was just listed as written by a contributor."

"Hmm..."

"What?" Wanda snapped at him.

"I'm just wondering who the contributor could be."

"Lincoln said there were at least twenty reporters at Kirby's this morning. It could have been any one of them."

"No," Andy mused. "It's written in the same tone as the others."

"Is that a problem?"

"It means that the same person who wrote the other two articles wrote this one. It means the writer couldn't have been Paulo." His speech slowed as he stopped at a stoplight.

"Cut to the chase, Andrew."

"It means..." He broke off as his eyes met mine in the rearview mirror. They widened ever so slightly.

Crap.

"It means..." Wanda prompted him to finish his sentence, but Andy was quiet, his eyes still locked with mine.

A loud horn startled us and we all jumped in our seats.

"Green means go," Wanda said unhelpfully. The driver behind us was laying on the horn, waiting for us to go and after another half second, Andy started to drive.

"Are you ever going to finish your sentence?" Wanda asked him a block later.

"What?"

"You said that Paulo couldn't have written the articles which means dot dot dot." She waved her hand in the air as if writing something off.

I could see his eyes narrow in the mirror and my heart beat a vicious tattoo against my chest. Was I having a heart attack? He couldn't know who wrote them just from the writing, could he?

"Paulo could file a wrongful termination suit," Andy said.

Wait, what?

Wanda groaned. "Why are you always so quick to find the negative side of things? If it becomes an issue, we'll get PR and legal to offer him a settlement."

Andy was silent. Wasn't he going to tell Wanda his suspicions about me? Maybe he'd wait until they were alone…

"As long as the articles continue to benefit us, it won't matter that Paulo didn't write them. The more the entertainment industry sides with us, the less they'll side with whatever loser reporter is following us trying so hard to get noticed."

I bristled through my panic. I was already noticed. That was half the problem. A company can't fire you if they don't know who you are.

"And when it stops benefiting us?" Andy questioned. "What then?"

"In that case, we'll just have to make sure that the last article will destroy his reputation."

I bristled again, but this time it was from Wanda presuming the "reporter" was a man.

"You do have to admit," she shrugged. "The articles are funny. And eerily accurate."

"They definitely give a unique perspective, that's for sure." His eyes locked with mine once again. I slithered down in my seat, wishing I'd ridden with Lars/Larry after all.

$$$

The second Andy pulled into the driveway of the estate, I was out of the car and heading toward the house. I made it all the way to the door and even had my hand on the doorknob before Andy said, "Paige" in a voice that made me screech to a halt and cringe.

"What's going on?" Wanda asked, immediately suspicious.

"Paige and I need to talk," Andy said. I still hadn't turned away from the door. "We're going to go on a drive."

"No, thanks," I squeaked.

"Paige." His voice wasn't gentle, but it wasn't harsh either. It was somewhere in the middle, like how James Bond might sound right before he killed someone. Deadly calm. I finally faced him.

"I'm too tired to deal with this," Wanda sighed and walked toward a red convertible on the other side of the garage that I hadn't noticed. "Whatever is going on between the two of you better be resolved by tomorrow."

"It will be."

Wanda sighed again, loud enough to send a soft echo around the garage, then she got in her car – at least I hoped it was her car – and drove away.

Andy jerked his head in the direction of the passenger side door. "Get in the car, Paige."

"Are you going to drive to the desert in Nevada, kill me, then bury the body?" I asked, only half-kidding.

"Get. In. The. Car." He bit out each word before he got back in himself, settling behind the steering wheel. I curled my hands into fists to try and stop them from shaking, and after several deep breaths, I slid into the passenger's seat. Andy didn't start the car, though. We just sat in silence in the dark, each waiting for the other to speak. The silence was taut as if our words were balancing on a tightrope and a single misstep would cause the rope to snap sending us to our deaths.

I was the first one to break. "What did you want to talk to me about?"

"You already know."

"Why don't you tell me anyway?" I folded my arms.

"You're a fraud."

I didn't disagree, but neither did I nod or show any sign of emotion at all.

"You wrote those articles. You're the mole everyone has been looking for."

I didn't speak, afraid I would say the wrong thing. As if there were a right thing to say.

"What about me, Paige? Do I know anything about you that's real? Or have you lied about everything? Your hair probably isn't even naturally red, is it?"

"Yes, my hair is naturally red," I said, defending the only thing I could. "It's just not quite *this* color red. They made me dye it a little darker before I came."

"I don't care what color your hair is," he snapped. "You lied to me. You lied to everyone. You exposed Amelia's sexual harassment case and revealed Bunny's blackmail scheme. The only one you haven't done something to is Peggy."

"And Carmen," I shrugged a shoulder.

"Who?" he asked, confused.

"Exactly."

"Why are we having this conversation?" He gave me a scathing look. "You're making jokes like you don't even care. Do you care about anything?"

Ouch. That hurt.

"Of course I care." My voice cracked. "Andy, please, it's not as black and white as it seems."

"Tell me the truth then. Did *Look!* send you here or are you selling your articles to the highest bidder?"

No way was I going to incriminate *Look!* but I had to tell him something. He deserved to know. He deserved the truth. Or at least as much as I could give him. "My roommate and I needed the money. It's insanely hard to get a job as a writer – especially one who wants to specialize in fashion. Without work, I wouldn't have been able to afford rent and both me and my roommate would have had to move home."

"Which is where?" he said harshly.

"Texas," I said with pleading eyes. "Almost everything I told you about me was true."

"Fine," he folded his arms. "You're an event planner. Truth or lie?"

I took a deep breath. "Lie."

"You live in New York City."

"Truth."

"You spend all your money shopping."

"Lie. I don't have any money."

"You have two brothers."

"Truth."

"Your best friend's name is Jemma."

"Truth."

"The other night you went to Lincoln's room, but were actually looking for mine."

My shoulders relaxed. "Truth."

Andy looked out the front window for a long while. The conversation, it seemed, was over. Andy studied the resting speedometer and then started to open the door.

"Where are you going?"

"To tell Wanda. Go pack your things."

"Wait, Andy, no!" I grabbed his wrist and pulled him back to me. To my relief, his grip on the door handle loosened as he focused his gaze on me. I scrambled to think. "I can't go home, Andy, not yet."

"I can't just let you stay and write more articles about us. You've already broken your agreement. We can sue you for this. Wanda's going to insist on it."

"I know, I'm sorry," I said, scooting as close as I could get with the console in the way. "I know how it looks, but I want to be here."

"That doesn't matter anymore, Paige. You're a liability." He huffed, anger stirred up inside him once more and moved to open his door. Desperation clawed at my skin and I said the only thing I could think of to keep myself here.

"I'll stop," I said and clutched at his shirt, tugging him toward me, begging him to listen. "I don't want to go home, Andy. I won't see you anymore. If I have to stop writing the articles in order to stay, then I'll stop."

He looked at me warily.

"I will."

"What about your career? What about New York?"

"You don't have to be in Manhattan to write about fashion." The words tumbled out of my mouth each word seeming heavier than the last. "I can get an apartment here in L.A."

"You would do that?"

"I can write from anywhere," I said with a deep breath.

I could tell he wanted to believe me. *I* wanted to believe me. I wished so much that what I was saying was true. I wanted to be the kind of person who would give up everything for even just a chance at love. And for one second, I was that person and I could practically taste what it would be like to have someone stand beside me. Someone to take care of me.

He ran a hand over his face. "I'll see you in the morning."

He didn't say anything more as he got out of the car, but I was sure I already knew his answer. At that moment, I convinced myself that it would be fine. I would quit *Look!*, move to L.A. and write for E! News or another major competitor. Andy and I would fall madly in love, get married, have kids and a white picket fence and maybe a dog and a goldfish I'd undoubtedly kill within three days and he'd go off to work in the morning and I'd have dinner ready when he got home complete with Tiramisu for dessert and it would be the picture-perfect life.

I desperately wanted to want that life.

But I didn't.

And I knew what I needed to do.

Chapter $20

The consultant held THE curtain aside for me, but I stuck my head out first, ready to duck back inside the dressing room if I saw Andy. Luckily for me, he wasn't anywhere to be found so I gathered the bottom of the gown into my arms and made my way to the mirrors. The consultant, Nancy, an older woman with a kind face, held the rest of the dress up off the floor until I was standing on a pedestal in the center of the room.

Today we were filming inside Panache Bridal in Beverly Hills, but my anxiety was so high I could only muster up little more than a half-hearted response of "great" when I'd been told we'd be visiting the luxury boutique. In ordinary circumstances, I would have been ecstatic to just drive past the store. (Of course, ordinary circumstances meant that Jemma and I would have gone inside Panache pretending to be wealthy tourists only to be kicked out the moment our half-priced shoes hit the floor).

The next elimination round was tonight and all the contestants were trying on wedding gowns. Based off what I'd heard last night, Bunny would be eliminated tonight, but even she was off picking out a gown. Each appointment was being filmed, but only the final two would have their first shopping trips broadcast. Only in TV land they could make choosing a wedding dress, getting fitted, figuring out hair and accessories last a total of five minutes.

"Paige?" Nancy asked.

"Oh, yes, this one is beautiful."

"That's the exact same word you've used for the last four gowns." She folded her arms.

"Well, it is." I fingered the lace and tried to focus on the movement of the fabric, the rosy color of the sash, but my gaze made its way to the entrance wondering if Andy would come in at any second. He was supposed to be here. He was attending at least part of each contestant's appointment and I was his last stop. This whole thing was a waste of time if he was going to expose me. I still wasn't convinced he wouldn't. He'd believed me so easily about moving here that it made me wonder if he was lying to me, just as I was lying to him.

Nancy sighed heavily and pursed her lips in thought. A moment later she brightened and held up a finger. "Give me a moment."

She disappeared into a back room and through the mirror's reflection I stared past the clearly bored cameramen, one of whom was on his phone, and focused on the entrance. I imagined a hundred different ways Andy might burst in and reveal who I really was and what I was doing.

Nancy got back a few minutes later. She was holding a gown covered in a black bag that made it impossible to have any idea what it looked like. I followed her into the dressing room and let her lace me up.

It wasn't until I was back on the pedestal ready to continue watching the door that my eyes froze on the dress reflected in the mirror.

"Let me guess, it's beautiful?" Nancy teased seeing my awestruck expression in the mirror.

"No, it's…" Beautiful didn't seem like the right word. "Beautiful" was too generic, too so-so. All the dresses she'd shown me so far were beautiful. This was…this was… "Whose is this?"

The cameramen hurried to start filming again upon hearing my stunned voice. Nancy fiddled with the fabric, fluffing the as she answered. "It's a Romona Keveza design."

Romona Keveza. That meant the dress was easily $15,000. Probably more.

I turned back to the mirror, inspecting every inch of myself in the mirror now that I knew whose design was wrapped around me. The fit-and-flare gown was strapless with a chapel train. A thin layer of lace cascaded over the ivory silk, perfectly fitting every curve and fold. I stared, forgetting about Andy, unable to think of anything other than the dress – and how breathtaking I looked in it.

Without asking, Nancy twirled my hair into an expert bun, so my shoulders were bare. She went to a nearby curio cabinet filled with tiaras and took one from the top shelf. It was small, no more than a headband really, but it was covered in diamonds that sparkled so brightly I imagined it was possible to see them from the sky. Her wrinkling hands placed it gently on my head and she stepped back to admire her handiwork.

"What do you think?" she asked quietly.

I didn't answer. I couldn't. I'd never been in a dress like this before. I finally understood what they said about wedding dresses – that you just knew. Your wedding dress was the dress that signified a life-changing event. It was the dress that made you feel like the most beautiful person in the world. A wedding dress was supposed to make you feel excited and awestruck and incredible. I'd always thought those descriptions put too much pressure on the dress. Until now.

I opened my mouth to respond to Nancy, but I still didn't know what to say. All thought escaped me and the only thing I could imagine was walking down the aisle toward –

Andy's face stared back at me in the mirror. I hadn't even heard him come inside. He was there, just behind me, looking over my shoulder at our reflections. I turned around so slowly I felt like a ballerina in a music box. The gentle *shhh* of fabric brushing across the wood floors was the only sound. Even Nancy seemed afraid to speak for fear of shattering the moment.

"You look –" Andy gulped, "—exquisite."

Exquisite. That was infinitely better than beautiful.

I wanted to cry.

"It's a Romona Keveza. It's practically a work of art." I said softly.

"So is its canvas," he replied so quietly I wasn't sure anyone besides me could hear.

The stretch of silence was broken by Nancy clapping her hands together. "It really is an incredible dress. Can I assume this is the one?"

Andy and I still stared at one another, unblinking.

"Yes," he said at the same time I said, "No."

I looked at him bewildered. Why would he want the show to buy this dress? We both knew I wasn't getting married. A strange sadness filled me at the thought, but I shook it off.

"Andy, I –"

"We'll take it," he said to Nancy without taking his eyes off me. "Paige, I'll take you home once you're ready."

My heart thumped frantically against my chest. "Home?"

He corrected himself without missing a beat. "Back to the estate."

Unsure what else to do, I nodded and followed Nancy back into the dressing room.

Thirty minutes later, after measurements and multiple promises from Nancy that we would have the dress within the next five days, we were in the car on our way back "home." I kept looking at Andy out of the corner of my eye. He'd insisted that he and I ride together without cameras because, according to union rules, the cameramen were overdue for a break. He told them he'd buy their lunch and handed them a hundred-dollar bill. They'd been only too happy to oblige. I'm pretty sure they were going to go to the most expensive place they could find. Like a strip club.

"Stop," he said with an exasperated sigh as he switched lanes on the freeway.

"Stop what?"

"Sneaking glances at me as if I won't see you."

And here I thought I'd been stealthy. I folded my arms. "You're supposed to be driving, not paying attention to whether or not I'm looking at you."

"Why do you keep looking at me?"

I shrugged but said nothing.

"Paige?"

"Why did you buy the dress?"

"What do you mean?"

"It makes no sense to buy the dress if you're just going to send me home."

He pursed his lips. When he didn't respond I turned to the window and watched the cars race past, wishing I was inside the ones going the opposite direction. We didn't speak for the rest of the drive. The second Andy pulled into the garage, I undid my belt.

"Thanks for the ride," I said and reached for the door.

"We need you for the show." I didn't turn to look at him, but I let my hand fall from the door handle. "You said you wouldn't write any more articles so I'm choosing to believe you."

"Does that mean you're not mad at me anymore?" I turned to face him then, focusing on his eyes, trying to foresee his response. It was an unrealistic hope, but my breath caught as I sent up a prayer that he'd give me the answer I wanted.

"Yes, I'm still mad at you, Paige." But his hand found my knee even as he spoke. "You lied to me. I'll be mad for a while. But I'm not so mad that I don't still find you to be the most brilliant and beautiful woman I've ever met."

I understood where he was coming from. I didn't like it, but I could understand it. My fingers intertwined with his still on my knee and I squeezed his hand. Hesitantly, he leaned toward me across the console. Almost unconsciously, I moved toward him as well. His hand cupped my cheek and he gave me a whisper of a kiss.

"Did you mean what you said yesterday? About quitting your job?"

No.

"Yes."

The lie came too easily. I wasn't an investigative reporter. I was a liar.

He pulled back and stared into my eyes. "I don't want you to quit your job."

I desperately wanted to believe him.

He kissed me again, deeper this time, and my anxieties of the day faded into memories.

I shifted closer, but my thigh dug into the gearshift. Balancing one knee on the seat, I moved as close as I could. Suddenly he hooked his fingers through the belt loops at my hips and pulled me across the console so I was straddling him. His fingers buried themselves in my hair.

I pulled back, breathing heavy. Andy's hand cradled my head as his thumb traced my parted lips. I leaned down and my hair fell over my shoulder, shrouding us behind a waterfall of lily-scented shampoo. I kissed his top lip first, taking my time. His teeth grazed my bottom lip right before our tongues found each other.

Kissing Andy was better than any number of cookies I could ever hope to steal from my roommate. It was better than kissing Joey Poulson, small-town Playboy, behind the bleachers after gym class. And it was a thousand times better than making out with Mark Hathaway after Homecoming in the 1998 Toyota Camry that his grandma's cats lived in. Kissing Andy was quickly becoming my favorite pastime.

I straightened when he started to leave a path of kisses across my collarbone. His hands gripped my arms and I let him push me back against the steering wheel.

A steering wheel that had a horn.

An extraordinarily loud, obnoxious horn.

We both jumped in fright at the world's most terrifying noise which, once my butt was off the steering wheel, was not at all terrifying. Andy and I let out awkward laughs, the moment broken, and I maneuvered my way back to passenger's seat. It was quiet for a moment, neither of us really knowing what to say after our *cough* conversation.

"I really am sorry." I finally opened my door.

He nodded. "I know."

"Oh!" A startled cry and childish laugh echoed through the garage. I twisted around to see Peggy standing at the door into the house. "I didn't realize anyone would be in here."

"Peggy!" My voice sounded too cheery even to my own ears. "Um…hi! How are you? We just got back. From our – my – dress appointment. How are you? How did yours go?"

Andy shot me a look and my mouth snapped shut.

How long had she been there? If she had seen us even 30-seconds before we would have been caught.

"I'm sorry, I didn't mean to interrupt." She'd seen us. It was something about the way she said "interrupt" made me think she knew exactly what she had interrupted, and she wasn't the least bit sorry.

Andy casually came to the front of the car. "How was dress shopping, Peggy? I believe Wanda went with you?"

In a way that would make even Ariel jealous of her hair, Peggy tossed back her thick mane and giggled. "Wanda did come with me and she was by far the best person to have around."

"Really?" I asked skeptically.

"She insisted I try on every dress in the store. And she was so complimentary."

I snorted. "The only thing she compliments me on is my silence."

Peggy looped her arm through Andy's as we all headed inside. I made a face at the way she clutched his arm.

"It was wonderful," she continued. "I could actually picture myself as a bride."

"Yes, wedding dresses tend to have a bridal effect." My snarky comment just slipped out. I didn't mean anything by it. Not really.

"Not all of us have a closet full of designer gowns, Paige. Some of us have to enjoy it while we can."

"Of course." The three of us slowed to a stop at the staircase to our rooms. "I didn't mean –"

"After all," Peggy folded her arms and blocked the staircase, but in true Peggy fashion there was still a smile on her face, "it might be the only chance I have to wear such an extravagant gown. You're more likely to get a proposal – at least from someone."

She looked pointedly at Andy who shuffled his feet. Yeah, she totally saw us in the garage. Great. Just great.

"Personally," she said in a conspiratorial whisper to Andy that I was definitely intended to hear, "I think it'd be settling, but it's really up to you."

My temper flared. "Better settle for sane than sleep with psycho."

Her mouth dropped open and she stomped her way up the stairs.

Andy ran a hand through his hair and let out a slow breath as she disappeared upstairs. He managed to spare me a glance, but I couldn't decipher its meaning. He left too quickly, heading back toward the garage.

It was only then I realized that Peggy had never told us why she'd been in there herself.

Chapter $21

Wanda had wanted Bunny's elimination to be a scene, but it was far worse than she could have ever imagined. It was a scene with a side of fiasco topped with a dollop of debacle. It was – for lack of a better word – ugly. Really, really, ugly.

That night we didn't stand around the pool (I assumed Andy was worried about getting pushed in again), instead standing around one of those fancy fire pits that held glass rocks instead of wood. Upon seeing the pit – which was really just a fancy hole in the ground with rocks stacked around it like a wishing well – I rolled my eyes at the absurd things rich people spent their money on.

Then again, if I had the money I would have paid more than $15,000 for a Romona Keveza gown, so who was I to judge?

Amelia, who was immediately called to Lincoln's side for winning the last round, wouldn't look at anyone except him. I think she was attempting to play the "I have stars in my eyes" card, but from the way she kept blinking I felt it was more like the "I have dust in my eyes" card. She must still be upset about the article I'd written. Lincoln and Andy stood across from Bunny, Peggy, and me, with Lincoln looking appropriately somber at the thought of losing another potential soul mate.

"Peggy, we're sorry, but you came in last place in Round 3," Andy said. "You've been eliminated."

My brow furrowed. Was Peggy being eliminated? I thought Bunny was being sent home.

Peggy started to cry, just as prettily as you'd expect a Disney princess to cry and threw her arms around me.

"We're not going to be roommates anymore!" She tightened her hold on me, pinning my arms to my sides, and I hoped she really was being sent home because this girl was *strong*. Her arms were like a boa constrictor, I began worrying she'd break one of my ribs if I let her hold on any longer.

"There, there," I said and tried to pat her back, but my pinned arms didn't allow for much movement. I shot Andy a frantic look, but his gaze was focused in the opposite direction on Wanda who was striding angrily toward us.

"This will not do!" Wanda bellowed, and I flinched at her tone. Even Peggy abruptly let me go and moved to stand just behind me as though I could protect her. Wanda stopped in front of us, and pointing at Bunny said, "I will not let you ruin this young man's quest for love!"

Oh, please. I fought the urge to roll my eyes again.

"What's going on?" Andy asked, coming between them. He was still in debonair host mode, so I knew this was part of the act, albeit he was convincing enough I think he'd fool the audience. "Wanda, why are you so upset?"

Bunny stuttered. "W-what did I d-do?"

Wanda produced a folded piece of paper. "Does this look familiar?"

Bunny paled even though I was fairly sure the only thing on that piece of paper was lorem ipsum. She must have an incriminating paper somewhere else. I wondered if I could find it before she left.

"What gives you the right? You signed a contract!"

Bunny's whole demeanor did a 180. Instead of a sniffling, timid woodland animal, Bunny was a ferocious beast ready to pounce. Both Peggy and I took an involuntary step back.

"I have the right to look after those I love!" Bunny snarled. "I did what was best for him! He'd never be happy with Paige."

Out of the corner of my eye, I saw Lincoln and Andy exchange a "how did we find another crazy girl" look.

"I love him." Bunny waved an arm in Lincoln's direction. Upon doing so, Lincoln's eyes widened, and he took a small step behind Andy just like Peggy had done to me. Amelia followed suit. It looked like Wanda, Andy, and I were the only ones not afraid of Bunny.

Yeah, who was I kidding? We were all terrified of the manic look in her eyes. I thought bunnies were supposed to be chill. For instance, Wanda was so taken aback by Bunny's reaction that she flinched and no longer looked the least bit upset.

Wanda's eyes kept darting to Andy to see what she should do, but his face was blank. I felt bad for her. Bunny just claimed she loved someone who she'd never actually been on a date with. "You, uh…"

"I, uh, what?" Bunny taunted.

Luckily her attitude helped Wanda gain back some steam. "You sold us out to the press! You risked both Lincoln and Paige's safety by telling the media where they were. And not only that but you cheated, tripping Peggy, so you could make it to the finish line before her."

"So? Everyone thinks Peggy is so nice, but she's got secrets. She's a conniving b—"

Slap!

Bunny's head shot to one side as Peggy's hand hit her cheek. Peggy's face was red but composed as though she'd just slapped aside a fly or a bee and not someone's face.

To Bunny's credit, she didn't seem all that surprised. Furious? Yes. Surprised? No. In a move no one saw coming, she wrapped her hands around Peggy's throat and started squeezing.

As soon as everyone realized what was happening – which, I'll admit, took a couple seconds longer than it should have – chaos erupted. Lincoln and Andy jumped to the women attempting to pull them apart only to stupidly let go of them two seconds later allowing the pair to start attacking one another once again. Princess Peggy got in quite a few good hits. The one to Bunny's face would most likely bruise. Bunny clawed at her in return, leaving scratches on her cheek so deep that they started to bleed.

At least now Peggy could say that she'd been clawed by a Bunny.

…too soon?

The cameramen proved their worth by filming the whole thing while Amelia and I…well…for once we were on the same side. Literally. We both stood on the opposite side of the fire pit, avoiding the fray, but unwilling to miss out on the drama by hiding inside.

"Hey," Andy casually said to me as he removed his tie, his chest heaving as he tried to catch his breath.

I jerked my head in the direction of the Princess vs. Rabid Animal show-stopper that he'd just abandoned. "Did you get tired or something?"

"I can't stop them," he said. Lincoln, upon barely missing a fist meant for Peggy, threw up his hands and came to stand by the three of us.

"You're giving up too?" Amelia asked him.

"They've lost their minds!" Lincoln said with one eye still on the pair.

"Well, someone should do something," I said.

"Wanda went for security."

I looked to where I'd last seen her standing, but she was gone. "Do you think they'll live until she gets back? They're drawing blood." I winced at Bunny's bloody nose.

"I guess we'll find out," Andy said. "Anyone want a s'more?"

We turned in tandem to see an array of graham crackers, chocolate, marshmallows, and other goodies spread out on a table a few feet away from the fire pit. Amelia and Lincoln immediately went to the food and started helping themselves. When Andy stuck a marshmallow on his stick and settled on a chair to roast it, I asked, "We're really going to roast marshmallows while two pageant queens beat each other up?"

Amelia at least had the decency to look somewhat ashamed, but it didn't stop her from sitting on the bench next to Lincoln. Lincoln and Andy didn't respond to my question, they just rotated their marshmallows so they'd cook evenly on each side. Andy patted the empty space next to him and, after throwing my already somewhat unreliable moral compass out the window, I shrugged and joined them.

Andy's marshmallow wasn't even done roasting by the time Wanda got there with security and broke the girls up. He handed me his roasting stick and went to meet them. The second the two were apart, it was if they'd flipped a switch turning on their normal personalities. Bunny gently touched Peggy's scratches and I thought I heard her apologize. I think Bunny might have even laughed at one point. I rested the stick on the cement and went to see what was going on. Andy's gaze darkened when I got there which stung a little, especially since I wasn't the one who'd tried to strangle someone, but he didn't tell me to leave. The smiles I could have sworn were on Bunny and Peggy's faces a minute ago were gone as soon as I walked up.

"You're both going home," Andy said to the pair. "Immediately. Pack your things."

"I'll make a plane reservation for each of you. You'll leave tonight." Wanda pulled out her phone, already on top of it.

Neither one of the women seemed particularly upset at this development, but Peggy (who still managed to look like a princess even with wildly frizzy hair, a bloody face, smeared makeup, and a torn dress) at least had the decency to look ashamed.

"I'm so sorry," she said to Andy, then turned to Bunny with a sheepish look. "I shouldn't have slapped you."

"Ehh." Bunny dabbed at her nose to make sure the bleeding had stopped. "I would have done the same thing."

Bunny's examination of her nose must have made Peggy aware of her own appearance. She tugged at her clothes and ran fingers through her hair trying to get rid of the tangles.

"Your flights are officially booked," Wanda chipped in, reaffirming they were going home just in case they got any ideas. "We'll have a driver take you to the airport. Get your things and be at the front door in exactly one hour."

"Yes, ma'am," Peggy said dutifully. "If you'll excuse me."

She went into the house with her head down seeming deep in thought. I was more than a little surprised she was taking this so well. A minute ago, she'd been attacking Bunny for even suggesting she was anything less than a saint. And now she was ready and willing to go home acting like she was a southern belle accepting a hand slap punishment from her mother?

"Me too." Bunny groaned, wiggled her nose and trailed after Peggy. "I need some Advil."

I narrowed my eyes as I watched their retreating forms. Something wasn't quite right.

$$$

I dreamed a monster crawled out from under my bed. It crept its way up and put its face close to mine. It was so close I could feel the warmth of its breath on my cheek.

I forced my eyes open and screamed.

It was a monster all right. Peggy's face was inches from mine.

My heart was in my throat, but I managed to play it cool by scooting back against the headboard and looking around the room for some kind of weapon. I ended up grabbing the lamp on the nightstand.

"What are you doing here?" I brandished it like a baseball bat. "You're supposed to be on a plane!"

"Relax, silly, I was just getting my flip-flop." She held up a flowery shoe. "It got under your bed somehow."

This calm, cheerful Peggy seemed like the normal, calm, cheerful Peggy instead of her normal, murderer-in-the-night self. I didn't trust her, but I put down the lamp anyway.

"You came back from the airport just to get your five-dollar flip-flop?"

"My flight was canceled, and Wanda felt bad so she said I could stay here one more night until the flight tomorrow."

"Did she actually say that or did she say you could stay at the airport and you intentionally misheard?"

Peggy sighed and sat on the edge of her bed. "I'm not crazy, you know."

"You do an award-winning impression."

"I'm a lot more like you than you think."

"Sure." I nodded with fake enthusiasm. "Like when you let birds do your hair in the morning or mice sew your clothes or when you stand over people and watch them sleep."

She raised her eyebrows. "Mice sew my clothes?"

"You know, because you're a Disney princess."

"Ahh," she nodded. "I've heard that before."

"I would think you were used to hearing the crazy thing too."

"I don't always act like this."

"I just bring it out in you, huh?"

Peggy's phone trilled, and she looked at the text. "Wanda said she found another flight that leaves in an hour. I should go."

I nodded. It didn't feel right to say a formal goodbye when she'd gotten kicked off the show only to return and have me accuse her of being psychotic and threatening her with a table lamp. Yeah, it was definitely better to nod.

"Oh, and Paige?" she peeked back into the room before she closed the door.

"Yeah?"

"I'm really sorry about tomorrow."

I furrowed my brow. "What's tomorrow?"

She gave me a half smile and closed the door behind her. I was too scared to follow.

I tossed and turned for an hour. My eyes never closed. Rather than counting sheep, I lay on my back as memories and daydreams painted their way across the ceiling. Andy was all I thought about. All I could think about. Every direction my thoughts turned he was there. Frustratingly, gorgeously there. Just the memory of his laughter made me smile like a third grader. I should not be thinking about him.

I groaned into my pillow. I needed a reality check. I texted Jemma.

HELP! Can't stop thinking about Andy.

An instant later I had her reply.

You've been thinking about him non-stop since day 1.

I bit my lip. She was right. My phone buzzed and I read her second message.

Maybe it's time you stop thinking. ;-)

And so I did.

$$$

It was, by far, the stupidest thing I'd done since I'd arrived.

I slipped around the corner, coming to a stop in front of a door. I knocked softly before I could chicken out. After a moment, shuffling sounds came from inside the room and I tensed as I heard him reach the door. I was so going to be sent home. For real this time.

Lincoln opened the door and confusion clouded his face when he saw me.

Wait...Lincoln?

Lincoln?

"Paige...is everything alright?" he asked.

"Lincoln." I couldn't get past the fact that he'd opened the door. Wasn't this Andy's room? "I'm sorry, I didn't mean to wake you."

The corner of his mouth quirked up. "Then why did you knock on my door in the middle of the night?"

Good question.

"I – I –" I traced the doorframe with my fingers and studied it as if it was intricate woodwork. And as if I cared about intricate woodwork. "I couldn't sleep and thought...um..."

My face was bright red. I was grateful for the dim hallway lights. Hopefully, Lincoln wouldn't be able to see how mortified I was.

"Yeah?" he prodded, amused once again.

I calculated how long it would take me to get back to my room and pack my bags.

"Um...I..." Alarms wouldn't go off for a few more hours. I could probably be out of the mansion before anyone even woke up.

"Paige?"

Think fast, Paige. Come up with some excuse. *Any* excuse! Why, oh why, had I done this at three a.m. when my brain wouldn't function properly?

"Lincoln," I finally said. "I'm sorry I woke you. I didn't really see you today and I...um..."

"I'm glad you came. I feel bad we haven't really talked since Kirby's."

We hadn't? I felt immediate guilt wash over me when I realized I hadn't even noticed.

He widened the door. "Do you want to come in?"

"No!" I said so quickly, his amused expression fell. "I mean, no, thank you. I should go back to bed."

He looked more confused than ever. "Okay...then why?"

"It's just...I didn't get to talk to you today," I repeated lamely. I might as well pack my things when I got back to my room. He was bound to tell Andy and there was no way they would keep me around after this fiasco. I wouldn't even keep me around. Showing up at a guy's bedroom in the middle of the night? The wrong guy?

The corner of Lincoln's mouth quirked up and without warning, he leaned in and gave me a kiss on the cheek.

"Goodnight, Paige."

"Goodnight, Lincoln."

He shut the door as I walked away. Halfway down the hall I stopped and banged my head against the wall – softly so no one would hear, and because, well, who needs the headache? – and turned to go back to my room. I'd only taken one step before someone yanked me through another door.

Andy held a finger to his lips and reached behind me. The door clicked shut. Instant, yet pleasant anxiety spread through me upon feeling him so close. I stepped past him further into the room so he wouldn't see me tremble. The room smelled faintly of Calvin Klein.

Like his sweater. The thought brought back the reasons I'd risked coming here tonight and my nerves hummed.

A king-sized bed faced a giant floor-to-ceiling window with a perfect view of the night sky. A door close to the window was open and I could see clothes strewn across a walk-in closet's floor. I desperately wanted to go inside and search for my – his – sweater. I shifted my focus so I wouldn't do something even crazier than I already had. I regarded his bed, far bigger and nicer than mine. It looked heavenly. Its puffy down comforter was covered in a brown duvet with a light-colored geometric print. The bed was still made from that morning and it was obvious it hadn't been slept in. Instead, a rumpled throw blanket was on one side next to two thick books, a corner of the blanket acting as a bookmark.

It was so easy to imagine him there reading, avoiding bedtime simply so he could enjoy some peace before he had to act as host again. Everything from the smell, to the view, to the books, made me wish I could stay here. We could lie on the bed, him reading about the history of the civil war and me reading the latest Liane Moriarty. Or we could ceremonially toss the books off the bed and…who am I kidding? I could never treat a book like that. I smiled at the thought. A smile which promptly fell when I saw the look on Andy's face.

His arms were folded, and his jaw clenched. "You know the rules, Paige. You're not supposed to be in the private wing of the house, much less sneaking into Lincoln's room. Haven't you broken enough rules? What were you thinking?"

"I wasn't sneaking into Lincoln's room!" I protested. "It just happened while I was –"

"For someone who keeps telling me you're not interested, you tend to spend a lot of time trying to see him."

"Yes, but –"

"What are you doing here, Paige?"

This was not going as planned. It was supposed to be like a romantic movie where I showed up and fell into his arms without a word. At the very least he was supposed to be happy to see me.

"Looking for you," I said in a rush, praying he'd believe me. "I was looking for you. The other night I thought you ran into your room when you went to get a sweater. I guess I took a wrong turn."

He used one hand to rub his eyes, surrendering. "Earlier this week I was in Lincoln's room talking and left my sweater there. I thought it'd be smaller so I went to his room to grab that one."

"Oh." I shuffled my feet. "I went to his room thinking it was yours."

"In the middle of the night?"

"Don't say that like it's unusual. We've been getting together in the middle of the night all week."

"That was until I found out you've been lying to me the whole time and selling the show's secrets to *Look!*"

I had nothing to say to that.

"Listen, Paige," he let out a deep breath. "We can't do this anymore."

I knew he was right, but it didn't stop me from asking, "Why?"

"You know why."

I did know why. "What do you want me to do, Andy? You said I could stay until we filmed the last episode. Can't we wait to stop sneaking around until we can actually stop sneaking around?"

"What happens when he chooses you?"

"He won't." I rolled my eyes.

"What if he does?"

"He doesn't love me."

"It's reality TV, Paige. He'll propose whether he loves you or not."

"Then he proposes!" I threw up my hands. "It doesn't mean anything. It's not like the wedding is real."

Andy was taken aback. "Didn't you read your contract?"

"Of course I did."

"Then you should know that it *is* real. You really will be married. Legally married."

I felt like I'd just been slapped in the face, then had a bucket of ice water dumped over my head. It wasn't supposed to be real. How could I have missed that? I wouldn't overlook something like that. Paige Michaels didn't *miss* stuff.

"W-What? That's…that's insane!"

"That's Hollywood."

"You can't be serious about this."

Andy's voice was soft but firm. "Paige, you and Lincoln will be married."

I ran my hands over my face, suddenly exhausted. I probably could have fallen asleep standing up. Stupid Peggy for waking me up. Stupid Jemma for telling me to do something about how I felt. Stupid Hollywood for being stupid. And stupid Amelia too, just because I was officially in that kind of a mood.

"It doesn't matter if it's a real marriage or not," I said, attempting to snap myself out of it. "Lincoln won't choose me. Even if he did, I wouldn't marry him. It's a non-issue."

"Paige, you don't understand."

"Look," I ignored him, "I didn't come here to argue."

"Then why did you come here?"

I made a sound of disbelief. "Isn't it obvious? I wanted to see you. Why else?"

"And what would make you think that was a good idea?"

"Right." My cheeks flamed with embarrassment and my eyes stung. What was I thinking? I was supposedly almost engaged to another man. I was a liar. I was a fool. Embarrassment was flush on my face and I took a shaky breath. "I must have been sleepwalking or something. Goodnight, Andy."

I took two long strides to the door, eager to leave before my tears fell.

But I never got there.

Andy had taken my hand and pulled me back to him. He backed me up against the wall. Resting his forehead against mine, he looked down into my eyes and said, "Lincoln would be an idiot not to choose you."

His breath was on my cheek and I pulled my head back to look at him. The usual traces of his laugh lines were nowhere to be found. I could feel his body heat, and then he was cupping my cheek with one hand and pulling me even closer with the other. Our faces touched. His breath danced across my skin as his nose brushed mine. His lips grazed my cheek, my jaw, the corner of my mouth. His kisses were so soft that if it weren't for the fire that lit up each touch, I could have been convinced they hadn't happened at all.

"I should probably go," I said, but made no move to pull away.

Andy nodded. "Probably."

Our mouths kept inching closer. Closer. Until I wasn't sure what air was mine and what was his. His fingertips traced my sides and my hand tangled in his hair. His lips were nearly as close as they could get, but they'd never seemed so far away. Every nerve in my body was singing with life, dancing in anticipation, waiting for him to finally close the distance. My eyelids grew heavier as every inch of our bodies touched. Everything except our lips.

Then it was over.

He stepped back so fast I almost stumbled.

Too disoriented to know what to say, I stared at Andy, back against the door, breathing heavily. He ran a hand through his hair and took a deep breath before he spoke.

"Goodnight, Paige," he said and opened the door. He wouldn't meet my eyes as I left. I stepped into the hallway, but when I turned back to say goodbye, his door was already shut and I was alone.

Again.

Chapter $22

A few hours later, and long before anyone else would be up, I was awakened by my phone ringing so loudly that I cried out and stuffed a pillow over my head. I blindly searched for my phone so I could stop the noise, but it fell silent the second my fingers closed around it. Through bleary eyes, I looked at my missed calls and groaned.

It was officially the world's longest day.

I called Carla back immediately. When she picked up she didn't greet me.

"We need proof." Her voice was commanding. Authoritative. It was one-hundred percent Carla.

"Proof of what?"

"Proof that everything you say is true. Our lawyers told us that in order to back up our claims we need to provide evidence. It's this whole 'intentional harm' thing they keep blathering on about. The lawsuit keeps building with every article."

"Carla," I rubbed my eyes, "to prove any of this I'll have to come out and say that I'm the mole."

I wasn't about to tell her that at least one person already knew.

"The final episode is next week. We won't need to reveal anything before then, but the lawyers need proof now. They can't prepare a defense if they don't proof."

"But I don't think –"

"Paige!" she barked.

"Fine!" I barked back. "I'll find something!"

I tossed my phone onto Peggy's now empty bed, buried my face in my pillow and screamed my frustration into the feathers. Once I was finished cursing my career choice, I got dressed in dark jeans and a black t-shirt and headed off to investigate. Although I wasn't quite sure what I was investigating, I knew the best place to start would be the private wing of the house.

Having made my way to the private kitchen multiple times, as well as Lincoln's and Andy's rooms, I felt fairly confident I could find the office Andy had led Lincoln and me into when he'd yelled at us. I made my way through hall after hall, turning left and then right, backtracking when I saw an unfamiliar statue and then backtracking my backtrack when I realized I'd seen that statue before. Six hallways, ten doors, and two bathrooms later I found the office. Only it wasn't an office I'd been in before. This office was a disaster zone. Papers were piled so high on a glass desk you could barely see underneath the clutter. The wires that hooked up the computer and printer were crisscrossed and tangled more than my grandma's bag of yarn she kept for the knitting she never did. One wall of the office was full of shelves, but there wasn't a book in sight. Each shelf was covered with branded swag and awards haphazardly strewn on the shelves. It was as if the International Entrepreneur of the Year award was nothing more than a participation trophy.

I grimaced as I stepped over a pile of old CDs. The other office I'd been in must have been Andy's because this was definitely Lincoln's. Andy's bedroom was spotless. No way would he let his office look like this. But why would Andy's office be here instead of at the studio?

The sun was starting to rise, casting an early morning glow through the tall windows that seemed to be standard in every room. If I hadn't been so paranoid about getting caught snooping – again – I might have enjoyed the way the soft light warmed my skin.

I carefully made my way over to Lincoln's desk, afraid I was going to step in a plate of moldy food or something equally horrifying. Lincoln's housekeepers must not have been allowed in here. Which meant I most certainly wasn't.

I fingered through a few of the papers on top of one stack but didn't see anything of interest. Several thank you letters from kids who went to the rec center, a certificate honoring him as an anonymous donor to California's foster system (um…if it's anonymous why would they send a certificate? Seems counterproductive), receipts from trips he'd taken, a photograph of him and Andy at a basketball court, a napkin with some girl's phone number… I sighed and chewed on my lower lip. Nothing here to suggest the show was rigged. Nothing to hint he was even on television.

A metal filing cabinet was against the wall opposite the desk and I was about to start opening its drawers when I heard someone humming. I couldn't tell where it was coming from, but it was getting louder. I ducked beneath the desk only to be reminded it was a glass tabletop desk with no back. I cursed and looked for another place to hide. Unfortunately, other than the desk and two metal chairs, everything was pushed up against the walls. The floor had piles of books, boxes, pictures and junk all over it, but nothing big enough to hide behind. If someone came inside the office I would be found.

The humming got louder and louder and I braced myself to get caught. I'd have to come up with some amazing lie about why I was in Lincoln's office and convince the person not to tell Andy and then we'd go get ice cream like we were old friends who occasionally lied for one another and…the humming quieted and seemed to get further and further away. I let out a shaky breath and resumed my search at a faster pace.

I opened the top drawer of the cabinet to find nothing but rubber bands. I rolled my eyes. Andy was right – Lincoln was like a child. But I struck gold in the second drawer of the cabinet. I took out the folder with the words Los Angeles County Registrar emblazoned on it. I flipped it open to see several forms about how to file an application for a marriage license. I continued to flip through the papers I was surprised to see the application was already filled out. Was Lincoln already married?

No. The next page revealed a reminder card that read "Please pick up your marriage license on or before…" The marriage date was listed. It was the same day as the final episode; the live broadcast. But it didn't make sense. They wouldn't be able to fill out the application without the bride's name which meant…

They'd already chosen the winner.

Yes!

I almost shouted for joy – this was better proof than Carla or her big shot lawyers would dare to hope for.

But then the same thought crossed my mind with an entirely different meaning: they'd already chosen the winner.

Lincoln sneaking me out to breakfast, saying that he wanted to get to know the person he was going to end up with? The abrupt silences between him and Andy anytime I was around? Andy's certainty that I would be Lincoln's choice? Suddenly it all made sense.

No.

No, no, no, no, no, no, no, no, no, no, no, no, no, no, NO! A million times no. I could not be the bride. I *would not* be the bride.

I started scanning the pages looking for any indication of the bride's name, but it was all background info on Lincoln.

"Hey, Andy!"

I froze. Lincoln's voice had come from just outside the door.

"What are you doing up, Linc? And going into your office? We both know you can't possibly be working. It's not even noon." Andy's voice had the teasing quality of a brother and Lincoln's responding laugh made me want to say "*aww*." Except I was about to get caught trespassing in a millionaire's office going through confidential information.

If the articles weren't going to get me sent to prison, getting caught rifling through Lincoln's private papers certainly would. I stuffed the papers back in the drawer as quietly as I could.

"I'm guessing you were working so long you didn't even go to bed." I heard Lincoln retort. "Maybe you should have a little fun once in a while."

I scoffed. Yeah, I thought so too.

"Yeah, sometimes I think so too." I almost laughed that we'd had the same thought, but I didn't. It wasn't funny enough to go to prison for.

I could practically see him rubbing the back of his neck as he said, "Can we go for a walk? We haven't talked in a while."

"Sure, bro."

I held my breath as their footsteps echoed down the hallway. I was tempted to go back to the drawer to look at the application again, but I didn't want to risk it. They were public records. I could easily access them online.

I peeked out the door and, upon seeing no one nearby, sprinted all the way back to my room. I waited another hour before I thought it was safe enough to go back downstairs. I texted Carla and told her to check the marriage license records for LA County. I got an immediate reply saying she was on it. When I finally dared to go back downstairs and walked into home base, Andy was already there.

"You're up early," I said by way of greeting. I had no idea how to talk to him anymore. Did he like me? Did he hate me? He knew I was the mole, but he wasn't sending me home – yet. We kissed in the car yesterday, but he shut the door in my face last night. Did he expect me to quit my job and join him here? Was I listed as the bride on the marriage license application? Had he been the one who had filled in the form? How was I supposed to talk to him when I had no idea where we stood?

"I should go," Andy replied.

Okay, it seemed we were going with the whole avoiding each other completely thing. At least now I knew.

Before I could respond – although I have no idea what I would have said – Wanda entered the room, her thumbs typing furiously on her phone. "Where are you off to, Andy?"

"Just to scout out the location for the shoot next week." He turned to leave.

"Take Paige with you," Wanda said without looking up from her phone.

"What? Why?" Andy seemed more annoyed than strictly necessary. It was like spending time with me was equivalent to spending time in a dentist's office.

"Because I don't want her to be alone in this house. Someone went through Lincoln's papers either late last night or early this morning and I'm not taking any chances. He went in there to get something and said things were out of place."

Andy shot me a knowing glare. I retained an expression much calmer than I felt. Inside I was freaking out like Brittney Spears in 2008. That office was a mess! How could they even tell? If I was a robber I wouldn't have even bothered with that room because it was too disorganized. Can anyone blame me for not leaving things *exactly* how they were originally? I mean, *come on!* How on earth was I supposed to put anything back to the way it was? A jury had to understand that, right?

"Amelia and Lincoln are going to be here alone," Andy pointed out. "What if one of the cameramen catches them doing…something? Isn't that going to be more of a PR nightmare than anything Paige could come up with on her own?"

"I don't trust either of our so-called contestants at the moment." Wanda looked away from her phone just long enough to give me a steely glare, but she spoke directly to Andy as if I weren't there at all. "But Lincoln and Amelia haven't gotten into any trouble so far and she has. Until we are sure the articles have stopped, I don't want to leave either of them alone. Take her with you."

Andy sighed heavily and with a "fine" that could have rivaled a teenage boy being told he had to shower, he ended the conversation. I followed him out in silence, partly because I didn't know what to say and partly because I was still upset they'd noticed I'd been through Lincoln's papers.

I mean, really.

I went to open the door to the garage, but Andy kept walking.

"Aren't we –" I started to ask.

"No, a car can't get us there." I could tell he was fighting back the urge to smirk and that made me smile. He couldn't stay mad at me forever. At least, probably not.

I furrowed my brow but continued to follow him. We walked past the pool, the private garden area where Lincoln had met with each of us, and a tennis court on the other side of the mansion. We stopped at a rectangular slab of concrete with a few white lines painted on it.

"What's this?" A loud buzzing interrupted my question. Andy pulled me back a few feet and I watched open-mouthed as a helicopter landed on the concrete slab. When Lincoln and I had gone bungee jumping we'd ridden in a helicopter, but we'd gone after dinner. We didn't leave from here.

I wanted to Andy if it was for us, but then got afraid that it would be one of those transplant emergency helicopters and they had to land here because they didn't have enough time to make it to the hospital and they had to do a kidney transplant next door and then I would be blocking their way and forever be known as the "girl who ruined lives by blocking the emergency transplant helicopter parking spot."

That would suck.

Luckily, the helicopter was for us. Andy handed me a jacket and helped me put on earphone things that kind of drowned out the sound of the propellers while making it easier to hear Andy. I started to get in first, but he held me back.

"Get in after me!"

"Why? So you can leave me?"

He rolled his eyes. "I'm not going to leave you. Just get in after me."

I nodded and after he'd gotten in he held out his hand to help me up. Once I was inside and we'd shut the door, the helicopter lifted off the ground making my stomach flip. We went higher and higher and higher. Fast. So fast. Was it this bad the first time around? The bungee jumping must have blocked it from my memory. I couldn't do it. Helicopters were not like airplanes. This was not exciting. This was going to be a horrible and fiery death. I suddenly wished I'd gotten caught in Lincoln's office. I squeezed my eyes shut.

"Open your eyes."

"What?" I asked with my eyes still closed.

"Paige." Andy's voice was calm and clear as he took my hand. "Open your eyes."

I did.

The view in front of me was incredible. It was almost a 360-degree view. From where I sat I could see practically everything. To my right was the ocean, a far off wide expanse of blue and green. Out the front windshield, I could see hundreds of rooftops from small homes to celebrity mansions. To my left were the mountains and rolling hills. Greens and browns and yellows of every shade covered the ground, a spectacular panorama of color.

"I wanted you to be able to experience it all." He squeezed my hand. "You can see better from that seat than you can from this one."

I knew I loved him then. I don't know why it took me so long to see it. I just know that it wasn't until that moment that I knew I was in love with him. Maybe it was something about the way he looked at me with such care in his eyes. Or maybe it was how his hand fit in mine, strong and stable, able to calm my nerves with a single stroke of his thumb. It could have been how he wanted me to experience something incredible or that he put my comfort and enjoyment above his own. I'm honestly not sure. But something about that moment made me fall in love with him and, for the first time, I actually wanted to give my career up for him.

Maybe I could do it – leave my job and move to LA. Maybe I could risk it all for a chance at love. Maybe I should. Maybe by not being willing to sacrifice my career, I was making a choice that would ensure my single status for the rest of my life. Could that be it? Could I not have a career and a family?

I thought of my mom, doing everything for her kids. I thought of the days she served as chauffeur to soccer and music lessons. I remembered how she would sit in the car and wait for us while my brothers and I participated in nearly every club school had to offer. She and my dad went to all my brothers' high school basketball games. They both came to my recitals. She was the perfect mom and he was the perfect dad. She gave up her whole life and career for her husband and family and she was happy. I could do that...right?

At some point, I stopped seeing the scenery around me and started replaying the past week in my mind. Meeting Andy in the driveway. Making grilled cheese in the middle of the night. Sneaking out to enjoy a fake lunar eclipse. Kissing in his car. I could spend my whole life doing anything and everything with him.

It terrified me.

It was the soft landing that broke me out of my reverie. I didn't expect the landing to be so smooth. I expected (besides us crashing, I mean) a much grander arrival. But when I stepped down out of the helicopter, I was once again in awe.

I turned in a circle to take it all in. We were on top of a mountain in a secluded area that looked like we were the first ones to ever set foot there. There was a small waterfall that cascaded down a mountain of rocks ending in the calming swooshing noise that came from water hitting stone. Trees of all kinds and all shapes surrounded us. Wildflowers blossomed around the bases of the trees and it was easy to imagine getting engaged here.

Or married.

My phone buzzed. It was from Carla.

Your name is on the application.

Chapter $23

I couldn't breathe.

"This is one of my favorite places," Andy said, but I could barely hear him above the buzzing in my ears. My mind was racing with the thought of marrying Lincoln.

They rigged the show. They rigged the show so I would be the one who ended up with Lincoln. They wanted me to marry Lincoln. Did Andy know? Did he want me to marry Lincoln too? I thought he wanted to be with me. My heart that had been so full of love and appreciation for Andy only moments before started to crack.

"This is amazing." I forced out a breath. I wanted to sob about everything I'd thought in the helicopter. How stupid was I to even consider the idea of marriage and motherhood? I couldn't believe that I'd spent my whole life intent to make it on my own and within a week of knowing a hot guy I had been willing to give it all up.

No. The helicopter ride was a fluke. It didn't matter if Andy had planned for me to marry Lincoln. I didn't want a relationship anyway. I could do it. I would do what I had to do to get the job done.

My career came first.

Andy must have thought I was in awe because he chuckled. "I'm glad you like it."

My heart hurt. I didn't know a heart could physically hurt from emotion. I pulled out my phone then hesitated, holding it up to him in question. "Can I record this?"

He laughed. "Of course."

I recorded the scene around me. I narrated the video, my anxiety growing to the point I couldn't even tell you what I said.

He must not have known about the application. He must not have known they were going to rig the show like this. He couldn't have. He didn't.

I was filming some rocks or something when Andy's arms wrapped around my waist. I leaned back into him and forgot about my phone. I twisted so we faced each other and snaked my arms around his back, my phone still in my hand. He was so tall my head fit easily under his chin as his strong arms pulled me closer. I let him envelop me and I buried my face his chest, breathing in his scent.

"Do me a favor?" I whispered, looking up at him. He nodded and brushed the hair off my face, his dark eyes concerned.

"Kiss me," I said. His eyes held mine for one long moment and then he kissed me. I desperately didn't want it to be the last time. It felt so good to be in his arms, the sun hot on my back, the only sound coming from the waterfall crashing against the rocks below. I wanted to stay like that – safe and warm and peaceful – forever.

"Come to New York," I blurted.

"What?"

What?!

"Come to New York," I repeated. "We can go now. Today. Forget the show. Come to New York and we'll be together. You can produce TV shows and movies there just as easily as you could here."

"Not exactly," he said, but not in refusal, more like he was in shock. I think I was too.

"I want to be with you." It wasn't until I said it out loud that I realized how true it was. I loved him and I wanted to be with him. And more than anything I wanted him to want to be with me too.

He looked pained. "I want to be with you too."

"So?" Hope surged through me. He couldn't have known about the application. I grabbed his hand. "Come back to New York with me."

"I...I thought you wanted to come here." He brushed the hair out of my face.

"I don't want to quit my job," I said. "My boss is...well, she's horrible, but I've learned so much from her already. I know I can't learn half as much from anyone else in the business. I have to learn from her."

"Why did you say you would quit then?"

"Because I was scared."

"I want you to be happy. I would never ask you to quit for me."

"Then you'll come?"

He opened his mouth, but upon seeing the look in his eyes every last ray of hope I might have had disintegrated.

"It's not that easy."

I stepped back so we were no longer touching. My mind was like a lens zooming in on the application from Lincoln's drawer. I wondered whose idea it was. Was it Andy's? Could he see how much I wanted him and decided he'd just give me to Lincoln rather than dealing with hard part of rejecting me? I tightened my grip on my cell phone, using it as an anchor to reality. "I see."

"I want to be with you. I just can't move to New York. It'd be different if you moved here."

Anger coursed inside me. "It's okay for me to quit my job and change my entire life for you, but it's not okay for you to do the same?"

"That's not what I'm saying!"

"Then what *are* you saying?"

"I'm saying that it's different, okay? You don't understand."

"Explain it to me."

"If I leave with you, I'd be writing off the entire show. My business. Lincoln's business. It would all suffer if I were to leave because of you."

"Wait, so you could leave, just not with me." I hated everything about this. I was hurt. I was angry. I wanted to throw things at Andy, make him realize how painful it was for me to ask him to be with me only to have him reject me. Most of all I was angry with myself for even entertaining the thought we could have worked this out somehow.

He growled in frustration. "You're taking this the wrong way."

"How should I be taking it?"

"I don't know!" We were several yards apart now, but I could still see his chest rise and fall with angry breaths. "I can't be with you while you're on the show. You're supposed to win! Lincoln's going to choose you!"

Tears sprang to my eyes.

"Then I'll go home! Kick me off the show. Eliminate me. Whatever. Just be with me."

Fight for me.

"You don't get it, do you, Paige?" His eyes were manic. "It's not just Lincoln I'd betray, it's the whole show. Do you realize the scandal this would cause? Everyone would lose their jobs and their credibility. It would ruin us. No one would get paid. The network would drop the show and no one would ever work with anyone on our team again. If I left with you now everyone would find out the truth."

"What's the truth?" My heart thumped as I prayed he wouldn't say what I knew would.

"It's rigged! It's all fake!"

There it was. I had it. I had proof. I had evidence. I had the one line that would make the whole series of articles credible.

"I helped you cheat your way through the first round because you were supposed to win. We planned on Amelia winning the second round, but we had no idea about Bunny's involvement to stop your progress to make you come in last. The grand ball was so easy we just expected you to find us first. You're clearly the most capable. Oh, and the fight between Bunny and Peggy?" He waved his arms in the mansion's general direction. "They knew they were both going to be kicked off the show, so we paid them to make their exit memorable. It was just more memorable than originally planned. Not all, but almost everything that has been filmed this past week is completely fake."

"Well," I held up my now trembling hand to display my phone – still in video mode, "this isn't fake."

It took only seconds for him to realize what I'd done. His mouth hung open and he had a look of complete pain and betrayal. A few tears escaped my stinging eyes, but I kept my phone's camera focused on him.

"This whole time?" He looked disgusted. "All that talk about being with me? About me moving to New York? About you moving here? You were recording the whole time?"

"I'm so sorry, Andy." I took a shuddering breath. "I'm sorry, but I won't sacrifice my career for anyone. Even you."

His jaw snapped shut and his whole demeanor shifted into the stiff professionalism reserved for someone you hate. He turned on his heel and headed for the helicopter. Every part of me wanted to fall to the ground and cry over what could have been. The only thing holding back my sobs was pure determination.

Andy was already holding the helicopter door open for me when I reached him. I got inside, but instead of climbing in after me, Andy yelled to the pilot, "Take her back to the house then come back to get me."

"But sir –"

"Do it!" He slammed the door. The wind from the propellers made his hair and shirt blow wildly, but he didn't hurry away. He walked tall with his head high. A rising sensation made me rush to fasten my seatbelt as the helicopter took off. Andy was already on the phone by the time I looked down at him.

The half an hour flight back to the mansion felt five times longer.

$$$

I emailed Carla the video while I was packing, except I'd edited out all of the parts about me and Andy. It wasn't her business. The revised fifteen-second version only contained the part where he'd agreed to be recorded and when he'd explained I was supposed to win. I watched Andy's reaction to my betrayal ten times before I deleted it. It was so much worse than I'd thought at the time. I never wanted to hurt him.

No. I had to stop thinking like that. It was him who betrayed me. *He* betrayed *me*. I was just protecting myself and my career. He was planning on marrying me off like I was property.

Carla didn't need to know about the two of us. Ever.

I'd was already in the foyer with my bag by the time Andy showed up. His gaze went from my suitcase to my eyes and back to my suitcase.

"I'll call you a cab," he said and brushed past me.

Always the gentleman.

"Andy, wait." I didn't expect him to stop, but he did. He didn't turn around, instead choosing to face the wood-paneled wall with his shoulders tense and fists clenched.

"What?" he growled.

I didn't know what to say. I thought he would have kept walking. I would have. I should have! He planned for me to marry Lincoln. He filled out a marriage license application with my information and just assumed I would go along with it when the final episode rolled around. And to top the whole thing off he'd made me fall in love with him, fully aware that he was basically selling me off to the highest bidder.

My tone was venomous as I called him a word my mom would be appalled was even in my vocabulary.

He whirled around and stalked toward me, anger making his whole body practically shake. "How can you say that? You've lied to me for days. You knew how I felt about you and you used my feelings against me!"

"You're such a hypocrite." I shook my head in disgust.

"How's so?" We were in each other's faces now.

"You rigged this whole show so I would have to marry Lincoln. You chose me as the winner before I even got here. You made me feel guilty for not quitting my job and moving out here when you weren't ever planning on being with me anyway! You never had real feelings for me, you were just using me to boost ratings."

Andy opened his mouth to speak, but a new voice joined us.

"That's why you tried to change the plan at the last minute?" Lincoln entered the foyer looking both confused and betrayed. I blushed, embarrassed at the things I'd said. How long had he been listening? "You didn't want me to have her."

"You don't love her anyway," Andy snapped and resumed glaring at me.

"That didn't matter to you when we started filming." Lincoln's voice was rising with every word, his face contorting in anger. "You pushed this plan on me and then went and changed your mind the second you realized you were in love with her."

"I had my reasons."

"Your reasons?!" My voice rising to match theirs. "You had your reasons for forcing me into an arranged marriage?"

"It was in the contract!" Andy threw up his hands, exasperated.

"You put it in the contract?" Lincoln was livid and before I realized what he was doing, he punched Andy in the face.

They both swore simultaneously, Lincoln cradling his hand in pain, and Andy doubling over holding his nose.

"You tried to force both of us into marriage!"

"What's going on?" It was Amelia. She'd come around the corner first looking confused and then alarmed upon seeing our expressions. The second she saw Lincoln shaking out his hand she rushed to him and put her arm around him in concern. "Are you okay? What did they do?"

"Stay out of this!" Andy yelled as best he could with a voice stuffy from holding his bleeding nose.

"Don't talk to her like that!" Lincoln snarled and moved toward Andy.

"You two!" Wanda stomped into the foyer.

The three of us stopped arguing long enough to yell "WHAT?!" clearly not knowing to whom she was referring.

She got in mine and Andy's faces, not seeming to even notice that Andy's nose was bleeding. Her jaw was clenched, and her nostrils flared as she held up her phone for us to read what was on its screen.

It was another article.

Only this time, I didn't write it.

CAUGHT CHEATING!

by Peggy Cochran

Paige Michaels, top contestant on WWTMAM, and Andrew Warner, the popular reality show's producer, were caught kissing inside Warner's car yesterday afternoon.

Who Wants to Marry a Millionaire? revolves around one of America's wealthiest bachelors, Lincoln Lockwood. Five lucky women were chosen to compete in an archaic game of "love" in order to become his wife. The winner was to be announced and then married to Lockwood in the final episode. Except marrying a millionaire on live television wasn't all Michaels had in mind.

After a morning of trying on wedding gowns at the high-end Beverly Hills boutique Panache Bridal, Michaels was found in the midst of a passionate tryst with WWTMAM's producer. Further evidence suggests the torrid affair had been going on long before that day. Pictures of the pair getting cozy in the middle of the night surfaced early this morning.

Based upon Michaels' hometown, one would think she had more traditional values. Raised on a cattle farm in Tennessee...

Chapter $24

Why can't anyone remember where I'm from? Is *Texas* really so difficult to remember? It's five letters for heaven's sake!

I shook my head. Now was not the time.

After having read all I could take I removed myself from the group. I now knew what Peggy meant last night when she'd said she was sorry about tomorrow. The funny thing was that I couldn't even blame her. Wasn't I doing the exact same thing?

Her article was complete with a disturbing number of pictures, one of which was taken in the garage where she'd caught us. In the car. Making out. Except the pictures made it look more like that one scene in the *Titanic* with the handprint on the buggy's window.

I guess I could always put "re-enacts famous movie scenes" on my resume.

A couple photos backed up her claims of the length of time our "torrid affair" had gone on. Two were of Andy and me in Lincoln's private kitchen. Peggy must have followed me when I'd not-so-sneakily left our room to go meet him. Another was of us at the foot of the stairs that led to my room. I was in the same outfit I'd been in when Amelia caught us. Peggy was the noise I'd heard. Turned out I wasn't paranoid after all.

"Do you mind explaining to me how our lead contestant and co-producer have been caught having an affair?" Wanda was clearly not interested in an answer and we didn't offer one.

"Paige isn't the lead." Amelia scoffed, and this time Lincoln was the one who told her to be quiet.

"How did this happen?" Wanda didn't bother keeping her voice low. I imagined she didn't want to disrupt the theme of the morning. Instead of pancakes and eggs, we were having yelling with a side of betrayal. She pointed at Andy like a mother scolding her son. "I would have expected this from Lincoln, but you were supposed to be the responsible one!"

"Hey!" Lincoln sounded hurt.

"I know," Andy said, a tie pressed to his nose. I really hoped it wasn't Hugo Boss. I doubted the fashion mogul would be happy to know how his design was being used. "I'm sorry."

"What were you thinking?"

Andy's eyes darted to mine, then quickly back to Wanda's. "I wasn't, I'm sorry."

"The network has already called. They're threatening to cancel the show." I was surprised to see Wanda near tears. "You promised me this would work!"

What would work? What was she talking about?

"I didn't expect..." Andy checked the disgusting tie and seeing that his nose was no longer bleeding he tossed it to the ground. "I didn't expect her."

"You messed up!"

"I know!" his voice was rising again. "If I could do it all over again, I wouldn't, okay? It wasn't worth it!"

That was my cue. I rolled my suitcase to the front door and pulled it open.

"Paige." It was Amelia who stopped me. I expected to find triumph in her eyes, but with a start I realized she looked...concerned. She didn't say anything else, just held up a hand in goodbye.

I gave her a half-smile and then left. I didn't look back.

$$$

"You're *firing* me?" I started hyperventilating. "But I got you your story."

Two days had passed since Peggy's article was released and I was back in Carla's office, sitting in the exact same spot I'd been in when I was fired – the first time. The article had gone viral in less than two hours. The whole ordeal was being called "Red Gate" cleverly referencing the Watergate scandal and my red hair. (Thank you, Amelia, for coming up with the idea and then Tweeting about it non-stop for two days.)

The past forty-eight hours had passed in a blur. The network aired the episode that night as they normally would have but added an extra thirty minutes at the end dedicated to Andy and me. Apparently, they were going with the classic PR move of using a scandal to their advantage. Millions of people had watched live. I even read in *People* that it was the most watched reality TV episode of the past five years. A YouTube star had even made a recap of the "sordid affair" (as the video was titled) complete with a parody and puppet show.

It was actually a pretty funny video. I'd watched it twice.

I hadn't seen or talked to Andy or anyone from the show for that matter. After storming off, I'd waited down the road for a cab to pick me up. It seemed the guard had been notified to let one in because no one tried to stop me.

I'd arrived back in New York only to find Jemma busy packing boxes. She threw her arms around me before I could even start to explain what had happened. I'd cried to her for over an hour before asking why she was packing boxes in the first place. She then told me that she'd decided to move back home because New York was too expensive.

"I'll never become a makeup artist anyway," she said with a shrug.

"What are you talking about?" I asked. "What happened to the Jemma who believed she could do anything?"

"I think it's just time I gave up the dream. It's been a year, Paige. It's not going to happen."

"But Jem," I plead with her, "you're my dreamer. You're the one who insists that the impossible is possible! You're the adventurer, the one who single-handedly took down that guy in the dance club when he got too close."

She let out a low chuckle. "I don't know if I'm that girl anymore."

"You're just having a crappy time right now because you lost your job. Things will get better. Don't move home. Not yet."

She sighed. "I'll think about it."

That had been last night. Between Red Gate, Jemma possibly moving home, and missing Andy more than I wanted to admit, I was ready for things to start looking up.

Except now I was losing my job. Again.

"I don't understand," I said, praying this was a nightmare, and repeated, "I got you your story."

"You were scooped. Peggy's article about your affair with the producer was ten thousand times more interesting than an insider's perspective of reality TV. Your story was obsolete the second she published her exclusive."

"That's not my fault!"

"It is your fault, Paige. *You* were the one having the affair. *You* were the one who had the producer eating out of the palm of your hand." She stood, jamming her desk with a finger each time she said 'you.' "*You* were the audience favorite. *You* were the one who knew the show was rigged and that *you* would win. The story wrote itself and *you chose not to use it.*"

"I didn't know I would win until the end," I snapped. "I told Andy that I refused to marry Lincoln."

"That doesn't change anything."

I'd never seen Carla so upset. I'd never seen anything rattle her this much. I didn't think it was possible. She'd always been stone cold and now she was a volcano.

My eyes stung. I was so tired. Tired of holding back tears, tired of pretending I was fine, tired of being someone I wasn't, tired of not getting what I wanted. I'd never been so tired. I wished I could go back in time to the park where Andy and I had laid looking at the stars. I'd felt so good then. Had it only been a few days?

Carla took a deep breath and sat back down.

"You've made it clear you don't have the ability to be a journalist. Maria will call you a cab and help you clean out your desk."

"You asked me to go on this show," I said sternly. "You asked me to lie about who I was. You asked me to do whatever I had to do to get the real story."

"Yes," Carla acknowledged. "But you didn't get the real story. You were the real story and you couldn't even write that."

She was right. I hated that she was right.

"Carla, please," my voice broke. I didn't want her to see me cry, but I couldn't leave here without doing everything I could to keep my job. I couldn't go home and tell Jemma to keep fighting if I wasn't willing to do the same. "I proved I could get the story. At least a story. I proved that I can be an asset to *Look!*"

"Yes, you did."

"Then why not keep me on as a junior reporter? I wrote what you wanted me to write. I wrote an exposé on reality TV. Give me another chance. I'll write whatever you want."

"Journalists don't have the luxury of writing what they want. Journalists write what needs to be written."

"Then I'll write what needs to be written!"

"You can't. You've proved that. A good journalist will do whatever it takes to get the story but has to have integrity along the way. Journalists who use people to get ahead in their careers might know important people and attend high-class events, but they're missing the most important part: integrity. Real journalists don't use people to get ahead."

I bristled at her tone. "I won't use people to get ahead."

"You already have. You exposed Amelia's sexual harassment lawsuit which will not only give the defense proof that she lied to get on the show but the publicity, however minor, will push the case back at least a year. You used Bunny and Paulo for an article and Paulo got fired for it. You cheated your way through each round. You betrayed Lincoln's trust. You lied to Andy about leaving the show for him and then recorded him admitting the show was rigged. You used every single person there to get ahead. The only person whose mistakes you didn't use were your own."

I flinched. I had done all of those things and more. I didn't have any excuses other than I was focused on myself, my own career. I didn't stop to think about what my actions might do to anyone else. "How did you know about me telling Andy I'd leave the show for him?"

"You're a crappy video editor. You sent me the whole file." She pinched the bridge of her nose before casually clasping her hands together and resting them on the table. "It's over, Paige. You tried and you failed. You're a good writer. You'll be able to get another job. Maybe one that requires less from its reporters."

I was dismissed. I walked to the door and slowly opened it, hoping beyond hope that she'd stop me.

She didn't.

$$\$\$\$$

"Carla was right," I said. I'd been whining to Jemma since the second she walked through the door over half an hour ago. Thankfully for me, she's a good sport and didn't complain about my complaints. "I should have written my own story instead of publishing everyone else's."

Jemma bit her lip.

"Just say it."

"I've been thinking about it and maybe it's time to write one last article for *Look!*"

"What do you mean?"

"You said it yourself, Paige. You should have written your own story. Write an exclusive interview of yourself and send it to *Look!*, then people would get your side of the story."

I scoffed. "Why? Carla won't publish it."

"You never know." Jemma shrugged. "People can surprise you. Even if they don't publish it, maybe it'll be therapeutic for you."

"I don't need therapy." I fell back onto my pillow. "I need Andy."

"Maybe this can help with that too."

I turned toward the wall, signaling I didn't want to talk anymore. I felt her get off the bed and a few minutes later I heard her grab her keys.

"I'm going for a walk," she said quietly. I knew she was trying to be respectful and give me space. That was one of the best things about having Jemma as a roommate. She always knew when to stay and when to go and was never upset by it. "Be back later."

The second she closed the door I laid on my back and stared at the ceiling. Tears dripped from the corners of my eyes as I wondered if Jemma was right, just like Carla. Was everyone right except for me? If I hadn't been so desperate to keep my job maybe I would have done things differently. Maybe I would have gotten a story worth printing instead of turning my perceptions into gossip fit for a super-market rag. Maybe I would haven't lied to Andy. Maybe Andy would have fallen in love with me for real.

I pulled my laptop out of my bag and pulled up a new blank Word document. I would take Carla and Jemma's advice. I wouldn't try and figure it out on my own this time. This time I would fix things – with their help.

$$$

For love or money?
EXCLUSIVE with Paige Michaels!

I read and re-read the headline trying to get it to sink in. My story, the Paige Michaels' story, was out there for the world to read. It had gone online early this morning. Alarmingly early since I didn't send it to Carla until almost 1:00 a.m. I'd gotten the world's shortest email in response.

6:30 a.m.

I was up by six, anxiously awaiting what would happen at 6:30. I assumed that meant she was publishing my article, but you could never be too sure with Carla. She might be sending Liam Neeson to assassinate me. Even though I'd spent almost the entire day before writing it and was pretty sure it was the best piece I'd ever written, I was chew-off-my-fingernails nervous. Jemma, being the best friend that she is, read it about six times, giving me suggestions about things to include and ways to incorporate my own personality. The results were fantastic.

Hopefully, the world thought so too.

Jemma was right beside me by 6:15 with a plate of Eggos covered in syrup and whipped cream and two forks. At 6:25, I pulled on tennis shoes and told Jemma I was going for a run.

"What?" Only it came out like "Waaa?" because her mouth was full of waffle. She swallowed and said, "You don't run."

"I do today," I said as I shut the door behind me. I couldn't sit there any longer. Even when, or if, the article was published it wouldn't get results right away. I'd have to wait a few hours until people got to work and finished going through the previous day's emails to see whether or not they were commenting or sharing it. I couldn't just sit around until then.

I ran for over an hour. (Okay, I ran one block and then while gasping for air I walked another two blocks to a coffee shop where I got a smoothie and a chocolate cake-like muffin for breakfast both of which were so good I might have gotten a second of each only to realize I would barely be able to walk home let alone run.) I thought I'd calmed my nerves – or at least eaten them into submission – by the time I got back to the apartment, but I turned the corner to my street and hit a wall of reporters. When the first one saw me, he shouted, "There she is!" and the rest came at me like a mob.

Petrified, I froze like Bambi's mom before darting into oncoming traffic. Thankfully, I didn't get hit by a taxi and the reporters weren't stupid enough to follow me. I weaved my way through the crowds of people heading to work for a couple blocks and then ducked into a crowded café, which I figured would be easier to hide in than an empty one. I hid there for a couple hours until Jemma called to see if I was okay. Kind of.

"Your article went viral!" she said. "I started getting texts from my friends barely an hour after it was published. Reporters have been knocking on our door all morning. Everyone's going insane over it!"

"Yeah, I kind of figured."

"Where are you anyway? Are you okay?"

When I told her about the gang of reporters she looked out the window, but only a couple were still there. She called the police and, knowing they would take a while to respond to a non-emergency, I waited for another hour or so until the last of the reporters would be asked to leave. By the time I walked through our front door I was three muffins, two smoothies, a bagel and a Danish heavier. And a whole lot calmer.

"Hey," I said to Jemma as I locked the door behind me. She dropped the book she was reading and pulled my computer onto her lap.

"You ready to hear what people are saying?" She didn't wait for me to respond or even to sit down before she read the first comments.

"JennyQ said, 'Huge thank you to Paige Michaels. I come from a large family with a stay-at-home mom and I've never been able to put into words how much a career means to me. My whole life I've felt looked down upon because of my aspirations. You articulated exactly how I feel and I'm so excited to have my family understand.'"

I settled down next to her on the mattress and rested my back against the wall.

"Tyrell said, 'I am so grateful to know someone else feels like this. Hit me straight to the heart.' Elizabeth said, 'Shout out to my girl, Paige, for putting into words my secret thoughts and feelings. I was too afraid to share until now.'"

Jemma continued excitedly, "*Who Wants to Marry a Millionaire?* even posted a link on their website."

My chest constricted. "They did?"

"Yeah, it's got an intro from this lady named Wanda who says that it's the most genuine and daring thing she's ever read."

"That's great," I said, but my words sounded hollow.

"Paige," she said, noticing the tears rolling down my face. "Why are you crying? I thought you'd be happy."

"If it's on the show's website that means they've seen it."

"Yeah…?" She didn't get it.

"That means Andy's seen it. And he still hasn't called."

Chapter $25

I was dreaming about the Romona Keveza gown I'd worn in LA, but in my dream, the gown was wrapped around me like a vice. I gasped for breath, but just as soon as my lungs felt slight relief my head was enveloped in lace and silk and I fought to escape. To top it off, Carla was screaming at me, her voice shrill, even through the fabric. It kept getting higher and higher pitched until it was unrecognizable, and then she started to hit me.

"PAIGE!"

I jerked awake and tried to untangle myself from my sheets. Jemma, eyes still closed, had one arm reached over the small separation between our mattresses and was slapping me.

"Ow! Okay, I'm awake!" I squinted at the clock. 4:00 a.m. I groaned.

"Will you answer your phone?" she snapped, her voice muffled by her pillow. "It's been ringing for like five minutes."

Sure enough, five seconds later my phone lit up and it started to ring again.

Determined to yell at whoever decided to call in the middle of the night, I picked up the phone then sat up straight when I saw Andy's name on the screen.

I started slapping Jemma's back and she swore rudely.

"It's Andy," I said. She was sitting up ramrod straight before I could blink. Our eyes were wide as we stared at the phone.

"Why is he calling me?" My stomach flipped over and I wondered if I was going to be sick. The irrational part of my brain started throwing around insane notions about prison. "What if he's calling to tell me the police are coming to arrest me?"

"Don't be ridiculous," Jemma said solemnly. "If the police were coming they'd just break down your door. They wouldn't announce themselves first."

We looked at each other and then stared at the door in fear.

The phone stopped ringing.

We both jumped when it started up again.

"Put it on speaker," Jemma commanded.

My thumb was unusually shaky as I answered on speaker. "Hello?"

"Where are you?" Andy practically yelled. "Wanda said your flight would get in late last night!"

"What are you talking about?" Maybe I was still dreaming. "What flight?"

"We're filming the final episode tonight and you're still not here."

"Are you sure you have the right person?"

"Paige, I swear if you don't show up –"

"Then what, Andy?" My exhaustion grew into anger. "What are you going to do? We both know there's no way in this world or the next that I'm going to marry Lincoln, so please, tell me your master plan. Why on earth should I come out there?"

"You're contractually obligated."

I groaned. "I am so sick of everyone saying that. I was contractually obligated to *Look!*, but they tore up that contractual obligation the moment I got fired, so excuse me if I don't trust your contract."

"You lost your job?"

"Yes, I got fired. I ruined lives with those articles and I still lost my job."

"But what about –" He broke off. "I'm sorry."

"Contracts can be broken. Unless we pulled a Snape and did an unbreakable vow without my knowledge, I'm not coming back."

"Paige." His voice was soft now. Almost pleading. "I know the last time I saw you that things didn't go well."

"That's like saying the Ice Age didn't go well."

"Okay, it was horrible. It was a miserable explosion of lies and miscommunication. But we need you."

"No." I shook my head even though he couldn't see me.

"Please."

"No."

"We can't do this without you."

I rolled my eyes. "I thought the show would be canceled by now anyway. After the scandal last week and everything."

And the article that followed.

"So did I, but people have been demanding the final episode. Ratings are higher than ever. If we hit tonight's goals then we'll be set."

"Why is everything about money with you people? Lincoln's a millionaire. He doesn't need the money."

"No, but the youth center does."

"What youth center?"

He sighed. "It's confidential."

"Andy."

He hesitated only briefly. "We're building another youth center. This one will be in Compton."

"That's...nice." My words felt inadequate, but I didn't quite know what to say. "I guess I thought Lincoln had enough money to do that on his own. Why does he need the show?"

"Half the money is going toward the youth center and the other half is going to build a rehab center for children with addictions. Anyone under age sixteen can go there to get help. For free."

I sucked in my breath. "How is that possible?"

Being a journalist, I'd read my fair share of news. Rehab centers cost millions of dollars to build, not to mention the tens of thousands of dollars it cost to treat a single person. Adding free care to that? It was going to cost billions.

"I'm not going to bore you with the business plan, but the main thing is that once kids are released from rehab they're required to go to the youth center. Projections show it'll majorly cut down on crime in the area and eventually end up saving the city money."

Guilt colored my cheeks for my assumption that Lincoln would just be making more money. "Oh."

"It's your choice, Paige, I can't make you. But if you don't come then the network will drop us. The studio will go under, everyone will lose their jobs, and we won't be able to build the youth or rehab center we promised. You said yourself that you've ruined lives with your articles. Don't ruin more by just not showing up."

I was silent and looked at Jemma, still listening in rapt attention. She gave me a look that said she couldn't believe I was even considering saying no.

"It's one night," he said after a moment.

I took a deep breath. "On two conditions: Jemma comes with me."

Beside me, Jemma squealed, jumped up in excitement and pulled a duffle bag from the closet.

"Fine."

"Second, I'm going to need you to get me a dress."

I could almost hear him smile. "Way ahead of you."

Fairly sure I was going to regret this, I said, "Email me the airfare confirmation. I'll see you tonight."

$$$

"You got me a wedding dress?! I screeched. I sounded like a banshee with PMS. Andy flinched, but Jemma, who was standing beside me, was too enthralled with the dress to notice.

"I've never seen anything so beautiful." If my voice sounded like a banshee, hers sounded like Gollum with the ring.

"Calm down," Andy said, hands raised as if I might take a page out of Lincoln's book and just punch him.

"Have you ever noticed that whenever someone says, 'calm down' it has the opposite effect?" If the fashion gods wouldn't curse me for life I would have torn the dress apart. Okay, I would never destroy a piece of art, but I was really *really* mad. Not even eight hours had passed since I'd gotten Andy's phone call and we were already arguing. Well, at least I was arguing. He was being annoyingly calm about the whole thing.

We were on the first floor of Lincoln's mansion in a room I'd never seen before. Like all the other rooms, it had floor-to-ceiling windows, but these windows retracted into the walls to create an open-air space. The only furniture in the room was a full-length paneled mirror, half-covered by the Romona Keveza dress. A cream-colored couch and flowered chaise faced the mirror as though admiring the display. The windows were retracted, the lightest breeze blowing inside, stirring the fabric of the dress so it sounded like waves. It would have been soothing if it weren't so infuriating.

"I thought we were going to film up on the mountain," I said. "That dress would never fit in a helicopter."

"Change of plans. If I never go back to that spot it'll be too soon." His words renewed my guilt.

"Oh my gosh, Paige! Can you just imagine?" I whirled to face Jemma, who was holding it up to her chest and staring into the mirror. She met my gaze and asked eagerly, "Can I try it on?"

"No," I snapped just as Andy said, "Sure."

"You don't get a say in this." I pointed a finger at him and turned back to Jemma. "Put that down. No one is trying anything on."

For a second, I thought she might break down in tears, but I was too furious to care. I turned back to Andy. "I am not wearing that. Get me a different dress or we're leaving."

"Jem," Andy said to her as if they'd known each other longer than 15 minutes. "Do you mind giving Miss Demanding and myself a moment alone?"

I fumed. "Jemma doesn't have to go anywhere –"

"Actually," she said with a huff. "I'm not particularly happy with you right now, Paige, so I would welcome the opportunity to leave." She folded her arms and left, closing the door behind her. I rolled my eyes, not believing for a second that she was actually mad at me. She was just trying to give us space.

"What is this, Andy?" I said, my anger fading into exhaustion. "I told you I'm not marrying him. I don't need a wedding dress. I'm here so you can film me saying goodbye or whatever and then I'm going back to New York."

"I read the article, Paige."

If he'd announced he was going to move to Idaho and become a potato farmer, I wouldn't have been more surprised.

"It was good."

Definitely not the reaction I was expecting. I could almost feel the rising smoke climbing up my neck.

"It was good?" I repeated. "I poured my heart into that article and I never heard from you. That article got over a thousand comments in the first 12 hours and you didn't even bother to send a text."

"I know, I'm sorry. I needed time."

"The whole world knows how I feel about you and you didn't even have the decency to send something as impersonal as an email saying you don't feel the same way. What? Was your assistant out sick that day or something?"

"How you feel about me?" he asked. I realized my mistake as he took a step toward me.

"Felt," I corrected myself, my voice barely audible. "How I felt."

I turned my back on him and made my way over to the dress. I promised myself I was just tired and overwhelmed by everything that had happened over the past week. I wasn't going to cry. Not because of him.

Crystals sewn into the gown's bodice caught the light and reflected it from the mirror onto the ceiling creating a firefly effect. It really was a remarkable dress. It would have been stunning on Jemma. Maybe I should have let her try it on. Maybe I shouldn't have argued when Andy told me that's what I was supposed to wear. Maybe I shouldn't have come back to California at all. Maybe then I wouldn't be standing here, shaking from the fear that my breaking heart was going to start sending shards flying across the room. My life was full of maybes and what ifs and if onlys. What must it be like to be certain?

"Paige." I hadn't noticed Andy coming up behind me. "Do you love me?"

I turned and craned my neck to look up at him. "Do you love me?" I asked in return.

He took a deep breath. "Will my answer change yours?"

Yes.

"No."

He saw the lie in my eyes. He stepped back, his expression hard. "Let me know when you're ready to be honest with me. Until then, put on the dress. The crew is waiting for you."

Jemma came in moments after he left. I hadn't moved since he'd closed the door behind him.

"I'm assuming you didn't tell him," she said with a sigh.

"Why do you say that?" I couldn't tear my eyes from the door.

"Because if you had, you two would be too busy making out right now to care about filming."

"He didn't say it back."

It was as if I'd thrown ice water on her. "What do you mean 'he didn't say it back'? You told him? You're telling me that you said, 'I love you' and he said, what? Thank you? That –" She balled her hands into fists and headed for the door.

"I don't mean that I told him today."

She stopped halfway to the door. "I'm confused. Did you tell him or not?"

"I told him. I said it in the article."

Jemma's shoulders drooped her indignant rage on my behalf gone. She gave me a half smile and said, "Writing something isn't the same as saying something."

"They're my words. It's the same thing."

She shook her head sadly. "Anyone can write the words, 'I love you.' But when you say I love you out loud there's emotion behind it, something palpable the other person can literally feel. Written words are beautiful, Paige, but sometimes that's all they are. Just words."

I took a shaky breath, biting back tears for the umpteenth time that day. "What if he doesn't say it back?"

"He will."

"But what if he doesn't?" I looked her in the eyes, searching for some sign she could see the future. She put both hands on my shoulders and gave me a tiny smile.

"Then I'll break his nose, effectively ruining his masterpiece of a face, and then come back to pick up the pieces of your broken heart."

I chuckled and wiped the escaping tears off my cheeks.

"Now let's get you into this dress," Jemma said. "Because if you're going get dumped you might as well do it dressed like a queen."

"Hey!" I glared at her.

"I was referring to Lincoln dumping you," she waved her hand dismissively, "not Andy. He'd be a fool to not choose you."

Andy had said the same thing, only he'd been referring to Lincoln.

He'd be a fool to not choose you.

The memory gave me hope.

Chapter $26

"Paige. I...I don't...you've never...I...oh, Paige!" Jemma threw her arms around me.

"Why are you crying?" I said patting her back.

She drew back and stepped at least a foot away from me. "You just look so beautiful!"

I chuckled. "Does that mean I can look now?"

Jemma had spent the last hour and a half helping me get ready. Andy had sent in someone to do my hair and makeup right after he'd left the room, but when Jemma saw the "monstrosity" they'd made me into, she insisted on redoing everything, kicking the makeup artist out of the room – making her leave the supplies of course – and refusing to let me look in the mirror the entire time. She had just barely finished lacing up my dress when she'd freaked out and started to bawl.

"Stop crying!" I demanded, my voice breaking. "You cry, I cry, remember?"

"Not as romantic as 'you jump, I jump,' but I'll take it," she sniffed and dabbed at her eyes with a tissue. "Take a look."

I took a deep breath and turned to the mirror. I barely recognized myself – in a good way. I looked like I was about to be featured on the cover of a major fashion magazine.

The dress looked better on than I remembered it. It hugged curves I didn't even know I had. The fabric hung around me in perfect waves, the color so pure I couldn't stop staring. Crystals I hadn't noticed before sparkled in the light. Jemma had done an amazing job on my makeup making it look natural enough that I still looked human, but still managed to enhance my features by highlighting my cheekbones and making my blue eyes pop. She'd pulled my hair into a bun at the base of my neck holding it place with several braids and only two bobby pins.

"Jem, it looks amazing," I said in a reverent voice.

"*You* look amazing." She took a few photos on her phone and stared at me for a minute more. "Are you ready?"

My heartbeat kicked up a notch. "Do I have a choice?"

"Sweetie," she said gently. "You always have a choice."

And, true to form, Jemma meant it. She didn't move to open the door and I knew that if I decided I didn't want to do this, if it was too hard, she'd help me sneak out of the mansion by faking a pregnancy or something equally unbelievable.

"Let's do it." I nodded for her to open the door.

With a small smile, she went out to get Andy. A few seconds later she returned with Wanda, not Andy, in tow.

"Where's Andy?"

"He's busy at the moment," she said. The look on her face was one of awe. "Paige, you look incredible. I can't tell you how grateful I am that you're here."

What?

"Really?"

"Really?" Jemma echoed.

"Really." Wanda put her arms around me in a quick hug which shocked me to the point I didn't hug her back. "Andy told me that you weren't going to come back but when you heard about what we wanted to do with the rehab center…well…you changed your mind. I can't tell you how thankful I am. My son has been into drugs for years and we couldn't afford to get him the help he needs. Andy was nice enough to pay for it."

"Andy paid for it? Not Lincoln?"

"When I told Andy I wanted to spearhead this new program for children in Compton, he and Lincoln were so supportive that they came up with the idea for the show, pitched it to the network, and figured out how to use the proceeds to start the new program."

"What are you talking about?" I asked, shaking my head. "Andy said this was your idea. He said you convinced him and Lincoln to do it."

"He was probably just being modest, but I did kind of convince them as to why we needed a youth rehab center program. Maybe that's what he was referring to?"

I shook my head in disbelief. "Why didn't you tell anyone?"

"We didn't want anyone to connect the proceeds from the show to the youth center. Hollywood has a bad reputation with drugs and we didn't want people thinking Hollywood was using this as a PR opportunity. We want positive press for the center and this show isn't exactly encouraging honesty and openness."

I nodded, unable to come up with any words to describe how I felt. I wasn't even sure I knew how I felt. It was as though everything I'd learned about Andy over the past two weeks had been barely scratching the surface.

"I don't understand. Why would he make me marry Lincoln if he's supposedly such a good person?"

"He tried to change the plan."

I remembered then, something Lincoln had said during our fight. *"That's why you tried to change the plan at the last minute? You didn't want me to have her."*

"Change the plan to what?"

"He tried to make it so that you would be able to accept a proposal from anyone on the show, not just Lincoln."

"That doesn't make sense. Why?"

Wanda scoffed, finally sounding like the woman I'd come to know instead of this soft, kind-hearted stranger. "Oh, Paige. Even you aren't that dumb."

She didn't believe Andy loved me, did she?

"But he lied to me. He was going to make me marry Lincoln. He put it in the contract."

"Did you even read the contract?"

I thought I had. Mostly. I'd been so focused on the confidentiality agreement that I skimmed over the part about marriage. That's why I thought it was fake.

"It stated that you were contractually obligated to finish the show until you were eliminated or married."

"Okay, but –"

"I'm not done." She glared, and my mouth snapped shut. "If you were to be chosen as Lincoln's wife, you would be obligated to marry Lincoln on live TV during the final episode."

"How is this helping Andy's case?" I snapped. "He rigged the show so I would be chosen."

"Because there was an addendum that said that if you were chosen you would have the option of refusing Lincoln's offer of marriage and walking away but would be subject to a fine of one million dollars."

"Are you kidding me? How on earth am I supposed to pay one million dollars? This has got to be illegal."

Wanda's voice rose. "The contract also stated that the winning contestant would be awarded a prize in the form of one million dollars. The prize would not be contingent upon her marital status."

Wait…what?

"You could have bought your way out of the marriage, Paige. Andy made certain that the winner would have a way out. It was in the contract."

Andy's words were now the ones running through my mind. *"It was in the contract!"* He'd repeated it so often it never occurred to me to go back and read through the contract. I'd just assumed it said exactly what I'd thought. The elephant that had been sitting on my chest since the moment I'd learned of my arranged marriage flapped its ears like Dumbo and flew away. I could breathe again.

"Paige," Jemma said, her eyes wide, "that means…"

I picked up the skirts of my dress the best I could and hurried to the door. At the door, I stopped.

"Wanda," I said.

She raised her eyebrows in question.

"Thank you."

"Meet in the foyer in five minutes." Her voice was clipped, but she smiled when she said it.

I rushed down the hall, scanning the rooms through open doors, looking for Andy. Almost unconsciously, I found myself in home base. Amelia was there in the second most incredible wedding gown I'd ever seen. It was strapless with a sweetheart neckline that showed off Amelia's tanned skin. The gown was blush-colored, but a traditional ball gown with a tulle skirt and lace bodice.

She looked exquisite.

"Paige," she said. "You look amazing." Her voice held no trace of sarcasm or malice, only pure admiration.

"Thank you," I said. "You look gorgeous. I love your dress. Monique Lhuillier's right? The new collection?"

"Yes," Amelia said and fingered the tulle.

I nodded.

We stood there for a moment, standing across the room from one another, unsure what to say or where to go.

Amelia was the first to break the silence. "I never hated you, you know."

I raised one eyebrow. "Really?"

"Really. In your exclusive you said that I did, but I didn't. Not really."

"But I published info about your lawsuit and set your court case back."

"Okay, yeah, you suck for doing that."

I totally agreed.

"I believe you, though. Not that it helps, but I believe that you didn't harass him. And I'm sorry I wrote the article. I would take it back if I could."

"Thank you." She cast her eyes down, seeming embarrassed and hopeful at the same time. "Lincoln said he'd help me get a better lawyer and after we're married…oh…"

She'd said too much. Except for this time, I believed she wasn't just bragging. She really hadn't meant to say anything.

"You're marrying Lincoln?"

"I'm sorry, Paige." She looked it too. "I know you and Andy are…whatever you are, but Lincoln and I really love each other. It's been a long time since I felt this way about anyone and…well…I think we'll be good together. We went and picked up the marriage license this morning."

"Tonight? Are you getting married tonight?" My heart skipped.

She bit her lip and then shook her head. "We want to date longer. Oh, Paige, please act surprised when Lincoln tells you on camera. I wasn't supposed to say anything and they're going to be so upset when they find out –"

"Find out what?" Andy entered the kitchen and I turned to look at him. He had stopped dead in his tracks, staring at me with admiration and then desire. His eyes scanned my body, slowly, appreciatively, and my nerves tingled. He cleared his throat and tore his gaze away to Amelia.

"Find out what?" he repeated with a hoarse voice.

"Nothing," I said. "Andy, I really need to talk to you, it's important."

He took my arm. "It's going to have to wait until after the show. Wanda was waiting for you in the foyer. When you didn't show up she sent me to get you. We'll have to go straight to where they're shooting."

"But –"

He led me outside and down the path past the pool and into the garden where I'd first spoken to Lincoln. As we walked I could hear Lincoln's voice and a few cameramen calling to each other, but instead of focusing on them I focused on the way my dress trailed on the ground. It wasn't enough to get dirty, but enough that the sound of it grazing across the grass calmed my nerves.

We turned past the trees and I gaped. It was incredible. They'd transformed the small garden into a wedding planner's dream. There weren't any chairs (this was supposed to be a small, private affair, viewed by millions from the comfort of their own chairs), but there was a canopy of lights strung up between the trees – so many they looked like stars. A sheer backdrop was a foot away from a pedestal covered in hundreds of rose petals. The natural flowers and trees surrounding the space provided an amazing atmosphere of peace. I was wrong about the mountain. This was the perfect place to get married.

"Andy, I –"

"After." He led me to my spot, just out of sight of the pedestal where Lincoln was standing. As he left he said, "When they signal, start walking to Lincoln."

I hated waiting. I wanted Lincoln to dump me already. I scanned the area, looking for something to focus on and I saw Jemma and Amelia standing several yards away behind the cameras, ready to watch the show. What was Amelia doing over there? Shouldn't she be getting ready to go on after Lincoln epically rejected me?

"In three…two…one…"

I spaced out during the intro and recap. I didn't care anymore. I started bouncing up and down on my toes, anxious to get the whole thing over and done. I looked behind me at the bright orange of the setting sun. That was one thing we didn't have in New York. Sunsets were hard to see when the skyscrapers blocked the light. I liked California sunsets. Now that I'd been fired maybe it wouldn't be so bad to move to LA. If Andy would give me another chance, that is…

A cameraman motioned for me to start walking. I made my way down the path to the pedestal and when I stepped on it and looked up into Lincoln's eyes, I was surprised at my reaction. I wasn't nervous, at least not for this. I wanted Lincoln to be happy. Knowing he was going to marry someone he loved – no matter how crazy she seemed to me – who would make him happy…it made me happy.

I must have looked like a fool smiling at him as I did. I was just so relieved he wanted to marry Amelia. Then there was the thought of Andy, putting in an addendum so the winner could "get out" of the contract easily. It made my heart soar to know what he was doing to help others. The way he and Lincoln had planned this whole game just to help kids who were struggling. How he'd held me in his arms that night in the park. The way he'd kissed me in the kitchen, at the swings, in the car. The way he kissed. The way he'd looked at me in the kitchen before leading me out here. I loved that man.

I took Lincoln's hand and he smiled as he looked into my eyes and I said, "I love Andy."

Well, that wasn't planned.

Lincoln's smile faltered. "What?"

I closed my eyes, praying that was only in my mind, but when I opened my eyes again Lincoln, and everyone else, was waiting for an explanation.

"I'm in love with Andy." I dropped Lincoln's hand and turned to look at Andy, standing over by the cameras. He looked like a breeze could have knocked him over. I looked back at Lincoln. "I'm sorry, Lincoln, but I love Andy."

"I know," he said with a shrug.

I wrinkled my brow. "It's okay?"

"Paige, you're incredible, but I'm not in love with you either. I love Amelia."

He left me standing alone on the podium and went to Amelia. The cameras followed him until he reached her, swept her into his arms, and kissed her deeply. He was holding her when he asked, "Will you marry me?"

Her grin was so wide it could have been seen from space. "Yes, of course!"

They kissed again, but I didn't have it in me to be happy because Andy still hadn't said anything. He just stood there, by the cameras, waiting for...what? I'd said it in an article and now I'd said it to the whole world, but I hadn't said it to him.

I started toward him and he met me halfway.

"Hey," he said it like we'd just seen each other on the street and wanted to acknowledge that we knew one another, but not that he was madly in love with me. "So I heard you've got a crush on me?"

"I'm in love with you, Andy. I love you. I'm sorry I didn't say it sooner. And it's okay if I'm too late, I get that. I'm just finally ready to tell you the truth. The truth is that I love you."

He stepped closer and took my hands.

"Do you remember when we went and played on the swings?"

"Swings?" Did he hear my confession or not?

"You really want to talk about swings right now?" I looked to see if anyone else thought this was weird, but the cameras kept on filming as though he hadn't just lost his mind. Maybe I'd spoken too softly, and they didn't know what I was saying. Maybe it was me.

"That's where we had our first kiss. That's where, as the sun rose, I realized I was in love with you."

"Wait, what?" My head jerked back to him. In a mix of awe, love, and horror I watched him get down on one knee.

"Paige," he said. "You are the most infuriating person I have ever known. But you're also the most caring and kind, driven and ambitious, brilliant and beautiful woman in the world. Nothing would make me happier than to stand by your side, holding your hand as you take the world by storm."

He pulled a tiny blue box with a white ribbon out of his pocket. The box sent my heart into a rhythmic dance as he knelt on one knee and opened it. The diamond inside caught the morning light and I was almost convinced he was sending an SOS signal instead of proposing. The gorgeous eyes I'd come to know so well were eager, ready for the question we both knew was coming. I could just imagine the look on his face – on my face. Everyone watching would expect me to cry and squeal with joy. They would cheer and clap and pour champagne to celebrate.

"Paige? Will you marry me?"

"Holy crap," I said.

I stared into his eyes, waiting for him to tell me he was kidding. He didn't.

"You're serious, aren't you?"

"I'm in love with you, Paige. I'm crazy about you. Marry me."

I was taking too long to answer. I knew exactly what to say, but I couldn't speak. I never expected it to go this far. I was supposed to get the story and get out. I wasn't supposed to fall in love.

He stood, eyes never leaving mine, took my hand and pulled me out of view of the cameras. I wasn't sure how they would manage that on live TV, but I guessed it wasn't my problem. When we were hidden in a copse of trees, Andy finally spoke. "Paige, what's wrong? You just said you loved me. I thought you'd be happy."

"I am…I just…it's so quick. It hasn't even been two weeks yet. We haven't talked about whether I'll move here or you'll move to New York or what we're going to do about our jobs or if you want to have kids and when or if that's going to happen and you haven't even met my brothers what if they hate you and you didn't ask my dad's permission and so he's going to kill you and there's so much –"

He kissed me.

If there's one way to tell me to shut up that won't make me angry – that's it.

"Paige," he said, my face cupped in his hands. "I'm not saying you have to marry me today, but someday. I love you. I love your quick brain and that you speak in run-on sentences when you're worried. I love every part of you and we'll figure it out. Say you love me and we'll figure it out."

My thoughts stopped racing all at once. "I do love you. I'm sorry I didn't tell you sooner, but I love you more than anything."

"So where do we go from here?"

For the first time in a long time, I didn't overthink it. I took his hands and led him back around the corner where Lincoln and Amelia were attempting to fill up time by doing an impromptu interview. The second we were within filming range they stepped to the side and everyone fell silent. Once Andy and I were back at our original spot, I said, "I'm sorry Andy, I went momentarily insane. Can you repeat your question?"

Andy's smile went ear to ear. "Paige Michaels, I love you. Will you marry me?"

My responding smile matched his. "Yes."

Opening the blue box for the second time, he took out the ring and slid it on my finger.

It was a perfect fit.

He kissed me then, deeply and with such love my heart was near bursting.

When we broke apart I said, "I love you so much, Andrew Warner."

He kissed me again and it wasn't until Lincoln tapped us on our shoulders that we stopped. We were surprised to find the cameras packing up. Apparently, they got bored waiting for us.

"You guys have got to come up for air," he said. "Show's over."

"Sorry, Lincoln," I said sheepishly.

Andy didn't stop looking at me. It seemed he wasn't sorry at all.

"Paige!" Jemma squealed and pulled me into a quick hug, before abruptly letting me go and yanking my left hand out of Andy's grasp.

She swore in awe at the ring. "Have you seen this? It's gorgeous!"

"I know my jewelry," Andy said.

I raised an eyebrow. "I'm not sure that's something you should admit minutes after you've gotten engaged."

He shrugged.

"I know now's probably not the time," Jemma said and held out my phone, "but Carla texted you a few hours ago letting you know you have a job with *Look!*"

"What?" I grabbed my phone and pulled up Carla's text.

> **Impressive work. Your exclusive proved to me you're through writing gossip columns and ready to move on to the big stories. You've got a job at LOOK! if you want it. Senior reporter.**

"Oh my gosh. She wants me to be a senior reporter." Just as I said this another text came through. It was from Carla.

> **Based off what I just saw on WWTMAM I'm guessing you'll want to stay in LA. We can work something out.**

I turned to Andy. "She said I can work from here."

"Really?" Andy looked at the text. "That's great, but I can move to New York too. I'll just fly back to keep ahead of the project."

"What project?" Jemma asked, but before we could answer Wanda was with us.

"The network just called. They're finalizing the numbers, but it's predicted that this was the most watched series they've had in the past two years. Based upon that our estimation is that we will have surpassed our goals." She was practically in tears. "More than double."

Andy had never looked so relieved. "That's so great, Wanda. I'm so happy for you."

"Couldn't have done it without me," Lincoln said and clapped Andy on the shoulder.

"We couldn't have done any of this without you," I said with a wink.

Wanda cleared her throat and was back to business. "Jemma, is it? Everyone was admiring your work."

Jemma looked confused. "What work?"

"Paige's makeup. Tons of people saw the photo you posted on Instagram. The video of her hair and makeup? You said in the description that you did it for her."

"Oh! Well, yes, yes I did."

"How would you like a job at the studio?" Wanda asked her. The two of them started to walk away, talking about a potential job.

"Did you...?" I turned to Andy wondering if he'd put the idea in Wanda's head.

"I didn't say a word. Jemma just does really good work. She was bound to get noticed."

The three of us left the crew to finish cleaning up and wandered back toward the mansion.

"What are you two lovebirds up to now?" Lincoln asked. "Want to go to a movie?"

Amelia came up behind him and hit his arm. "They want to be alone."

"As do we." He wrapped one arm around her back and kissed her neck.

"Linc?" Andy asked, slinging an arm over my shoulder. "Why don't you and Amelia go somewhere to celebrate?"

"Are you saying you no longer want the pleasure of our company?"

"That's exactly what I'm saying. Make yourself scarce."

"Sure thing, boss," Lincoln said. He took Amelia's hand, she wiggled her fingers at us in a goodbye, and they disappeared.

"Why did he call you boss? Is that a joke between you two?" I asked as Andy and I walked down the trail, the flowers seeming to glow in the moonlight.

"He likes to tease me. He knows too much about me. He's never been able to take me being his boss seriously."

I stopped in my tracks and Andy faced me, concern on his face. "You're his boss?" I asked. "I thought he ran his own company."

"He does," Andy shrugged, "but my company owns his company."

"But that means –" I said, realization dawning. The one-million-dollar addendum. It was to be paid by Andy. "Oh my gosh. You're a millionaire too."

"Nah, I'm not a millionaire," he said with a shake of his head. I furrowed my brow, thoroughly confused. He wrapped his arms around me and pulled me close. His eyes sparkled with mischief when he said, "I'm a billionaire."

His lips met mine and I smiled against them.

You know, it's true what they say. You can't buy love. But you can buy a Romona Keveza dress and a plane ticket to honeymoon in Fiji.

So we did.

About the Author

Jessie J. Holmes is a professor of social media marketing, an avid reader, and self-diagnosed Reese's addict. When she's not training her students to laugh at her jokes, she can usually be found taking marathon-level naps in the world's comfiest bed. She currently writes from Utah while (unsuccessfully) attempting to keep her Reese's addiction under control. She is the author of Who Wants to Marry a Millionaire? and the young adult novel, Twisting Fate.

Visit her at jessiejholmes.com and follow her on Facebook @authorjessiejholmes.

CPSIA information can be obtained
at www.ICGtesting.com
Printed in the USA
LVHW05s0517100518
576606LV00008B/33/P